SHADOW OF THE PHOENIX

The Sons of Jacob
Book I

THE SHADOW OF THE PHOENIX

The Sons of Jacob
Book I

J.B. Vosler

The New Atlantian Library

THE NEW ATLANTIAN LIBRARY
is an imprint of
ABSOLUTELY AMAZING eBOOKS

Published by Whiz Bang LLC, 926 Truman Avenue, Key West, Florida 33040, USA.

The Shadow of the Phoenix copyright © 2018 by J.B. Vosler. Electronic compilation/ paperback edition copyright © 2018 by Whiz Bang LLC.

For information contact:
Publisher@AbsolutelyAmazingEbooks.com

ISBN-13: 978-1945772863 (The New Atlantian Library)
ISBN-10: 1945772867

"I can no other answer make, but, thanks and thanks."

-William Shakespeare

For all of you who have helped me, supported me, and sat by patiently while I read you my words, I thank you.

THE SHADOW OF THE PHOENIX

The Sons of Jacob
Book I

"Which came first, the Phoenix or the flame?"
- J. K. Rowling

Prologue

Ventspils, Latvia, Friday, November 28th, 2003

Lili remembered the day Martin Henderson died. Though it had been over three years ago, she recalled every detail ... the explosion, the screams that filled the fiery ballroom, and the pain ... especially the pain. She had been only five at the time, but it had stayed with her. She had felt it. As if the flames had burned *her* skin instead of his ... the embers feeling like hot pokers as they scorched his hands, his cheeks, his hair. It was as if she had been there, as if she had somehow traveled thousands of miles and crossed two oceans, and had landed in his very heart.

It was her gift. One of them anyway. Lili could see things others could not. Not visions of the future; more like feelings of what was about to happen with images to match. She had *felt* the man perish under the weight of a fallen pillar as the flames had come and taken him alive.

But there was more ... more to what she had seen and felt, and now, as she lay in her bedroom and stared out the window at the Baltic Sea, she was seeing it again. Only this time, maybe because she was older, she saw it more clearly.

It hadn't started with the fire. No, it had started with a conversation ... a talk she had overheard between her papa Albins and her Uncle Mart. Martin Henderson wasn't her real uncle; she just called him that because they were close ... closer than friends. *"We're family,"* he used to tell her when he read to her at night. Or when he walked her and the sled he had built to the snowy hill a mile away. *"We're family, Lili, so you can always count on me to be there for you."*

Lili wiped a tear. She missed Uncle Mart. Taller than her father, but with the same golden-blonde hair, the two men had been friends for as long as she had been alive. It was getting harder for her to see either one of them, which was unusual ... Lili remembered everything; every word, every deed, even the feelings – good and bad – that accompanied those moments from the past. It was her other gift. *Eidetic memory*, it was called. Did she like it? No. But there was nothing to do about it. As her mother had often told her, *"You don't choose your gifts, Lili ... they choose you."* And so, not only had she been forced to sense the awful events that had taken place so many miles away, she was then compelled to remember them in agonizing detail. The present memorialized into the past ... neither one shaded by the thoughtful prism of time.

That was what happened with Uncle Mart. But, though she was the one with the special gift, it had been her father who had seemed to sense what was to come....

"Have you ever wondered, Mart, when the first moment of a battle begins? That instant when suddenly you're at war?"

"I can't say I have," Uncle Mart replied, as he stood next to Albins on the second-floor balcony. "I suppose you don't know until it's over."

Albins said nothing as he looked down at Lili and smiled. She was playing in the garden below and she looked away, pretending she hadn't seen him.

"She looks like her mother, you know." Lili's heart broke as she thought of her mother Clarissa who had died four months ago.

"Yes, I know." Said Uncle Mart. "She'll be fine, Albins."

"What if she's not? What if something happens to me today?"

"Nothing will happen to you; I've got your back."

Albins paused. "You don't know that. No one knows when they're going to die."

Lili ran to the other end of the garden, covering her ears so she wouldn't hear them. But it didn't work; she could hear every word ... as if they were standing right next to her.

"That's true, Albins. But, even if something was to go wrong, there are so many people who love you both. She would be well taken care of."

Lili waited. Finally, she heard Albins choke up as he said, "Promise me something, Mart."

"Anything."

"If something happens to me, will you make sure she is cared for?"

"Of course."

"I don't mean food, clothes, and shelter ... I mean loved and cared for."

"Yes."

"Promise?"

"I promise, Albins Platacis, if anything happens to your sorry ass today, I, Martin Henderson, will not only provide for your daughter, Lili, but will make it my personal mission to love her and ensure her safety and happiness for a lifetime."

"That's a big promise."

Uncle Mart grinned. "I'm a big man..."

Lili leaned back on her bed. Tears stung her eyes as she stared at the ceiling. She often thought of that moment ... those words between the two soldiers, especially after her papa died on that very same day. Had he foretold the future? Or was he simply aware of the fact that every time he walked into battle, there was a good chance he might not walk out? She would never know. All she knew was that he had died honorably; he had died saving his friends. It was all she had been told of the battle, and – though she was able to see so many sad events – for whatever reason, she couldn't see that one. Maybe it was God's way of letting her sleep at night.

But she remembered his burial. It had been later that night, after the sun had set. The sky had been clear, the night air cold and damp.

The moon seemed brighter than usual as Mart and Danil buried Albins at the back of the compound where all the soldiers were laid to rest. In spite of being told to stay at the manor, Lili had crept to the site, and she watched now as they tossed the last bit of dirt on his grave and then covered it with stones. She shivered, but not from the cold as she saw them put a cross of wood at the head. Mart said a prayer, and, when he had finished, he turned to Danil. Fighting tears, he said, "I need a favor."

"Anything, Mart."

"Lili is playing at the estate." His voice broke. "I ... I promised Albins, if something happened to him, I would care for her, and I have every intention of doing so." He closed his eyes. "But first, I need to go home ... to America. I have an obligation to fulfill, but I'll be back by the weekend. I'll take her with me then. Can you watch her until I get back?"

"Certainly, Mart. For as long as you need."

Mart nodded. "I should return by Friday ... Saturday at the latest."

"What shall I tell her?"

"Just tell her she's coming to visit you for a few days, and that I'm bringing back a special lady to meet her so we can take her home."

"And this 'special lady;' will she be willing to help you care for a little girl?"

Mart closed his eyes. "I think so ... I hope so..."

It wasn't until months later that Lili learned who that 'special lady' was. *Maddi ... from America.* Lili would see her ... feel her grief as she mourned the loss of Martin Henderson. Her sadness was different from Lili's; it had more layers. Lili had done all she could to reach out to her ... and she would continue to try, for she knew, the people who loved Uncle Mart should be connected.

She turned over on her bed. As she recalled that night in the ballroom – that horrible night when Uncle Mart was killed – there was a part of it that upset her almost as much as feeling him burn. It was the men who had come for him at the end. They had not been warriors like Uncle Mart and her papa ... No, they had been dark and scary. And they hadn't wanted to do it. Whatever had made them risk their lives to save Mart, it hadn't been done out of nobility. And so, of course, they had failed ...

"Just grab him!"

"He won't move. We have to get this beam off his legs!"

"How the hell did we get roped into this job?"

"I don't know."

"Why this guy? Who is he?"

"Just shut up!"

"You shut up, Simeon!"

~ ~ ~

Lili grimaced. She remembered Simeon. She would often see him in her nightmares. His hair was black, his eyes blacker still. His face was long and etched with fine lines. He had pushed the pillar from Mart's legs, and

Mart had cried out as the man had grabbed him by the ankles. The other man had lifted him by the shoulders, and they had carried him out a back door, past charred bodies to the outside. Lili trembled and wrapped her arms around herself. Even now, over three years later, she could feel the pain of the night air on his skin as if it was her own ... like bayonets piercing each follicle, searing every tiny hair.

She closed her eyes. She was seeing it again. They were carrying him through the trees to a black sedan. They reached the car and shoved him in back. Simeon pulled out a syringe, filled it, and stabbed it into Mart's thigh. Whatever it was, it worked almost instantly. Lili flinched. She felt it; she felt *him* ... leaving, a sense of peace surging through his entire body as the pain faded, and euphoria – and death – took its place.

She sat up. She was crying. She wiped her eyes. She smelled pancakes. Danil was in the kitchen making breakfast. Her heart was heavy as she looked out the window. It was November. Snow was falling. It reminded her of sledding ... with Uncle Mart. The tears kept coming and she wiped them away.

She had never felt Mart leave ... not completely. But she knew he had ... no one could survive what he had been through. She missed him. And, though it was getter harder and harder for her to see him, she would make a point of remembering his face, his smile, his hair ... even his swagger as he and Albins prepared for battle. But, most of all, she would try to do good ... like he had. He had once told her, *"Touch as many lives as you can, Lili ... they eventually touch you back."* Lili would do that. She would touch as many lives as she could ... for her father, Albins ... for Uncle Mart ... even for Maddi, the 'special lady' she had never met.

She looked again at the snow outside the window. She stood, walked over, and put a hand to the glass. It felt cold. Sometimes she could sense Uncle Mart's presence; as if he was with her, only a breath away ... *like the snow.* But then he would vanish and she would be alone. It had happened more lately; the sense that he was disappearing ... getting harder and harder to feel. *Don't leave me, Uncle Mart.*

She left her room and went to the kitchen. She took her seat at the table and tried to imagine him sitting next to her. She couldn't; she couldn't see him, she couldn't feel him, and it made her heart hurt. As she prepared to dig into pancakes and eggs, all she could think was ... *Where are you, Uncle Mart?*

Chapter 1
NEW YORK CITY

Saturday, November 29th, 2003

Martin Henderson was cold. He was always cold. And it hurt worse because of the scars. He pulled his scarf tighter around him as he stood outside the restaurant in downtown New York. The scarf stayed with him ... as if it was sewn to his neck. It hid the scars; some of them, anyway. He patted the gun tucked in his pants, comforted by the thick barrel pushing against his groin. He had grown used to it; the feel of a pistol next to him, like an extra arm, ready to fight when the need arose. *Or a lover ... caressing me when no one else will.*

He was wearing a disguise; a full beard, a mustache, and a pair of wide, horn-rimmed glasses, tinted to hide the scars. He adjusted the lapels of his Armani jacket and walked into the restaurant. He smiled at the maître d', who led him to a corner table he had reserved earlier that day. It would allow him to see the other guests as they arrived. It would also give him the proper trajectory. He needed this hit – the angle of it, the forensics – to be tied to someone else.

He sat down, lowered his scarf only slightly, and ordered a glass of Chianti. He leaned back and waited. He watched each guest as they walked in. It was the "Who's Who" of New York City, but Henderson didn't care. The thought that, a few short years ago, he would have been one of them was quickly pushed aside.

He was there for one purpose only; to kill the Yemen leader Abdulkarim Al-Gharsi. He didn't know why; it didn't matter. *"You do what I tell you, or the little girl dies."* Henderson shifted in his seat. The threat was like a refrain stuck in his head. And he knew the man meant it. *Morningstar always means what he says...*

"Pretty soon, I'm going to need you to do a few things you're not going to like." Short, impeccably dressed Edward Morningstar turned to look at Henderson, who was lying in bed with an IV in his arm. *"Do you hear what I'm saying?"*

Henderson tensed, eager for Morningstar to inject him with the drug that would ease his pain ... at least for a while. He had been in the hospital outside Novosibirsk, Russia for weeks, and, though the man with a limp was his ticket out of agony, Henderson had begun to think Morningstar was crazy.

Morningstar bristled. "I said ... do you hear what I'm saying?"

Henderson closed his eyes, stuck out his arm. He needed his medicine.

"It doesn't matter," Morningstar said as he ignored him and walked to the window. "I'm sure you'll comply." He pointed out the window. "See that cardinal, son?"

Henderson looked through a barely-opened eye at the bird perched about 200 yards away. All he could see was a splash of red against the snow, and the gray of the trees as they blended with the sky.

Morningstar inched open the window. "Such a lovely creature ... so perfect, so ... innocent," he said wistfully. Without warning, he pulled out a pistol and shot the bird dead.

Henderson watched, stunned, as the magnificent bird fell from the tree and was buried by the snow. Yes, Morningstar was crazy ... and cold...

Henderson had thought many times about killing Morningstar. But always, without fail, as if he had read his mind, Morningstar would pull him aside and whisper, *"Remember, Henderson, if anything happens to me, Lili Platacis dies."*

Henderson stiffened as he unfolded his napkin and laid it on his lap. And he knew; Morningstar would do it. Either he or one of his men would be quite willing to kill an innocent little girl ... *which is why I'm sitting here with a gun in my pocket.*

The wine came and he sipped it slowly. Just after 7:00 he saw a group of Omani leaders enter the restaurant. The day before, he had sent them an invitation on behalf of the Yemen Council. He had informed the restaurant, requesting that the two groups be seated next to one another. The Omanis were led to their table.

Minutes later, the Yemen leader, Al-Gharsi appeared at the door, flanked by bodyguards and guests. Henderson reached for his wine and was about to take a sip, when he stopped. Al-Gharsi had leaned down to speak to one of his guests ... a woman Henderson hadn't seen – not that close anyway – for nearly four years. He was having a hard time catching his breath. *Maddi.* She looked thinner, and her blonde hair was a few inches shorter, but the eyes were exactly the same ... blue eyes that had stayed with him when everything – everyone – else had vanished. She was laughing at something Al-Gharsi had said, and the very feel of that laughter hurt him. He tried to look away but he couldn't. She was so close. He took a swig of the wine. *How does she know Al-Gharsi?* She had never mentioned him. Then again, they had only had the one weekend together. There was plenty he didn't know about Maddi. *It doesn't matter; nothing's changed.*

A hostess led them directly past him to their table in the center of the room. Maddi didn't seem to notice him, but he could feel his temperature rise as she passed so close he could smell her hair. He turned away, trying hard to refocus his attention. His heart was racing and he had begun to sweat. *Calm down, Henderson!*

He watched as Al-Gharsi and his guests took their seats at the table next to the Omani. The two leaders exchanged nods. A waiter handed out menus, another filled water glasses, and a third brought in a bottle of wine and was preparing to open it.

Henderson felt for his gun, a .45 caliber USP, with silencer attached. *How does Maddi know him?* He frowned. *I can't do this ... not to a friend of hers.*

But he had to. A little girl's life depended on it.

Maddi ... my Maddi ... less than ten feet away. He had not been that close to her in so long; he felt like his heart was about to explode. He put his hand to his chest and closed his eyes. He wanted to go to her ... forget about the hit on Al-Gharsi ... forget about the last three years of his life.

He thought of Lili. *"You do what I tell you, or the little girl dies."*

He tightened his jaw and pulled the weapon from his pocket. He used his napkin to hide it as he laid it on his lap. He looked down and noticed his hand shaking. *Do it, Henderson ... it's just another hit.* He checked his watch: 7:22. He pulled on a pair of black tactical gloves, and then wiped his prints from the gun. He took a breath, raised the napkin, and grabbed the pistol. He could barely feel his fingers on the grip. The nerves in his left hand had been destroyed by the fire. He gripped the gun tighter. *Do it!* With one fluid motion, he lifted the gun, aimed at Al-Gharsi, and fired a shot directly into his forehead. He shoved the gun in his pants. The man fell forward onto the table. There were shouts, followed by screams of hysteria. Chairs were overturned as guests either fled the restaurant or tried to help the fallen leader. Bodies collided, dishes crashed to the ground. Henderson, pretending to try to help, moved next to the Omanis' table, grabbed their leader by the arm, and pulled him under the table. He placed the gun in the man's hand and forced him to shoot himself. He slid from under the table, smoothed down his jacket, and became a part of the crowd. He edged his way to the back of the dining room. He was about to disappear into the kitchen when he stopped. He looked back. He saw Maddi ... staring at her dead friend. The look in her eyes was devastating. Henderson's heart broke; he could feel her despair. *What have I done?* He forced himself to keep moving.

The kitchen had cleared and he hurried out the back door. He checked his watch: 7:29. When he was far enough away, he removed his glasses, the beard, the mustache, and then stripped off his dress clothes. He had on a pair of Neoprene running tights and a long-sleeved shirt. He pulled a skullcap from inside the waist of the tights and put it on. He ran a bit further, and then tossed the clothes and the disguise in a dumpster. Ignoring the cold, he jogged down Fifth Avenue, staying in the shadows with his head down. No one gave him a second look as he headed west on 50th Street to the Hudson River and on to Central Park. With every step, he saw her ... Maddi, the shock in her eyes, and the hurt as she watched her friend fall forward onto the table. It was completely his fault; he alone had made her witness the evil she would never forget.

As he sprinted to the rundown hotel room at the north end of town, he tried to remember how it felt to think of Maddi without guilt or shame. He couldn't. They were all he knew. They had replaced honor or decency; they had replaced hope. He had nothing left. He was an assassin ... the Phoenix ... whose only lover was a pistol ... his only friend, the monster who had created him, Edward Morningstar.

Chapter 2
WASHINGTON, D.C.

11/29/03

Edward Morningstar stretched out his legs and leaned back in his chair. He was in his study, where he had been for the past three hours, waiting for the call from Henderson, from Phoenix, telling him he had completed the hit on Al-Gharsi. In all their time together, Henderson had never missed a call.

Morningstar sipped a glass of wine and closed his eyes. *He'll call.* He tightened his silk robe over his pajamas, pulling an afghan from the chair beside him and laying it across his legs. After a minute, he picked up his leather-bound Bible from the coffee table and set it in his lap. It had been given to him by his mother, Marianna, when he was just a boy. He sighed. *How old would I have been?* Was it before or after she had gone crazy? Before or after his brother Timmy had died in a street fight in Laredo, Texas? Before or after his father had beaten him so badly with a belt that his butt had bled for three days straight? He tugged at the collar of his robe. He couldn't remember. Did it matter? No, all that mattered was that his mother had etched – in the leather cover of that Bible – her name next to his, with a heart in-between. *"Marianna and Edward ... mother and son."* He touched the inscription and felt a stab to his chest.

Though he preferred the feel of the book sitting in his lap, he often referenced an online Bible for his day-to-day planning. The online version had only one purpose: to record changes to his master plan. Using the same font and tenor, he would insert his own words where appropriate as a way of communicating to his followers. It was as if he was one of the disciples ... *or God Himself, penning a blueprint for the future.*

This Bible, on the other hand, was his blueprint of the past. He had altered it, as well, but he had used bold red ink to make the changes. He caressed the leather as he opened the cover to the Book of Genesis. The pages were worn, the corners bent, and he went easily to the 49th chapter. He looked at the words of Moses and grinned. The iconic prophet was telling the story of Jacob and his twelve sons; the boys who became men and then colonized the world with Jacob's seed.

He had written beside the scripture using the red ink, noting the moments when history and the present day collided. *Jacob's sons ... my sons ... in the very same order, by the very same God.*

Five years ago, almost to the day, Morningstar had been given a challenge ... an ordinance by God. And the Big Man had delivered it personally. It had been Morningstar's fiftieth birthday, a cold November night in 1999, and he had been standing at the window of a shabby hotel room on 13th and Girard, where he had spent nearly every Monday night for the past decade. He was celebrating. His boss of twenty-seven years, General Alexander Daniels, had just been appointed to the Joint Chiefs, which meant that Morningstar had been promoted along with him. He had gone to the Breezeway Inn to celebrate. He had just finished a bump of cocaine, when, from nowhere, he heard a voice. He had ignored it at first, ascribing it to the effects of the cocaine, but then, the more he listened, the more he knew ... God was speaking to him. *"I've been waiting for you, Edward, for quite some time. I needed you to be ready ... to be well positioned for what I have planned. You are finally there."* The voice had become louder, almost bellicose, as God had added, *"You will become Jacob. And, like Jacob of old, you will find twelve sons. With their help, you will reshape this world ... and compel the nations to comply with my wishes."*

And he had done it ... the first part, anyway. Starting in January of the following year, Morningstar had taken the steps necessary to find the twelve sons.

He looked down at the Bible and grinned. He was staring at the first name, *Abid Mensa,* written in red next to the scripted words. Beside Abid's name, and also written in red, was *Reuben, January 2000.* Morningstar had found Abid in West Africa, on a fact-finding mission for General Daniels. A destitute fisherman, Abid was ideally suited for what was about to take place. *I'll need you soon, son.*

He looked at the next entry written in red, *James Roberts, Simeon, February 2000.* A mercenary from the first Gulf War, Simeon had brought a considerable amount of color to the family with his tendency for cross-dressing and late-night carousing. But no one was more loyal, or better with a disguise. Simeon had become his right-hand-man.

The third entry, *Clint Molinaro, Levi, March 2000* had been added soon after the first two. Morningstar had been thrilled to find someone not only gifted with a rifle, but so remarkably well-connected. Molinaro had worked as a driver for Martin Henderson, the man the world now knew as Phoenix, just before Henderson was altered forever by a hotel blast in May of 2000. Though Morningstar wasn't yet sure how to take advantage of that bond, he felt certain an opportunity would present itself soon.

He looked at the next five entries and nodded approvingly.

Judah, April 2000

Dan, May, 2000
Naphtali, June 2000
Gad, July, 2000
Asher, August 2000

It had been The Year of the Sons, and, up to that point, those sons had served him well. His first disappointment had come with the next entry: *Curt Simpson, Issachar, September 2000*. The name had been crossed through. Morningstar had been forced to eliminate Issachar soon after 'adopting' him. The man had been a coward, failing at his mission, and then running from a bar fight in his hometown of Cleveland, Ohio. It had been intolerable. A son of Jacob needed to show valor and strength ... at all times. Morningstar sneered. *Adopted in September ... dead by Christmas*. He had yet to replace him.

The next entry, *Vladimir Karev,* was written in the same red ink, followed by *Zebulun, October 2000*. Morningstar smiled. Of all of his sons, Zebulun was the one who needed him – and therefore trusted him – the most. The young Russian had been betrayed not only by his father's weakness, but by the arrogance of his country. Morningstar had readied him for a vital role ... a sacrificial role ... and he felt confident the loyal son would do whatever was asked of him.

He looked down at the last entry and sighed. He hadn't written a man's name; the eleventh son's identity was too sensitive to even put in the Book. The man had three titles by which he was recognized. He was Martin Henderson to those who had known him before May of 2000; he was the Phoenix to those who knew him now, and, finally, he was a son of Jacob to God's ordained king, Edward Morningstar.

Joseph, November 2000

Conceived in May in a hotel fire, nurtured for months under Morningstar's watchful eye, and then released to the world three years ago, he had made his mark as a top-notch assassin. Not one of the other sons had even come close. Prestigious and wealthy prior to his transformation, Henderson had been his greatest acquisition. And, like the Biblical Joseph, he was the best of the sons, " ... *the prince among his brothers.*" It was his phone call he was waiting on. *Where are you, Joseph?*

There were no further entries; he had yet to find Benjamin. For whatever reason, God had told him to wait. *"It is not time for your final son to be chosen."*

Morningstar closed the Bible, and then carried it to the closet. He placed it in a safe at the back, careful to lock it when he was done. The truth was in that book ... not only God's truth, but Morningstar's ... his truth, his sons, and all that had happened up to that point.

He walked to the window. It was getting late and he was becoming impatient. *Why haven't you called, Joseph?* Had something gone wrong? The assassin had never been late with a call. He looked out at the stars as they filled the night sky. They reminded him of Ferris wheels, cotton candy, and the Laredo County Fair, 1960. He licked his lips, the taste of sugar lingering; the stickiness clinging to his face and hands. He raised the window, ignoring the cold as a stiff breeze blew back his hair. The call would come soon ... it always did. Henderson had never let him down. And the hit on Al-Gharsi was only the beginning. What was hidden in Morningstar's Bible was a blueprint ... a story of Revelation ... *his* revelation ... his pathway to a future kingdom on earth. *And it all begins tonight ... with you, dear Joseph ... and the destruction of the Middle East.*

Chapter 3

NEW YORK CITY ... WASHINGTON, D.C.

11/29/03

"My darling Maddi ... I'm sorry. As the stink of this city devours me, I mourn. Not just for the lives I took tonight, but for all the lives I've taken ... and the loss of virtue on every count. I know now that it was your friend I killed, and it's unforgiveable. You'll learn of it someday and I beg you, don't hate me. Though you should, it would be unbearable ... to live, to die knowing you despise me. I'll do what I can to turn this around ... to make right what went so wrong. But, in the end, there's no changing what I've done; there's no going back ... who I am is irrevocable."

Henderson laid down his pen and pushed the journal aside. He ran his hands through his hair as he checked a clock on the wall. *Eleven-thirty.* He was amazed he could write so soon after the hit on Al-Gharsi. But he had to; he had to tell Maddi how he felt.

It was often that way. Late at night when he hurt the most, he would sit down, write to her, and pretend she was there ... sitting next to him, listening as he confessed his sins. *So many sins.*

He was supposed to call Morningstar, but he couldn't bring himself to do it. Why? He wasn't sure. Something had changed. *He* had changed. He needed to do it soon, however, or Morningstar would follow through on the threat he had held over Henderson's head since the beginning..."*You do what I say or I'll kill her.*"

He slid from the bed in the Bronx hotel room and

stretched his thick arms in the air. They hit against the blades of a dirty ceiling fan, and he pulled them to his chest. He rubbed them, ignoring the scars on his left forearm. He walked to the window and opened it, welcoming the cold air on his face. He breathed in the soot of downtown and sighed. He should have left New York by now. He knew better than to linger in the city where he had just carried out a hit. But, for whatever reason, he couldn't leave. Was it because Maddi was there ... staying in a downtown hotel?

He coughed and stepped back from the window, putting a hand to his chest to brace for the pain from ribs that had been cracked too many times. He hated New York in the winter ... then again, he hated about everywhere anymore. The mountains in Utah, the ocean along Cape Cod; he hated every bit of it. It was all part of a happy past ... a history he could barely remember, a life he would never have again.

He closed the window and walked to the bed. *Just call him ... buy yourself some time.* He rubbed his eyes, angry as his fingers brushed over his misshapen jaw. It had been crushed by a piece of plaster. Though it had been nearly four years ago, it felt as if it had happened yesterday; as if the heat was still smothering him and the flames were about to burn him alive.

His stomach growled and he grabbed his belly. He couldn't eat ... but not because of his scarred throat or disfigured mouth. He had overcome those wounds years ago ... at least to the point where he could swallow food and drink water without choking. He couldn't eat because he was ashamed. *Call him.*

He hung his misshapen legs over the side of the bed and rubbed his thighs. He was still wearing the running tights from the hit on Al-Gharsi, and his scarred hands caught on the neoprene. He refused to take them off; they were a symbol ... a marker of the moment only hours ago when he had finally seen what he had become.

He needed to get away ... not only from the hotel, not even from New York ... he had to get away from himself. *I can't do this anymore.* That was what he had decided in those lonely hours in the Bronx hotel room. Regardless of the consequences, it was time for him to leave Morningstar.

But not until I know that Lili is safe. He walked to the window and once again stared down at the alley. He imagined her ... reading her books, writing her poetry *... or playing in the garden beneath my bedroom window.* Over the last several months, he had begun work on a plan to keep her safe. He wasn't sure why he hadn't done it sooner ... maybe because it had seemed hopeless; she was so far away. Or maybe he was afraid. Of Morningstar? No. Of himself. Of what he would do to Morningstar – and then to himself – once she was safe. *Regardless, the time has come.*

He walked to the sink and splashed water on his face. He stared in the mirror, bothered by what was looking back. *You'd think I'd get used to it,* he thought as he rubbed a towel over his face. But the scars and crushed jaw had only been the beginning; nothing about him was the same. The damage inside was even greater, and it showed in the mirror like a spotlight on his soul. He had allowed a tyrant to change him and, though he tried to blame it on fate or bad luck, he had had a choice. In that moment when he had been asked to show courage, he had failed.

Or had he? The choice he had been given was impossible. The safety of a little girl thousands of miles away relied solely on his compliance. And the man who had asked it – no, who had *demanded* it – had come to him as a friend. Edward Morningstar had saved him from the fire, only to send him to a different sort of hell.

"You do what I say or I'll kill her." And there had been nothing he could do; Morningstar's reach was endless. *But it stops here ... it stops today.*

~ ~ ~

"Have you found him, Simeon?"

"Not yet, sir. I have Naphtali looking for him in New York City."

Morningstar frowned. "What if he's already back in D.C?"

Simeon shook his head. "I doubt he would have had time, Father."

Morningstar nodded. It was true. The trip from New York took at least three hours. *So, why hasn't he called me?* Morningstar sighed as he combed his fingers through his well-styled hair and tugged at the lapel of his Caraceni suit. He had just arrived at the warehouse north of town, the secret location where he met up with his sons. He bristled as he paced back and forth, his limp – a relic from childhood – more pronounced the angrier he became. "No one does this to Jacob! Did you have Naphtali check the hotels near the restaurant?"

Simeon nodded, his thin features almost skeletal. "Yes sir ... I even had him check some of the homeless shelters in Queens. Joseph's not at any of them."

Morningstar was seething. It had been two days since he had spoken to Henderson ... two days since his best assassin had agreed to the Al-Gharsi hit. And tonight, he had completed it ... flawlessly. The murder of Al-Gharsi was being blamed on the Omani leader, and the reaction by Yemen fighters had been fierce. It wouldn't be long before the other Arab nations would take a side, and the whole Middle East would blow up like a powder keg.

Al-Gharsi's assassination was Henderson's fourteenth since becoming the Phoenix three years ago, and always he would finish with a phone call saying "It's done." But not tonight. *Where are you, Henderson?*

Morningstar waved a hand in the air; a silent order for Simeon to leave. The man ran out of the warehouse, leaving Morningstar alone to consider his options. As the door closed behind him, a rush of air doused the only light, a candle sitting in the middle of an old oak desk.

Morningstar walked to the desk. He was about to re-light the candle when he stopped. The moonlight through the window was enough. He hung his head. What if Henderson had decided to leave? *He wouldn't ... he wouldn't risk Lili's life.* But what if he had? What if he had decided that Lili's life was no longer worth what was being asked of him? Would Morningstar be able to handle it? *Of course I would!* But it incensed him to think that the man he had saved had had the nerve to leave him.

Then again ... it's only been a few hours since the hit. Henderson might have gotten into a jam. He might have been unable to get to a phone. Any number of things could have happened. *At least he completed the hit.* Morningstar raised a triumphant fist, but it was an empty gesture. Henderson was gone ... he could feel it.

He rubbed his neck as he stared down at two pieces of paper. He had saved them, knowing someday he might need to use them. They had been his power over the man he called Phoenix. Pieces of his history, secrets from his past ... and a threat against a special little girl, which had turned the sainted Martin into a sinner.

He walked to the only window, staring out at the moonlight as it shone on a patch of overgrown brush. He would wait a bit longer. He watched the brown grass sway with the wind, and he could feel his throat tighten. In all their time together, Henderson had never missed a call.

"It doesn't matter," he said aloud. "Al-Gharsi's dead; the hit was a success." But the absence of the phone call was a sign. Either Henderson had betrayed him, or he was about to. Morningstar bristled. *No one betrays me ... and gets away with it!*

~ ~ ~

Henderson had returned to the window. He shivered as he stared up at the moonlight. The heartless cold of the New York winter seemed fitting. It sent chills through his aching body, and the scanty hotel heat had done little to take it away.

He grabbed a sweatshirt hanging over the back of a chair. He had picked it up at a thrift store, along with a pair of sweats, a couple of scarves, and a backpack. He put on the sweatshirt and sweats, and pulled his cap over his head. He had calls to make. Deliberations were over; he knew what he needed to do.

But he couldn't use the phone in his room; someone might be listening. He walked out the door and down the stairs, the cap pulled low, one of the scarves wrapped around his neck and face. He walked outside, a sudden torrent of prickly sleet underscoring what he was about to do. He went to a phone booth less than a block away, dropped in coins, and, with shaking hands, dialed the number he had put off calling for the past three hours.

Morningstar answered after only one ring. "Yes?"

Henderson could barely say the words. "It's ... done."

He heard a pause. "What took you so long to—?"

Henderson hung up. His hands were still shaking; he felt like he was going to be sick. He had done it; he had called Morningstar. But, in spite of it, he knew ... *I still need to move Lili ... and soon.*

He checked his watch. *Midnight in the U.S. ...*

seven a.m. in Latvia. He put in more coins and dialed a number he knew well. An operator came on the line. "Your overseas call must be made collect."

Henderson cursed. "Just tell whoever answers that I'm a friend of Mart's." He could hear the beeps and buzzes of the overseas connection and he waited, praying Danil would accept the call. Soon he heard the voice of his old friend. "Hello?"

Henderson nearly wept.

The operator said, "Yes, I have a collect call from a gentleman who says he is a friend of Mart's. Will you accept the charges?"

There was a pause. Henderson held his breath. *Please Danil ... say yes!* Finally, the sleepy voice said, "Yes, okay."

The operator said, "You have three minutes, sir."

Henderson hated to talk; he hated the sound of his voice. It reminded him of tires on gravel, and it took all his energy to say more than a few words at a time. He closed his eyes, took a breath, and said, "Danil, my name is ... Jerry ... and I'm calling on behalf of Martin Henderson."

Cold, almost angry, the voice said, "It's seven in the morning ... and Martin Henderson is dead."

"Yes, I know; I'm sorry. But Mart and I were close. I spoke to him before he died. He told me about Lili."

A pause. "So why have you waited nearly four years to call?"

Good question. "I have received important information."

"Go on."

"Lili is in danger. I can't say more, but I'm prepared to help you keep her safe."

"How is she in danger?"

"There's a man in America who has vowed to kidnap her. I'm guessing it has something to do with

19

her unique ... abilities. Regardless, I know he's capable of it. You need to move her to somewhere safe and you need to do it now."

Another pause. "This is crazy. How do I know you're a friend of Mart's?"

Another good question. "What if I was to tell you something only you and Martin shared?"

"Go on."

"I know that on the day Albins was killed, you agreed to not tell Lili about her father's death. Mart insisted you wait until he was flying her to America."

Another pause. "Who did you say you were?"

"My name is Jerry."

"Jerry who?"

"I'm sorry, I can't say."

Again, a pause. "So, what do you have in mind ... *Jerry?*"

Henderson was getting tired. It hurt to talk; it took all he had to keep the words coming. "I've arranged for a trust to be established in her name. It will provide for her for the rest of her life, and it will also provide for you and your sister, Anna."

"How do you know of Anna?"

"As I said, Mart and I were close. Anyway, the money is available through the Uzava bank that sits on the corner of Lenik and Petrovsky in the south end of town."

"I know of it."

"Good. You are to ask for Alise, and the only thing you'll need is valid ID and the following account number. Do you have a pen and paper?"

Henderson heard him rummage through a drawer. "I'm ready."

Henderson rattled off a series of numbers.

"That's it? A pot of money? How do I keep Lili safe with nothing more than money?"

"I have also arranged for you to move."

There was a pause. "Move? I don't want to move."

"I know, but you must. And you have to leave soon; within the hour. There's a place outside Riga. It has a secured entrance, as well as a team of soldiers prepared to watch over the three of you twenty-four hours a day. This will be your new home." He heard a sigh. He understood. Danil had lived in Ventspils his entire life. "I know this isn't what you want. But you must believe me; Lili's life depends on it."

The operator interrupted. "Your three minutes is up, sir. Would you like three more?"

Danil yelled, "Yes!" There was a pause. "Jerry, I'll need an address ... for the new house."

Henderson gave him the address. "It's a few miles south of Riga."

"Is there a way for me to reach you ... if I have any more questions?"

"I'll give you my email address. The only thing I ask is that you make any message you send as vague as possible."

"You say you are doing all of this because of Mart?"

"Yes, it's the least I can do. He was a good friend to me when he was alive."

Henderson heard a break in the man's voice as he said, "He was a good friend to many, I think."

Henderson pulled away the receiver. He couldn't let Danil hear him as he choked back tears. He managed to say, "Here it is." He gave him the email address and then hung up before Danil could ask anything more. He stood in the booth, one hand on the receiver, the other on the cord that connected him to his past. His eyes burned. Slowly, with his fingers still gripping the cord, he hung up the phone.

~ ~ ~

Morningstar stared out the window as he rubbed

the back of his neck. Something was wrong. Yes, Henderson had finally called, but he had sounded different ... hesitant ... maybe even a bit unsure. *And the bastard had the nerve to hang up on me!* He walked to the desk and relit the candle. He needed to do something ... something to make Henderson more certain of his role, and remind him who was in charge. *He must know that I own him ... no matter what.*

He stared down at the two documents on the desk. The one on top was a summary of a Henderson family secret. He shoved it aside. *I'll wait on that one ... the implications would ruin the man I hope to save.* He looked at the next one, grinning as he read about the nine-year-old girl from Latvia, Lilija Platacis. The paper listed not only her name and address, but her unique qualities ... attributes that would make her remarkably useful. He chuckled. Perhaps there was something he could do. A move he could make that would not sever ties completely, but would underscore his hold over Phoenix ... *and give me something in return.*

He pulled out his phone and dialed, drumming his fingers on the desk as he waited. After the sixth ring, a crisp Asian voice said, "Yes?"

"It's me."

"Hello, sir."

"Take her."

"Now sir?"

"Yes, now."

"Is she still in Latvia ... outside Ventspils?"

"Yes. Where she's been for the last three-and-a-half years." *Dumbass.*

"I have men nearby."

"Good. Do it." Morningstar hung up. He grabbed the two documents, walked to a rusted cabinet in the corner of the room, and opened it. He pulled out a lock

22

box and, using a key from his key ring, he opened the lid. The box was full of papers and various keepsakes. He folded the documents and laid them aside. He rifled through the contents until he found a gold Rolex watch. He pulled it out exultantly as he ran his fingers over etched writing. *"To Martin, from Mom and Dad."* He grinned. *Perhaps now you'll think twice about putting me off, Phoenix ... son of mine.*

~~~

Henderson finally let go of the cord, struggling to breath as he left the booth and stole back to his hotel. He prayed that Danil would follow his instructions. He went to his room and pulled his computer from his backpack. He turned it on, went to his email account, and typed a message: "Juris, it's time. I need to know the Riga estate is ready." He sighed as he remembered the conversation with the man he had contacted three months ago. *Juris ... Juris Poliks ...*

"So, what's your name?" the man asked over the phone.

"I'd rather not say." Henderson was doing his best to use a normal voice.

"Okay. Why do you think I can help you?"

"Because I know what you do ... for the Latvian cause. Besides, you haven't got a clue who I am, yet you've taken my call."

He heard a sigh. "What do you need?"

"A safe house ... for a dear friend and his family."

"Where?"

"Near Riga."

"How soon?"

"As soon as you can."

There was a pause. "Will it need to be protected?"

"Yes ... around the clock."

Another pause. "That will take money."

"I have money ... a lot of it..."

And that had been the end of it. Juris had come through. He had put together a safe house for Danil, Anna, and Lili. In return, Henderson had placed a large amount of cash in a bank at the edge of town. The money, received over the last three years as "operating expenses" from his boss, Morningstar, had finally come in handy.

Henderson frowned as he stared at the computer. He had been preparing for months for a way to keep Lili safe, but had not expected to need to move on it so soon. Then again, he had not expected to assassinate one of Maddi's friends.

He stood and paced the room, running a hand through his hair as he fought the urge to punch the wall. He walked to the bed and fell on top of it, exhausted.

He heard a beep; Juris had replied. "Everything is in order. We will be ready for them."

Henderson shoved the computer to the side and lay back on the bed. It was done; Lili would soon be safe. Never had he felt so tired. But he knew he wouldn't sleep. Whenever he closed his eyes, he saw Maddi and the shock on her face as she stared at Al-Gharsi facedown on the tablecloth. *Sleep Henderson ... you need to sleep.* He tried again and the pictures kept coming; images of Maddi, followed by snapshots of Lili playing in the garden beneath his bedroom window. His friend, Albins, was standing beside him, foretelling his death on the battlefield. Then he saw his parents; his remarkable parents who had probably not slept well since the hotel explosion. How many times had he wanted to call them and tell them he was alive? But he couldn't; he couldn't tell anyone. To tell them was to let them know what he had become. *And to say it aloud is to confirm the truth ... yes, I'm alive, but Martin Henderson is dead.*

Chapter 4

VETSPILS, LATVIA ... NEW YORK CITY

Sunday, November 30th, 2003

"But I don't want to leave. It's so early in the morning, Uncle Dan."

Short, stocky Danil Latkovskis shook his almost-bald head and said sternly, "We must, Lili, and we need to go soon. We are going to a new home outside Riga."

"But I've lived in Ventspils all my life!"

"As have I, Lili. But I'm sure we will like it." He paused. "It's in the country. There will be so many places for you to play."

Her nine-year-old eyes lit up. "Like Uncle Mart's house?"

He grinned, sadly. "Yes, like Uncle Mart's."

Lili jumped out of bed and stepped onto the cold floor. It was winter and it was cold. "Negative one Celsius," she announced, as she looked at a homemade thermometer she had built from scratch only days before. "Is it snowing, Uncle Dan?"

"Yes. We must hurry before the storm worsens. Pack a bag and we'll go."

She found her slippers and shuffled to the closet, excited about the trip. Lili liked to travel. Though she knew of the world from the many books she read, it was much better to actually see it. Danil was still standing in the doorway. With wide eyes, she said, "Is our new house big, like the Neuschwanstein Castle outside Munich, Uncle Dan?"

His eyes softened. "I'm not sure." He looked away and said, much quieter, "I've not seen our new home, Lili."

She frowned. Danil would never take them to a strange place and call it home ... unless something was wrong. "I see," she said knowingly.

He looked at her and tried to smile, but his brown eyes were filled with worry and they gave him away. She had seen those eyes before. After her father's death, after Uncle Mart's disappearance; whenever there was something bad, she would see that same look; those same dark eyes that would change from kindness to concern in a flash. He said weakly, "It's going to be fine, Lili."

That confirmed it: the move was not a good one. Danil walked away before she could ask more questions. She pulled a bag from the closet and filled it with clothes. She was about to zip it when she stopped. The feeling was back. Not really a feeling ... *a sense of foreboding*. That was what her mother had called it when Lili had shared it with her. *"Mama, I feel like I know what is going to happen before it does."* Her mother, Larisa, had looked at her sadly. *"I'm sorry, Lili ... I share that gift, as well."* Lili had frowned. *"Why call it a gift if it saddens you?"* Larisa had shaken her head. *"Because not all gifts are good, my dear."* That was all she had said, but now Lili knew what she meant. To know, or to even guess the future often predicted pain, and – just as she had known when her mother would die and when her father would be killed in battle – she now knew ... *something is about to happen to me.*

She turned from the window, shuddering as she zipped the suitcase and carried it to the bathroom to pack her toothbrush and comb. She ran the comb through her hair, staring at her eyes in the mirror. *"As blue as the Baltic Sea,"* her father used to tell her. But she knew that blue eyes weren't really blue; she had read it in her science book...

"There is no blue pigmentation either in the iris or the ocular fluid ... blue eyes are nothing more than a genetic mutation ... likely from a single individual that lived near the Black Sea over 6,000 years ago..."

She had been fascinated by the thought that she might have ancestors from so far away. She had asked her parents to take her to Romania so she could explore their lineage, and they had promised her they would. They had not had the chance. She was transfixed as she stared at her eyes, remembering the day she had asked her father, Albins, about the fact that they were not really pigmented. He had simply chuckled. *"I don't know about those things, honey. You will have to ask your mother."* And, of course Larissa had known; she was smart like Lili. They were *"extra-special smart"* Larisa used to tell her. Suddenly Lili's genetically-mutated eyes filled with tears. She missed her mother and father. Though they had both died years ago, she remembered them as if she had seen them yesterday ... the way Albin's eyes crinkled when he told her stories at night, or how his soothing voice would lull her to sleep. Her mother's face; the wrinkles that had begun to appear around her eyes ... the smell of her hair, and the way her mouth turned up when she was thinking hard about something. Even the sound of her laugh. Yes, Lili remembered every detail because that is what she did; she recalled every gesture, every word, every line on every page she had ever read. And, though it, too, was considered a gift, sometimes it felt more like a curse. For though she had lived only nine years, in that time there had been things she wished she could forget. Like the day her mother died and she had been forbidden from hugging her goodbye. *"It will be too much for you, Lili."* Or the day Albins had been killed in battle, and neither Uncle Mart nor Danil had let her know. But she had watched them bury him; through a hole in a barricade of rocks nearby, she had seen her father lain to rest. She recalled the smell of the dirt as it was piled high over his grave, and the mist in the air as Uncle Mart said kind words, his own voice breaking at the end. She would give anything to not recall those moments, or the feelings and smells associated with them. But she remembered every last bit of it, even down to the roughness of the rock she had been sitting on ... and the agony she had felt when she realized her parents were gone. She was forced to relive it, over and over again. *Don't think about it,* she often told herself. But it wasn't an option; she had to think about it. It had become a part of her. The future and the past; Lili suffered all of it with absolute clarity ... and absolute pain.

She wiped her eyes and sighed. She was about to brush her teeth, when she stopped. Something was wrong. She stared in the mirror, stunned to see that the images behind her had changed. Instead of a flowered shower curtain and the blue painted wall of her bathroom, she saw a row of shower stalls. The walls were gray cement and the room smelled like anesthetic. She closed her eyes and waited, knowing the image would disappear if she kept them closed long enough. After a full minute, she opened them, glad to see the familiar bathroom with the blue walls. She brushed her teeth, her hand shaking as she held her eyes open to stave off the vision. *"Not all gifts are good, my dear."*

She rinsed her mouth and threw the toothbrush and comb in her bag. She returned to her room and changed into pants and a sweater. She pulled on a pair of boots and shoved her pajamas into the bag, which she tossed over her shoulder as she walked to the kitchen. She smiled as if nothing had happened ... as if she hadn't seen another vision ... as if she hadn't figured out a thing. "I'm ready, Uncle Dan," she said as she set her bag on the floor. She looked at Anna, Danil's sister. The woman's back was to her, her eyes fixed on the counter, where she was quickly packing sandwiches into a bag. Lili loved Anna; the woman had been the closest thing she had had to a mother in over three years. "Good morning, Aunt Anna."

Anna tossed her long brown hair over broad shoulders as she turned and gave a weak grin. "Good morning, Lili. Are you ready to go?"

"Yes, I am. And I'm hungry!" Lili smiled; she knew that's what Danil and Anna needed. It would bother them to think she had sensed the uneasiness in the room, or the ominous nature of their trip. She skipped to the table, pulled out her chair, and sat beside Danil. He was frowning, though he wasn't even aware. She looked at him and, with the hint of a grin, she said, "So will I have to feed the cats at our new house?"

He patted her shoulder and smiled. "Yes, I'm afraid so. All four of them."

"It's okay. I can handle it. After all, I'm best at it, don't you think?"

He chuckled. "Absolutely."

Anna offered her a Kaiser roll with butter and jam, and a glass of juice.

Lili frowned. Where were the eggs and bacon ... the hot breakfast that had been a part of every morning since they had taken her in? There was no doubt about it; something was wrong.

Danil said, "Eat quickly, my child. We need to go."

She couldn't eat the roll, and was only able to drink half the juice. She was about to take the cup to the sink, when Danil said, "Don't bother with it, Lili. We need to go."

She frowned. Not only were they in a hurry, it was likely they weren't coming back. She would never again smell the lilac bushes in the backyard, or feel the breeze from the Baltic as it greeted her like a best friend's smile. Though everyone she loved – including the cats – would be going with her, she was about to say goodbye to the only world she had ever known ... the world where her parents had lived and died; the world where she had learned the difficult lessons of life. *And if that's the case, I need to get my picture and my book.* She looked at Danil, fighting a sudden urge to cry. "Is there time for me to grab a few more of my things, Uncle Dan?"

He frowned. "Quickly, Lili. We'll be out in the car."

She ran back to her room and stared at a framed picture on the table by the bed. It had been taken outside their home in Ventspils when she was barely four. She was sitting between her parents. All three of them were laughing. The Baltic was visible behind them, the sun reflecting from the waves, casting a soft blue tint to the entire photograph. With tears in her eyes, she picked up the photo, saying softly, "We're going away." She then raised the mattress and was about to grab her journal, when she heard a noise. She looked up but saw nothing, laughing at herself as she heard the wind whistle through the trees outside the window. She reached under the mattress, comforted as her fingers brushed against the leather-bound book, which had been given to her by Uncle Dan. She grabbed it just as a thick arm wrapped around her, and an oversized hand covered her face. She tried to scream, but the hand was covering her mouth. She could taste the man's sweat. She hugged the picture and the journal to her chest, hoping to hide them. She went to kick whoever was holding her; he had pinned her legs against his body, and she tried to pull away, but he was so strong ... she could barely move beneath his grip. She was scared for Danil and Anna. What had happened to them? Why weren't they coming to help her?

She was being carried, but her eyes were covered so she couldn't see where. She felt cold air; she was outside. Heavy drops of snow were falling on her cheeks and hands. She felt the prickles of pine needles from a grove at the edge of the farm, and her heart sank; she was being taken away. All at once she heard whispers; Shenyang Mandarin from what she could tell, and they were arguing over where to take her. She felt another pair of arms grab her legs. There was a brief flash of light as her captor removed his hand from her face, but, before she could adjust her eyes, a thick piece of cloth was pulled over the top half of her head. She tried to scream, but the hand was still covering her mouth. She could barely breathe. She kicked as hard as she could, but her legs wouldn't move. The last thing she remembered was pain as a heavy fist pounded her on the cheek. She went limp as she fell against a cold, hard surface, thinking, *Please, don't hurt Uncle Dan or Aunt Anna.*

~ ~ ~

Henderson awoke with a start. He checked the clock by the bed. It was nearly two a.m. He pulled his computer close and saw that a new message had come through only seconds ago. No sender was listed. He opened the message.

"She is gone. Lili has been taken."

Henderson closed his laptop and slid it in his pack. He walked to the bathroom and grabbed his toothbrush. He picked up the pants and sweatshirt from a table by the bed and shoved them in the bag. He pulled on his jacket, his hat, his scarf, and then checked the room to be sure he had left nothing behind. He threw his pack over his shoulder and ran out the door

31

and down the street to the same phone booth he had used earlier that night. He pulled coins from his pocket and dropped them in the slot, his rapid breaths clouding the dirty glass. He dialed the number he had hoped never to call again. After two rings, he heard a terse, "Who is this?"

"You took her."

There was a pause. "Well, well now. Hello, Joseph."

"You took her, dammit!"

"I took who?"

"Lili."

Another pause. "What are you talking about?"

"She's gone, Morningstar. I know you took her."

"Why would I do that?"

"Because you're insane." Henderson heard a soft chuckle and he wanted to jump through the phone and strangle the man.

"Again, why would I do that; she's my insurance policy."

"It wasn't enough for you to stalk her in Latvia; you needed to have her ... to hold her over my head."

"My dear Phoenix; as much as I wish it were true, I have done no such thing. If Lili is missing, it is no fault of mine. However, it does change things a bit, now doesn't it?"

Henderson frowned. "What do you mean?"

"You need my help to find her. You certainly can't do it on your own, now, can you? After all, look at you."

Henderson bristled as he put a hand to his battered jaw. "I don't need you. I have never needed you." He paused, trying to catch his breath. "If you touch a single hair on her head, Morningstar, I will hurt you so badly you will beg for death."

"Now, now; don't get all excited."

Henderson knew he had to hurry; Morningstar was likely tracing the call. "I'm leaving. Don't come looking for me; you'll never find me."

"You can't leave. We have a deal."

"No, what we had were your threats."

"And they're still in effect."

"Lili's gone. You can't threaten me with her anymore now, can you?"

There was a sigh. "You're a fool, Phoenix. She's gone, but she's not dead ... yet."

Henderson screamed into the phone, "Don't you touch her!"

"Now, now, my son."

"I'm not your son!" Henderson hung up the phone and threw his pack over his shoulder. He walked down the street and away from the phone booth, the hotel, and the last three-and-a-half years of his life. He reached the corner, crossed the street, and flagged down a cab.

"Where to?"

"The bus station."

The cabby nodded and Henderson leaned against the seat. What now? He had left Morningstar and Lili was missing. Did Morningstar take her, or was he only bluffing? *There's only one way to find out.* He leaned forward. "Tell you what; take me to the shipping docks instead."

Chapter 5

HENDERSON ESTATE, UZAVA, LATVIA

Three Weeks Later, Wednesday, December 24th, 2003

Henderson could hear them. He could hear the staff and his parents singing carols inside the manor and it brought tears to his eyes. He tried to put himself there ... to place himself between his mother and father as they sat on the blue loveseat in the drawing room, while Emek and the guards stood on one side and Ina and the charwomen stood on the other, near the tall fir cut from the forest bordering the Baltic Sea. With lights, a star, and bulbs saved through the ages, he imagined the tree looking on as the carolers toasted one another, their stations forgotten as they shared a moment of Christmas cheer. Though it would normally be Anna Latkovskis playing the piano, Henderson knew, tonight she wasn't there. She and Danil hadn't come this year; their devastation over Lili's kidnapping had crippled them both. Henderson knew it because he had seen them only hours before. Through high-powered binoculars, he had watched them in their home outside Ventspils as they ate quietly, alone, not a word said between them. There was nothing to say; Lili was gone. Though Danil and his friends had searched everywhere, they had found no trace of her.

Neither had Henderson. He had left New York on Sunday, November 30th, and had crossed the ocean holed up in the bilge of a shipping liner. He had arrived in Spain four days later, and, from there, he had smuggled his way north in the back of a pickup truck carrying fresh fruit to Eastern Europe. The truck had taken him as far as Klaipeda, Lithuania, and he had then hitched a ride to Ventspils. It was there, where Lili had been taken, that he had begun his investigation, and he had spent the last two weeks scouring every part of Latvia, Lithuania, and Estonia looking for any trace of the little girl he had vowed to look after. But he had been hindered by his appearance. Though he had hidden most of his scars with a low-riding cap, a scarf, and a pair of sunglasses, he had seen the disgust in the eyes of those he was asking for help. The cash he had offered was no match for their revulsion. He had gotten nowhere.

A loud chorus of "Deck the Halls," forced him to train the binoculars on the large bay window that covered the east wall of the drawing room. He watched as his mother and father raised their glasses. How he longed to rush through the doors and hug them ... forget everything – the killing and the lies – and slip into the magic of a Christmas celebration. But he couldn't; it was best they never learn what he had become. He stared through the lens, refusing to look away, though his heart was breaking. Everyone was lost to him. His parents – only yards away – were gone. Lili had been taken and was nowhere to be found. The woman he loved was in D.C. and – even if he were sitting beside her – she, too, would be gone. But they hadn't left him ... he had left them ... the first time he pulled the trigger for Edward Morningstar.

He bristled. He would make it right. He would somehow find a way to do what he should have done years ago.

He stared at the mansion in the distance. He wanted to stay in Latvia, and keep up the hunt for Lili. It was his fault she was missing; he should be the one to find her. But he couldn't stay. He had duties to take care of ... debts to pay. So, he had made plans for someone else to take over. Juris Poliks, the man who had helped him secure the Riga safe house, had told him of a private investigator, Dain Rozenblats, who lived in nearby Uzava. Juris had assured him that Rozenblats was not only trustworthy, but was also alone. *"He has no one an enemy can use against him."*

Henderson had contacted the man and they had met at a rest stop early that morning. Henderson had towered over the short, stocky Rozenblats, but there was no question the guy was tough. His dark eyes were seasoned with insight, and his square jaw and graying hair revealed wisdom aged over time, like the fine wines in the Henderson cellar. Henderson had handed him an envelope filled with cash, and had said, *"Spare no expense, Mr. Rozenblats."*

"Thank you, sir. How shall I reach you to let you know what I find?"

Henderson had pulled a cellphone from his pocket. *"Take this. I'll call from a phone booth every day at six a.m. your time."*

Rozenblats had nodded and had stuffed the phone in his pocket, along with the cash. *"I'll find her, sir."*

Henderson stared at the carolers through the bay window and sighed. *Find her, Dain.* He looked up, spotting the Northern Star as it shone brightly over the Latvian estate where he had spent much of his childhood. He whispered, "...and on earth peace, good will toward men." All at once he grabbed his backpack, unzipped it, and rummaged past the pistol, the clothes, and the computer, until he found what he was looking for; the plain black journal with no title. He pulled it out along with a pen, and, using only the light from the North Star, he wrote,

Merry Christmas, Maddi. I love you.

Chapter 6
WASHINGTON, D.C.

12/24/03

"There is a tide in the affairs of men, which, taken at the flood, leads on to fortune. On such a full sea are we now afloat. And we must take the current when it serves ... or lose our ventures."
~ William Shakespeare ~

Morningstar laid down his copy of Julius Caesar and paced the floor of the abandoned warehouse outside D.C. The book was old and worn; he had carried it with him for the past four years. Though it was dark in the warehouse, he had memorized the words, and needed only the moonlight to read the parts that mattered. It had served as a blueprint ... a guide to how a ruler leads a kingdom. *Except for the part about getting murdered by his friends.*

It was suitable reading for this challenging Christmas Eve. It calmed him ... reassured him that he was on the right path. He was feeling edgy ... like a cat in a dark alley. It had been over a month since he had talked to Henderson. And that conversation had not gone well. Henderson had been angry. Morningstar's kidnapping of the little girl had gotten his attention. But, in spite of it, he had wanted out. Morningstar felt confident that it would be only a matter of time before he would come crawling back, if for no other reason than to make sure the girl stayed safe. It was what he had done for the past three years. *But never has he taken it so far.*

So, what had changed? What had made his son, his Joseph, suddenly defy him? The very thought of it unnerved him. He continued to pace. *It is merely a matter of waiting*. But was it? He had already waited nearly four weeks. Would Henderson come back? Or had he left forever ... like Morningstar's mother, Marianna, when he was just a boy. He slammed his fist against the wall. "I don't give a damn whether you come back or not, you ungrateful prick!"

He walked over to the rusted cabinet and opened it. He pulled out a bottle of Courvoisier VS cognac and, with a shaking hand, filled a small tumbler sitting next to it. He swallowed it in one gulp. "In ... the words ... of the Bard," he said, as he poured another glass, "'if I do lose thee, I do lose a thing ... that none but fools would keep.'"

He carried the liquor to the window and stared out at the dark night. He felt better. *There is far too much to do to allow one imprudent son to get in my way*. He pulled out his phone and dialed.

"Yes Father?"

"The time has come. What we've been planning for the past four years has finally begun, my son."

"Wonderful, Father! What do you need me to do?"

"Because of the untimely death of the Yemen leader at the hands of his Omani counterpart, the Middle East has fallen into chaos. As such, there will soon be a shipment sent out from Miami. I need to make sure it leaves the country without a problem, Simeon."

"How soon, Father?"

"Three weeks."

"Certainly Father."

"You also need to check in with the boats from Africa. It is imperative they leave by the first of the year." He paused. "Have you inspected their shipments?"

"Yes Father. I was over there last month.

Everything is in order."

"Good. I'll be in touch." He ended the call. He strode to the cabinet and poured another glass of cognac. His hand was steadier now. He grinned. For four years he had plotted and planned, and finally it had begun. Henderson's murder of Al-Gharsi had gotten the ball rolling. Within a matter of weeks, what had only been imagined would become a reality. *Whether you're with me or not, Joseph.*

He chuckled as he walked back to the window. "Let it be known on this holiest of days in December of the year 2003, that you, Martin Henderson, are the one who got it started." He opened the window. The wind swept back his hair and he breathed in, embracing the cold air. He could see the Washington Monument in the distance and he raised his glass. "Because of you, Henderson ... Phoenix ... Joseph," he polished off the drink, "this town, this Washington, D.C. will soon be mine." He threw the glass out the window and laughed as it broke against a rock. "Your murder of Al-Gharsi marks the beginning, my son ... the start of the New World Order."

MONDAY, JANUARY 5ᵀᴴ, 2004

"Scratch the ice, let the telephone ring
Sense of time is a powerful thing..."

"Start of the Breakdown"
~ Tears for Fear

Chapter 7
WASHINGTON, D.C.

1/5/04

"So, Cynthia, how are you this morning?"
*How do you think I am? One of my best
friends was murdered while I sat right next to him ...
Nothing has changed, Claire ... nothing will.* "Fine, I
guess."

"You don't seem fine."

Cynthia Madison, Maddi, stared at her therapist.
"I'm okay."

Claire Porter nodded. "Let's go back to what we
were talking about last week."

"What was that?"

Claire checked her notes. "The Senate chambers."
Her voice was comforting as she placed her hands on
her generous lap.

"The Senate chambers?" Maddi's arms were
crossed in front of her.

"Yes. You were sitting in the chamber, and
someone brought up Marker Health."

Maddi brushed a strand of shoulder-length blonde
hair behind one ear. "It was no big deal."

"No big deal? You've already told me that a man
you cared for – deeply, from what I can tell – *created*
Marker Health. I'm guessing your thoughts turned to
him?"

Maddi shook her head. "No ... they didn't. That was
a long time ago. I've put it behind me."

Claire said quietly, "We put nothing behind us ...
we pull it along."

Maddi looked at her and frowned. "I'm here to talk

about my friend's murder. I don't see what Marker Health has to do with it."

Claire nodded. "Martin Henderson created Marker Health. He is now dead." She paused. "And, from what you've told me, there've been a few men in your life who have experienced untimely deaths."

Maddi flinched. "'Untimely deaths' is one way to put it."

"How would you put it?"

"They were murdered ... every one of them."

"How many?"

Maddi counted in her head. "Five. Five men in my life either gunned down or blown up."

"And Henderson was one of them."

"Yes." Maddi sighed and looked away. After a minute, she turned to the therapist. "Did I ever tell you about him?"

Claire smiled. "Yes, but I'd like to hear more."

Maddi cleared her throat. Though part of her longed to talk about Martin Henderson, another part hated to even think of him. But this was Claire, the counselor she had hired to save her ... right? She wrestled with another strand of hair. "From the moment I met him, I knew he wasn't ... ordinary."

"What do you mean ... *ordinary*?"

"You know ... just another guy ... charming, handsome, brilliant. He was all those things, but he was so much more."

"In what way?"

Maddi looked out the window. It was early morning and the sky was still dark. "He had these incredible blue eyes ... like the Caribbean ... a blue that takes your breath away." She grinned. "But it was more than their color ... it was as if they could see right through me, past the walls ... to a place where lies can't live." In a whisper, she added, "And it was *okay*. No judgment, no shame; as if I'd been ... *forgiven.*"

"Forgiven for what?"

Maddi said nothing, staring down at her crossed hands. After a minute, she said, "There was only the one night together, you know."

"All these feelings ... after only one night?"

"It was actually a weekend." She grinned. "And I wasn't interested in him; not at first. He seemed arrogant ... rough around the edges. Out of character with where he'd come from." She paused. "But that all disappeared after that first night in Providence..."

"You have revealing eyes."

Maddi grinned. "I do? What do they reveal?"

Henderson stared at her and her heart began to race. "It's like they're telling a story ... your story. Like I know you without you saying a word."

She looked away. She didn't want him to know her. They had finished dinner and had toured the city, and were now sitting in his limousine outside her hotel. The driver came around and opened her door. She stepped out, shaking as she walked toward the hotel. She turned to wave goodbye, and suddenly he was beside her, opening the front door. "I can't let you walk these dangerous streets alone, can I?"

She tried to laugh, but only managed a weak grin. She was still shaking as they stepped into the lobby. Henderson nodded at the concierge and held her arm as they walked to the elevator and waited. The doors opened, she stepped inside, and, just before they were about to close, she grabbed his hand and pulled him in with her. With a trembling finger, she pushed the button to the top floor. Henderson placed his hand on her back and looked straight ahead. Maddi did the same. She was certain he could feel her heart beating out of her chest.

The elevator came to a stop and she stepped out; he was right behind her. They walked to the suite and she rummaged through her purse for the key card. She pulled it from her bag, fumbling as she tried to unlock the door. Henderson gently took the card, inserted it in the lock, and escorted Maddi inside...

Maddi closed her eyes. After a minute, she said, "It seems foolish; one weekend and I've allowed myself to feel all this pain."

Claire shook her head. "I don't think feelings are on a time continuum."

Maddi frowned. "Maybe not." She paused. "Death is."

Claire raised her eyebrows. "What do you mean?"

"Death ends time." She stared at her hands.

Claire said softly, "Tell me again about the night in the ballroom."

Maddi didn't look up. "I'd prefer not to. It ended ... badly."

"I know. But it's important. It was your last night together, wasn't it?"

Maddi nodded, fighting a sudden wave of nausea. "It was a week later. We were back in D.C., and had arranged to meet at a downtown hotel where a gala was being held to celebrate the passage of the health care bill." She paused. "Henderson and I hadn't seen each other since Providence. I walked into the ballroom and there he was, smiling, talking; he was hypnotizing. I grinned and he waved." She paused. "I wanted to run up and throw my arms around him, but I couldn't. We were still involved in the negotiation of a government contract. It wouldn't have been appropriate." She sighed. "I get tired of that sometimes."

"Tired of what?"

"Worrying about whether I'm conducting myself

properly. Always on display. Never able to do anything impulsive."

Claire nodded. "You can, you know. You simply choose not to."

Maddi shook her head. "You don't get it, Claire. I couldn't. It might have compromised the legislation."

With a gleam in her eye, Claire said, "But, wouldn't it have been fun?" She paused. "Tell me more about that night."

Maddi frowned. "As I said, I saw him..."

Henderson's face lit up and she was about to walk over to him when she stopped. He was with Hank Clarkson. She stared at them both, unable to look away. Hank turned to her and smiled, and she wanted to cry. Though she and Hank had spent the past two years together, it suddenly felt as though she barely knew him; as if they were nothing more than friends. She felt guilty as she smiled back and then looked away, grateful when she spotted her friends on the opposite side of the hall. She hurried toward them, and had gotten halfway across the ballroom when she looked over her shoulder. Her eyes met Henderson's and she stopped. It was if they were the only ones in the room. She had never experienced anything so powerful. She wanted to go to him, grab his hand, and pull him away. But she couldn't. Not yet. She turned away, but not before she saw Hank glance first at Henderson and then at her. He had seen it; he had seen the look between them. She threw him a quick smile and, though he smiled back, she saw the sadness in his eyes. She knew those eyes well; she had seen them nearly every morning and every night for the past two years. And she could see that he knew what had happened ... he had been replaced ...

47

Maddi stopped.

"What's wrong?" Claire asked.

She shook her head. "I don't like to talk about Hank."

"Why not?"

"I don't know ... guilt, maybe?"

"Tell me about him."

Maddi grinned. "Hank Clarkson is probably one of the finest men I've ever known. He's been with me through so much." She turned to Claire. "He even stayed with me – *actually helped me through it* – as I grieved for Henderson." She looked down and whispered, "He shouldn't have done that."

"Why?"

"No man should be that ... kind." She paused. "If I had never known Henderson, I'd be content to think that Hank was the man for me." She shook her head. "It's like Henderson ruined me for anyone else."

"How?"

"I ... loved him ... so much; it's like he carved a place for feelings that hadn't been there before. And now, no one can fill it."

Claire said softly, "Maybe something else carved that hole."

Maddi frowned. "What do you mean?"

"Maybe something else put the hole there, and Henderson simply allowed you to forget it; to cover it up with the intensity of your feelings."

Maddi shook her head. "What else would have put that hole there?"

"Our life – our *past* - consists of the holes placed by others."

Maddi said nothing.

Claire nodded. "Okay. Go on with the night in the ballroom. The last night you saw Henderson."

"Why? Why do I need to go through it again?"

"I thought you wanted to."

"Of course I don't want to. He died, alright? He died. He was blown to bits by a crazy man's bomb and I never saw him again." Maddi looked down at her shoes. Quieter, she said, "We ran into the burning building together, but I came out alone."

Claire frowned. "Why did you run into a burning building?"

"Have I never told you this?"

"No, you haven't."

Maddi sighed. "Maybe I didn't think it was important. Henderson's dead either way."

Claire said, "Cynthia, I think you should tell me."

Maddi tightened her jaw, trying to decide how much to share. *Share it all ... that's why you're here.* She sighed. "Henderson and I went back inside the hotel to find Hank. He hadn't come out with the rest of us and, if we had left him in there, he would have died for sure." She whispered, "I couldn't let him die."

"That's remarkably brave ... of both of you."

"Brave? Ha! Foolish, is more like it."

Claire frowned. "Either way, you could have lost one of them."

Maddi stared at Claire. "I never thought of it that way."

Claire asked, "Do you regret it? Do you regret saving Hank?"

Maddi closed her eyes. Never had that tragic night been framed more perfectly. Did she regret it? *No ... yes ... but what else could we do...*

"Where's Hank?" Maddi shouted to Henderson as she looked to be sure her friends had made it out of the ballroom.

"Didn't he come out with the rest of you?" Henderson had followed them through the door,

barely getting out before the blast.

Guests were running from inside, bloodied, panicked; like something from the Apocalypse. "I thought he did, but I don't see him." She did a quick search of the survivors; her brother Andrew and his girlfriend Amanda – both physicians – were a few yards away. She ran over to them. "Are you okay?"

Andrew nodded. "Amanda's a bit scraped up, but she's okay. We'll do our best with the injuries until the medics get here."

She frowned. "Where's Hank?"

Andrew looked around and frowned. "He was right behind us."

Maddi nodded. "I'll find him." A second explosion sent flames through the doorway, and even more screams from inside. Maddi had to fight not to scream herself; it was as if they had all been thrown into a giant incinerator, and only a few of them – the lucky ones – had managed to escape. She saw the back of a tall man with dark curly hair, and she ran up to him. "Hank!" He turned to face her; it wasn't Hank. He was bleeding from a cut to his forehead and Maddi helped him to a bench. She tore away a piece of her gown and put it on the cut. "That will hold for now." He was shaking, so she helped him lay on the bench. She pulled off more of her gown to cushion his head. Sirens blared as two police cars pulled to the curb. Officers jumped out and did their best to control the crowd, while hotel staffers tried to comfort those who had made it out alive. Maddi turned to find Henderson. He was helping a couple who had struggled through the doorway, burns over nearly every part of them. He wrapped the woman in his jacket to protect her from the cold as he walked them both to a bench. He saw Maddi and waved. She ran over to him. "Have you found him?"

He shook his head. "No."

There was another blast from inside the ballroom. Henderson ran to the door.

Maddi followed him. "I'm going with you!"

"No! You need to stay out here with the others."

"I'm going with you!" But he didn't hear her; he had already shoved his way into the ballroom. She pushed past those trying to get out. Flames and black smoke made it almost impossible to see. The heat was unbearable. Smells of burning wood and singed flesh made her want to vomit. 'This is what Hell is like,' she thought, as she tripped over a pile of debris. Cries were coming from all directions; she didn't know who to help first. She saw an older woman on the floor. She knelt beside her. "You okay?"

The woman nodded, tears streaming from her frightened eyes. Maddi helped her up. "Can you walk?"

"I—I think so."

Maddi bent low so the older woman could use her for support, and then walked with her, pulling her out of the way as a chandelier crashed to the ground. The woman flinched and Maddi held her tighter. "I've got you." They trekked to the doorway, the thick smoke making it nearly impossible to find the entrance. Maddi finally found the door, opened it, and walked the woman to a grassy area, several hundred feet from the building. She helped her to the ground. "Are you okay?"

The woman nodded, tears in her eyes. "Y—yes, I … I think so." She grabbed Maddi's hand and squeezed. "Thank you."

Maddi nodded. "You'll be fine. Wait here." She stood and was about to run back inside when she heard someone yell her name. She looked over her shoulder; it was Amanda. She and Andrew were huddled near a group of injured guests. Maddi did a quick scan of the faces to see if any of them were Hank. They weren't. Amanda waved and Maddi looked away, pretending she hadn't seen her. Two fire engines pulled to the curb, their sirens deafening. Maddi covered her ears. She ran to the door, just as crews of firemen grabbed hoses and ran toward the building. She felt the mist from the spray as she pushed her way into the ballroom. "Henderson! Hank!"

"Here!"

The hoarse cry belonged to Hank. Maddi held her breath as she ran toward him. Smoke was everywhere. She practically had to swim through it to reach him. He was buried beneath a pedestal. Henderson had already removed a chunk of it from across his chest and was working on another piece that had pinned his right leg to the floor. Flames surrounded them. Maddi was having a hard time seeing. Henderson had taken off his vest, wrapped it around his hands, and was holding the beam. He coughed as he tried to wave. He gestured to the beam, and then to Hank.

Maddi nodded. She stared at Hank. The flames were about to reach him. She looked at Henderson. "Hurry! You ... you can't let him ... die!"

She knelt by Hank's head. He looked at her, and then at Henderson, the man who had stolen her away. The two men locked eyes. But it wasn't anger or hatred she saw as they looked at one another ... it was respect. Facing death as rivals, Hank and Henderson shared an oddly profound regard for one another.

She wrapped her arms under Hank's shoulders. She waited as Henderson used all his strength to lift the beam. She pulled as hard as she could and felt Hank's body move at least a foot, but she couldn't hold *on as a coughing fit forced her to the floor. It was enough; Hank was able to twist from under the beam. He crawled to her side. "You okay?"*

She nodded. The roar from the fire had gotten louder. There were cries from every part of the room. Maddi stood and reached for his hand. "Let's go!"

He gripped her hand and tried to stand. He stumbled. Maddi grabbed him around the waist and put his arm over her shoulder. She turned to look for Henderson. A cracking sound filled the air; a table had split into pieces, and several windows had broken from the heat. There was a bang as bottles of liquor exploded into a fireball coming straight toward them. She spotted Henderson. He had shoved the pedestal out of the way, and was dodging flames and leaping over debris. She pulled away from Hank and was about to go to him, when Hank tugged her arm.

"Maddi, we have to go!"

Henderson waved her on. "I'm coming!"

She couldn't move. Hank tugged again, this time harder, and they fell over a pile of debris. Hank helped her up and they ran to the door. Once outside, she gulped in the cold night air and coughed. She kept coughing ... she couldn't seem to stop. Smoldering ash hung in the air. The sirens had quieted, but ambulances filled the lot as medics did their best to stabilize those who had made it out alive. People were laying everywhere, and the cries, though less frantic, blended like catcalls in the night. Hank started to fall. She grabbed him and walked him to a patch of grass.

"Are you okay?" she asked, as she helped him to the ground.

Coughing, and then choking, he nodded. "You?"

She nodded. "I'm okay."

He frowned. "Where's Henderson?"

"Right behind us." She looked over her shoulder,

waiting to see him burst through the doors. He didn't. She began to shake. She looked around. She didn't see him. She was finding it hard to breathe. She left Hank on the grass, and dodged bodies, medics, and police as she looked everywhere for Henderson. She ran to the ballroom and reached the doors, now sealed tight from the pressure of the flames.

Hank yelled, "Maddi ... stop!"

She barely heard him; she couldn't hear or see anything. It was as if the flames were gone; the cries silenced. She put her hand on the knob, and quickly pulled it away; it was scalding hot. She tore off a piece of her dress and wrapped it over her hand. She tried again, this time shoving the door with her foot. It wouldn't budge. She could see flames through the glass, and could feel the heat from inside. The screams were gone; those behind the doors had perished. Her eyes were watering and a coughing spasm nearly brought her to her knees. She clung to the knob as she stared through the glass. 'I ... I have to help him!' She pushed as hard as she could against the door. "Henderson!" It gave way, but she was pushed back by a wall of flames. She fought them as she tried to take a step. "Henderson!" She was halfway through the doorway when she felt strong arms pulling her back.

"Maddi ... No!"

It was Andrew. She tried to get away. "Let me go!"

"Maddi, you can't go in there."

"I'm ... not ... leaving him!" She fought Andrew's grip. "We have to get him, Andrew!"

He held her tight. "Get who? Who's in there, Maddi?"

"Martin Henderson. He went in to save Hank and he hasn't come out."

Andrew lifted her and carried her from the

doorway to one of the ambulances. He forced her into the back seat next to Hank. "Don't let her leave."

Andrew ran toward the building and was about to go inside, when another explosion brought the framework to the ground. He stepped back just in time. He looked over his shoulder and shook his head. It was too late. Maddi tried to pull away from Hank, who had his arm around her, holding her in the seat. "Let me go, Hank! I have to go to him." She tried again but his strong grip held her in place. She shoved him and then punched his chest as hard as she could, but he didn't move, he just held her tight as he looked at her with tears in his eyes. Neither one said a word; they both knew what had happened. Martin Henderson had risked his life to save Hank, and was now inside the hotel ballroom, burning to death...

Maddi looked at Claire, her eyes stinging, though she hadn't let herself cry. "Do I regret saving Hank?" She looked down. "Regret isn't the word I would use."

They sat quietly, slivers of light stealing into the room as the sun rose through the trees. Claire's eyes were kind as she said, "What word would you use then?"

Maddi rubbed the back of her neck. She whispered, "Rage." Louder, she said, "Rage at the fact that any of us had to die." She looked away. "If the roles had been reversed; if Henderson had been trapped and Hank and I had gone in to save him ... if Hank had been killed instead ... I think I would feel just as bad."

Claire looked her straight in the eye. "Would you?"

Maddi stared at her. *Would I?* If Hank had died and Henderson had lived, would she feel just as bad; just as empty as she had for the past three-and-a-half years? She replayed Providence ... the passion, the joy, the unbelievable rightness of that night carved in her mind like a favorite album, the same skips and crackles. *Like Sinatra on vinyl.* Would she feel just as bad?

"I would ... but for different reasons."

"What do you mean?"

"My heart would still hurt, and I would be just as angry..."

"But?"

"The hurt would be different. The way I feel about Hank isn't at all what I feel for Henderson." Maddi looked out the window at the early morning frost coating the trees. The sun reflected from the iced branches and her eyes filled with tears. Her love for Henderson hurt like the beauty of morning ... *so breathtaking you want to cry.*

Claire said, "Tell me about that; how your love for the two men is different."

Maddi sighed. "I don't know that I can. I love Hank; there's no doubt about it. But my feelings for Henderson ... they're not even in the same arena. It's as if I need to come up with a different word for how I feel about him."

Claire smiled. "You talk as though he's still alive."

Maddi nodded sadly. "Yes, I guess I do. I need to stop doing that, don't I?"

"Maybe he's still alive to you."

Maddi stared at Claire and then looked again to the trees beyond the window. They were now nothing more than brown sticks. The sun was hidden behind clouds and the frost had vanished; the trees looked dead. She glanced at a clock on the wall. *Seven-fifty ... time to go.* She stood, picked up her purse, and threw it over her shoulder as she walked to the door. She put her hand on the knob, looked back at Claire and said evenly, "No, he's dead alright."

Chapter 8
WASHINGTON, D.C.

1/5/04

Henderson shifted in the heavy brush, fighting to stay warm as he adjusted his binoculars. *One last look before I go.* He had watched Maddi and her bodyguard enter the one-story Knox Professional Building on Southwest A Street fifty minutes ago, and had then searched his laptop to find out who she might be going to see. He had pulled up the name of the building, and had scrolled through the short list of tenants. There was a surveyor whose office didn't open until 9:00, a hairdresser who didn't work on Mondays, and a psychotherapist who had apparently been at the site since the building's construction nearly twelve years ago. There was no doubt about it; Maddi was seeing the therapist. And it made him feel sick inside. He wasn't sure why Maddi felt the need to speak with a therapist, but he had a pretty good idea. *Watching a person you care about get shot in the head right next to you ... it would drive most to the counselor's chair.*

He had then spent the next several minutes sifting through all he could find about the therapist, Claire Porter. There wasn't much. She had been in practice for about twelve years, had gotten her undergraduate degree from Villanova, and her doctorate from Brown. She had published two papers early in her career, but had done little else to earn notoriety. She was forty-two, not married, and had no children. She seemed innocuous and low-key ... a good fit for Maddi.

He slid the binoculars in his pack, and checked his watch. *7:50 ... Maddi should be leaving soon.* He wanted to wait and follow her to the Capitol, but there wasn't time. He had a meeting to attend. He shoved his laptop into his backpack, threw it over his shoulder, and then ran through the woods to the nearest bus stop. He was still wearing the skullcap pulled low on his forehead, the sunglasses, and the scarf which covered his neck and much of his face. He reached the sidewalk, and did his best to keep his distance from passersby ... partly to avoid being identified; partly to avoid their reaction when they saw his scarred cheeks. Though he had put up with it for years, he had never gotten used to it.

He arrived at the stop and slipped into a nearby alley to wait for the bus. He had gotten back to D.C. only two nights ago, sailing into the Jersey port well after midnight, buried deep in the hold of a European shipping vessel. The fact that he had not found Lili weighed heavy on him. But he had left Rozenblats in charge; if anyone could find her, it would be Rozenblats.

Sitting in the hold of a boat crossing the Atlantic had given him plenty of time to think. Except for sipping a canteen of water, or digging in his pocket for an apple or a scone and then turning over to relieve himself when he could hold it no longer, thinking was all there was. So, he had thought ... about Maddi, about his parents, about Lili, and about Morningstar. It was the first real thinking he had done since the fire nearly four years ago. He had not had the courage to do it up to that point. But it was time. Time to think ... *and time to plan.* He had risked Lili's life to leave Morningstar behind ... he had to make it count for something.

But the thinking had been hard; it had made him physically ill. But he had had to do it ... he had *made* himself do it. He had started with Maddi. He wanted to see her. Now that he wasn't an assassin, he wanted to see her. But then he had realized, though he was no longer killing, he was still a killer. *And I killed her good friend.*

He pulled his coat tighter around him, and tucked his hands in his pockets as a cold wind swept through the alley. He had gone from thinking about Maddi to thinking about his parents ... maybe he could finally talk to them. *There's no way,* he had finally concluded. They were upstanding members of the Boston elite ... it would kill them to see what he had become. He had tried to imagine telling them what he had been doing for the last four years; plotting the deaths of vital leaders, assassinating honorable men. He had decided that they were out, as well.

He moved further into the shadows as a burst of sunlight shone on the alley. He watched a little girl walk past holding her mother's hand and he flinched. Though her hair was brown instead of blonde like Lili's, she had the same smile, and his heart broke. Albins had asked him to watch over Lili ... to love her and keep her safe ... and he had failed. He bristled as he thought of Morningstar's gibe. *"She isn't dead ... yet."*

Henderson had spent a lot of time on the boat thinking about the man who had saved him ... the bastard who had had him pulled from the fire, only to turn him into his personal hit man. He hated Morningstar. But thinking about him had been far easier than thinking of the people he loved. It had felt better somehow ... less emotional ... more invigorating. *Hatred is a vital fuel.*

He saw the bus in the distance and walked from the alley to a patch of shade near the stop. He held his backpack tight to his chest. Inside that pack was some of the army's most sophisticated surveillance equipment. He had gotten the gear from Morningstar years before, when he had been on a reconnaissance

59

mission in Libya. After the mission, he had told Morningstar it had been destroyed in a battle outside Benghazi, and – as far as he could tell – Morningstar had believed him. *And now I'll use your own weapons against you.* There were satellite jammers, a pair of night-goggles, and a computer chip that could extract data from any nearby device. There was also a scanner that could intercept private email and cellphone conversations, as long as the user had access to the name of the sender, the location of his computer, and the server he was using. Henderson had uncovered Morningstar's server ID, but had still been unable to intercept any of his correspondence ... *which means the man is doing all he can to keep it hidden.*

He had managed to acquire one vital piece of information, however ... Morningstar was about to attend a meeting. Henderson had learned that if he hacked into Morningstar's laptop deletion site, he had about a one-minute window to sift through all recently dumped emails. He had made a point of doing it every hour on the hour for the last day-and-a-half, and had found nothing of interest until late last night, when he had picked up an email from someone named Chief. *"I have something important to discuss. Make sure everyone's there. See you tomorrow morning at 8:10 ... and get there on time!"* Henderson had been unable to find an 8:10 meeting listed on any of the Pentagon websites, and there was no mention of it in the daily agenda. *Which means this, too, is a secret.*

The bus pulled to the curb. Henderson stayed in the shadows while the others climbed aboard. At the last minute, he ran up the steps, paid the fare, and hurried down the aisle to the back, all the while keeping his right hand – the unscarred one – over the only part of his face that showed; his mutilated cheek. He had learned that it was easier for those on the bus to not have to look at him.

He found an empty seat in the last row and sat down. The ride to the Pentagon would take about fifteen minutes. He put his pack beside him so no one would sit there, and then leaned back and stared outside. The sun coming through the window warmed him, reminding him of better days ... joyful afternoons on the ocean by his home in Boston ... vigorous morning hikes in the cliffs near the compound in Latvia ... good days with a happy heart. He closed his eyes. His heart was no longer happy ... ever. He ached for Maddi ... but, even more, he ached for Lili.

He had known Lili Platacis her entire life, and had watched with joy as she discovered her unique mind ... her *'special gifts,'* as Lili's mother had liked to call them. She had perfect recall. She could see the past in her head like a manuscript. Not with the faded changes caused by time and emotion, but with the permanence of a piece of text. And she could sense what was about to happen ... miles away from where she was. Not the specifics ... the what or the where ... but the *essence* of it ... the way it would affect the people she loved.

He tightened his jaw, recalling a conversation he had had with Lili only a few months before the battle in Ventspils. Even then, she had known what was coming ...

"Uncle Mart, I need you to know something."
"What's that, Lili?"
"You mustn't worry about me."
Henderson frowned. "What do you mean?"
"When things seem dark, when you're hurting, I don't want you to worry for me."
The two of them had been building a sled in a small workshop outside the manor. He stopped what he was doing and looked at her. Had she had one of

her visions? "What did you see, Lili?"

She shook her head. "Nothing. It's just a feeling, Uncle Mart. A feeling that you are going to spend far too much time worrying about me."

He put down his hammer and nails, walked over and gave her a hug. "It would be an honor to worry about you, Lili. So ... if the time comes for me to worry about you ... let me do it, okay?"

She grinned as she hugged him back. "Okay, Uncle Mart ... I will..."

He stared out the window. His eyes burned. He couldn't think about it ... about her. *Where are you, Lili? Are you safe?* The bus made a sharp turn and then pulled to a stop. He grabbed his bag, waited for everyone to get off, and then walked to the front and hurried down the steps. The Pentagon was less than a mile away.

He looked around for a good spot to carry out his reconnaissance. The surveillance protecting the Pentagon was some of the best, especially since 9-11. He would need to be careful. He saw a coffee shop a hundred yards away and walked inside. Keeping on his glasses, his hat, and even his scarf, he found a table in the back. A waitress came by and he ordered coffee and eggs. It was early morning and the place was busy. Good. He waited for her to bring his coffee, and then pulled out his laptop. He plugged it into an outlet next to the table to charge it; he did that every chance he got. He logged on and went to a popular webpage, which would serve as a cover screen whenever anyone got close. When he was sure no one was looking, he opened a separate site, which showed aerial footage of the entire Pentagon complex. He plugged in several numbers, and the screen focused on the northwest sector. He pushed a few more keys, and was now looking at the inside of the building. He guided the camera to Morningstar's office. He spotted him at his desk. He watched with disgust as the man sipped his coffee and rifled through paperwork. He saw him log onto his computer. Henderson pushed a few keys to hack into the computer.

The waitress brought his eggs and he switched the screen to the cover page. He smiled and waited while she walked away, pretending not to notice when she gave that second look as she spotted the scars above his scarf. He resumed his surveillance. He stared at the screen and frowned. Even with the Army's most sophisticated spyware, Morningstar had been able to keep him out. The man had clearly gone to great effort to protect whatever he was working on. *Which means it's important.*

He tweaked the site with a few keystrokes, but he couldn't break through the firewall. He watched a while longer, and then saw Morningstar close the laptop, slide it in his briefcase, and lock the case. He saw him stand and grab his coat. Henderson switched to the aerial view. He focused on the exits, and saw him leave through the southwest door. He was expecting him to get into one of the black sedans parked outside, and was surprised when the man walked right past them. *Where's he going?*

He closed his computer, shoved it in his bag, and threw a ten-dollar bill on the table. He left the diner and sprinted to where he last saw Morningstar. He rounded the corner and slowed to a walk as he fell in with a group of tourists. He looked everywhere for the small man with a limp, finally spotting him two blocks in front of him. He was approaching a cab. *Wherever it is, he doesn't want anyone to know.*

Henderson picked up his pace, practically running as he hailed a taxi. "Fifty dollars if you can stay with the yellow cab three cars in front of us." The driver nodded and jerked into the left lane. He sped in and out of traffic for about six blocks, and then slowed when Morningstar's cab turned right onto Morgan Street. It stopped in front of a nondescript building. Henderson had his driver go a half-block further and turn down a side street. "Let me out here." He handed the man a fifty-dollar bill and jumped out of the cab. He ran back to Morgan Street and found a secluded spot among a clump of bushes. He watched as Morningstar climbed the steps and walked into a five-story building on the corner. His telltale limp was barely noticeable.

Henderson waited and, when he was sure no one was watching, he pulled out his laptop and turned on the surveillance software. He tweaked it to focus on the inside, but couldn't see a thing. The entire building appeared to be protected from any type of reconnaissance. *He's gone to a lot of trouble to keep this meeting a secret.*

Henderson closed his computer and shoved it in his bag. He pulled out his binoculars. He put the bag on the ground and sat on top of it. He would watch the exits, wait for Morningstar to leave, and then he would look to see who, if anyone, left either right before or right after him. *Maybe if I figure out who he met with, I can learn what the bastard is up to.*

Chapter 9
WASHINGTON, D.C.

1/5/04

Morningstar had arrived at the Morgan Building at 8:10 sharp. The driver had slid the cab into a spot in front of a tall building on the corner, and Morningstar had handed him the fare with an additional hundred-dollar bill. *"Wait for me."*

As he walked up the steps to the front door, his phone vibrated. He opened it and checked the message. It was an alert from a surveillance program. He grinned. *Welcome back, Henderson.* He walked inside, skirted the lobby, and hurried down a corridor to an alcove near the elevators. He opened his phone and dialed. Without waiting for a hello, he said, "He's back in D.C. Somewhere near the Pentagon. Go!"

He walked a few steps to the far elevator. It was open and empty. There were buttons for each floor, but he ignored them as he pulled out a key, slid it into a slot to the side, and then waited as he was carried to the top floor. The door opened to a well-appointed room with no windows and no exits, other than the elevator and a set of stairs off the back. Scrolled cornices edged the ceiling and floor, with Picasso originals adorning the walls. There was a leather couch in the back, and several overstuffed chairs scattered throughout the room. A chandelier hung over a large round table; it gave off a yellow glow, softening the faces of the six men seated around it. The smell of furniture polish blended with the rich aromas of coffee and high-priced cigars. Morningstar nodded at two agents standing by the door. "Jones. Johnson." They said nothing, simply nodding in reply. Morningstar hung his coat on a rack by the door, and then walked to a sideboard, where a pot of coffee was brewing. He poured a cup, added sugar and cream, and then carried it to the table and sat down next to a large man smoking a cigar. The man's name was Conner, but everyone referred to him as Chief.

"Ya' want one?" Chief asked, offering a cigar.

"No, thank you." He set his briefcase on the floor.

Chief cleared his throat. "Now that Morningstar's here we can get started. Let's begin with the Phoenix."

A man across the table said, "He's gone. We can't find him anywhere."

Chief frowned. "Gone? What do you mean, gone?"

"He is no longer responding to CIA inquiries."

Chief shook his head. "The CIA can't find him?"

"No sir." The man paused. "He's good, Chief. Probably one of the best."

Another man joined in. "That's why he was so useful."

Morningstar grinned, saying nothing.

"When was he last seen?" Chief asked.

"The Al-Gharsi incident. About a month-and-a-half ago."

Chief smacked the table with his fist. "Holy shit! You're telling me that no one – not even the CIA – has seen or heard from Phoenix since *November?*"

"No sir."

"We have to find him." Chief rubbed his neck. "He knows way too much."

Morningstar cleared his throat. "Excuse me, sir, if I may?" Six pairs of eyes turned his way. "I have some information which might be helpful."

Chief snorted. "What are you talking about, Morningstar?"

Morningstar laid his briefcase on the table and

opened it. He pulled a piece of paper from a binder and began reading.

"Surveillance of the Phoenix, in response to a request by Edward Morningstar for the purpose of National Security: Phoenix was recently spotted near Jersey's north harbor."

Chief fumed. "Why the hell didn't you just tell us that?"

Morningstar ignored him and read on.

"Two nights ago, Phoenix was spotted at the pier, sneaking out of the hold of a European shipping vessel. He evaded surveillance once he left the dock."

Morningstar laid the paper on the table and looked at the faces of each of the men. He could see the respect in their eyes. *I am the one in charge of this meeting.* He turned to Chief and said proudly, "And I've just learned that our elusive Phoenix is now in the D.C. area."

Chief frowned. "How do you know that?"

Morningstar grinned. "He's using a surveillance program I gave him years ago. He told me it had been destroyed, but, because I trust no one," he glared at each of the men, "I decided to keep it active. It has a reverse sensor beam that is activated any time he uses the software. It won't tell me his exact location, but it gives me his general vicinity, within a few miles."

"So, were you able to apprehend him?"

"My man is looking for him as we speak." He paused. "But Phoenix is good ... my guess is he'll be long gone by the time my guy gets there."

Chief frowned. "So how will you find him?"

Morningstar grinned. "Don't worry. The fact that

he's still in D.C. makes me think he's not going anywhere soon."

Chief narrowed his eyes and exhaled, making his full cheeks even bigger. "Who do you have looking for him?"

"A guy that works for me."

"What do you mean, he works for you?"

How could one man be so stupid? "He's not with the Pentagon," he paused, "or the CIA."

Chief's eyes widened. "Ah, I see. That's good. The fewer who know about our tie to Phoenix, the better." He frowned. "I think we need to eliminate him."

Morningstar bristled. "No, we're not 'eliminating' him. We trained him well. He's the best we've ever had."

"No ... *you* trained him. We know nothing about him ... remember?"

"And we need to keep it that way. The less you know the better. Which is why he's perfect. Don't forget, gentleman, everyone who ever knew him thinks he's dead. It's like he's invisible. It would be a shame to get rid of him now."

"But he's no longer under our control. I think he could hurt us."

"He won't hurt us ... he has too much to lose."

Chief growled. "He's got nothing to lose!"

Morningstar had to work to stay calm. "Trust me, he has plenty to lose. Besides, I have a plan to get him back. Let's just watch him a while longer."

Chief sneered. "You've got to find him first."

Morningstar tightened his jaw. "Like I said ... not a problem."

Chief stared at him and then sighed. "Whatever you say, Morningstar." He leaned closer. "But hear this: Once you find him, you better not lose him again."

Morningstar had to fight not to strangle the man.

He said nothing.

Chief leaned back and took a sip of coffee, followed by a long drag on his cigar. "We've got another problem. Apparently, the Senate Majority Whip, Cynthia Madison, has requested documents related to Silverton."

Morningstar frowned. "Why?"

Chief shook his head. "That's what I want to know."

One of the men at the table, Senator Dan Lawford from Texas said, "I'll bet I know why. About two weeks ago, the bitch was put on my committee." He took a drag on a cigar. "And she can be kind of pushy, if you know what I mean."

Morningstar did know. Less than a year ago, Madison had pulled Morningstar before a senate subcommittee that was investigating foreign arms trades. Though she had not implicated him directly in the deals, she had clearly suspected him. Nothing had come of it and no one at that table was aware; it had been behind closed doors.

"What's the big deal?" he said with a shrug. "She's nobody." He combed his hand through his hair. "Don't worry ... I'll make sure she doesn't find anything."

Chief looked at him and frowned. "You better, Morningstar. If she figures out what we're doing with Silverton, we're all in trouble." He took a gulp of coffee, followed by a drag on his cigar. He exhaled, filling the air with thick white smoke. "Speaking of Silverton, how are we doing with the Syrian arms deal?"

A man to the right of Lawford said, "Right on course, sir. The shipment will leave New York's Inner Harbor tomorrow afternoon."

The man across from him said, "Has America weighed in on the conflict?"

Chief answered. "No. Not publicly, at least. And we aren't likely to. Dragging our feet ... it's our new foreign policy." He sighed as he rubbed the back of his neck. "What about the Yemen insurgency against the Kurds?"

Morningstar said, "We have a shipment heading there in about eight days. Out of Florida."

Chief nodded. "Good."

Morningstar said nothing, simply sipping his coffee as the men discussed the Middle East for the next twenty minutes. Nearly every region was immersed in some sort of conflict. And, with every new outbreak of violence came a request for arms that Silverton was then hired to fulfill. He took a last sip of coffee and grinned. Things were going well.

Finally, Chief put his hands on the table and said, "I guess that covers it, boys." He looked at Morningstar. "We'll count on you to take care of Madison ... and to keep an eye on Phoenix." He pushed back from the table. "We'll meet again next week." He struggled from his seat, his large belly bumping against the table. He stood and straightened his jacket as he walked to the elevator. The two agents at the door fell in beside him, while the other men waited behind.

Chief would leave first; that was how it had been since the beginning. Morningstar had to hide a sneer as the pompous man placed a Fedora over his wild hair. The door opened and the three men stepped inside, disappearing as the others waited and then, two by two, did the same. Lawford and Morningstar were the last to leave. They stepped into the elevator, each one staring straight ahead as it carried them to the lobby.

"So, what's your plan, Morningstar? For Madison, I mean."

"Don't worry about it, Lawford. I've got it handled."

"I sure hope so. She's one pushy bitch."

Morningstar glared at the man. "Like I said, I've got it."

When they reached the lobby, they got off the elevator without a word and left the building through separate doors.

Morningstar walked to the cab and slid in back. "Let's go."

The car pulled away, the D.C. shadows growing taller as the sun rose higher in the sky. Morningstar looked over his shoulder at the Morgan Building and its undisclosed room at the top. The secret of the Bentley Group had been well kept; none of them could afford to share what went on in that room. To talk would be suicide; both politically and – for some – in the flesh. The men were important; they were responsible for much of the nation's wealth and they oversaw nearly all of its wars. The business they conducted would dictate American policy for months, maybe years, to come. Morningstar chuckled as the building faded from view. *Those men have no idea what I have in store for them.* He pulled a cigar from his pocket and lit it, ignoring the pasted sign on the seat that said "No smoking." *I smoke when I want.*

He leaned back, watching as Washington came to life on an early Monday morning. *"And the world shall know that it was Jacob who saved them; who rebuilt them ... one nation at a time."* He chuckled as he blew a puff of smoke. *Don't worry, D.C., all is well. Jacob has everything under control.*

Chapter 10

WASHINGTON, D.C.

1/5/04

Henderson ran in place and then pulled out a thermos of coffee to try to stay warm as he skulked outside the Morgan Building. He had gotten the coffee from a nearby vender, who had added in the thermos for an extra five dollars. It was worth it. It was a frosty 27 degrees in D.C., and he was cold. The running in place helped, but the coffee helped even more. He stared at the building, and then looked up and down the street. It wasn't the busiest part of Washington, but there was plenty of street traffic. He shrunk even further into the brush.

He opened the thermos and poured another cup of coffee. He took a sip and stared through the trees at the building where Morningstar was meeting with ... who? *What is he up to?*

Henderson thought back to his role within Morningstar's organization. He had never completely understood how he fit into the man's plans; only that he was one of several men, soldiers Morningstar referred to as sons, who killed people whenever the man asked. He was aware of Morningstar's Pentagon ties; he had assumed that their role was to serve as a covert arm of the already-covert CIA. And it had made sense ... until the Al-Gharsi hit. Prior to that, the assassinations Morningstar had made him do were predictable, consistent with America's goals. Imperious dictators were making the world a terrible place ... and they needed to go. Though Henderson hadn't approved of the killing, he could at least take comfort in the fact that bad men had been removed from their post, and good men would hopefully take their place. But the hit on Al-Gharsi had been different. Abdulkarim Al-Gharsi had not been an overbearing dictator; he had been a hero to many, including the United States. So why had he needed to be taken out? Henderson frowned as he thought back to what Morningstar had said to him only days before the hit. *"It all begins with you, dear Joseph. You will put into motion what no one can undo."* Henderson had given it little thought at the time; Morningstar was always making dramatic proclamations. But, as he thought of it now, he realized ... the death of Al-Gharsi had ignited something far bigger. *And I'm guessing it has nothing to do with the CIA.*

He checked his watch. *8:42.* Morningstar had been inside the building for over forty minutes. *Hurry up ... before I freeze to death!* A minute later, he saw the front door open. He reached for his binoculars. He looked at the face of the first man to leave, and his jaw dropped. *What is Jim Conner doing here?* Two bodyguards walked on each side of him; hardly the full armament to accompany a man in his position. *Which suggests that his presence at this meeting is a secret.* Henderson waited. Soon he saw four more men leave, one at a time. He didn't recognize any of them. Using a telephoto lens built into his binoculars, he snapped photos of each one; he would know everything about them by the end of the day. A minute later he saw the senator from Texas, Sam Lawford, leave the building through a side door, and, within seconds, Morningstar walked out the front. He seemed to be the last of the group. *If it is, in fact, a group.* Had those men met together inside the Morgan Building? If so, why? How were they connected? Was it a government seminar of some sort? If so, why all the secrecy? It wasn't a sanctioned meeting; that much was clear. Whatever those men had discussed in that building, it was meant to be a secret from the world.

Henderson put away his gear and threw his backpack over his shoulder. He knew what he had to do. Whatever Morningstar was up to, it had something to do with the other six men who had just left that building. Henderson would learn about each one, and then – once he knew how they were connected – he would be one step closer to learning what Morningstar was planning. Then, hopefully, he could stop him before he could carry it out. *And my first task will be to figure out why – and how – Morningstar pulled Jim Conner, the Vice-President of the United States, into his web.*

Chapter 11
WASHINGTON, D.C.

1/5/04

D*amn ... no Miami hockey.* Dr. Hank Clarkson was searching the sports page, trying to find news about the hockey games in the CCHA. His son, Roger, had played in college and Hank had become a fan. But it wasn't well covered in the D.C. newspaper, and he often suffered this same frustration.

He poured a second cup of coffee, resisting, once again, the urge to light up a cigarette. He had quit several years ago, but he often longed for a smoke, particularly with his coffee while he was reading the morning paper. He leaned his six-two frame against the back of the chair as he thumbed through the basketball scores, looking to see if Ohio State was fighting their way through the challenging Big Ten schedule.

Although he was glad to no longer work for the Marker Health Insurance Company, he did miss the Chicago newspapers and their sports coverage. It was no secret that an East Coast bias existed and, since moving to Washington, he had had to adjust to more politics, less Midwest sports.

He folded the paper, leaving it on the table as he carried his coffee to the bedroom. He looked at his running shoes sitting by the closet and debated whether he should take a jog to clear his head, or work on reports due for the Department of Homeland Security. He had taken the morning off specifically for that purpose, but, as he thought about the mound of paperwork, he sighed and reached for the shoes.

He put on sweats and a sweatshirt, and slipped on the shoes. He grabbed a jacket from a hook on the door, along with a stocking cap. He put it on over his thinning brown hair, which, for the last several years, had been fighting for a place on his scalp. *And losing the fight,* he thought, with a grin. He stepped outside, the cold air jolting him as it filled his lungs and chilled his face and hands. He fell into his stride, heading south toward downtown, past the Capitol and along the Mall.

He had been in D.C. for less than a year, and had worked at the Department of Homeland Security for only the last seven months. His title, Deputy Director, told little of what he actually did. He led a team of agents that investigated the credibility of all bioterrorist threats that came through the Department. He had been amazed at how many there were. Hundreds a week; thousands over the course of a year. He was required to oversee written summaries of each and every one of them, credible or not. He saw no point to it but had learned quickly; the Government loved its reports.

He had tried to talk Maddi into staying the night and taking the morning off so they could sleep in and go to breakfast, but once again she had been "too busy." Hank wasn't sure what that meant. He wondered if perhaps he should just buy her a mood ring, knowing his radar about women was way off, at least according to his ex-wife, Jenny, who had pointed it out many times.

He glanced at the Capitol building. *What's going on with you, Maddi?* She had told him over the weekend that she "*...just needed a little time.*" He knew she was struggling. The recent murder of her friend at the New York restaurant had affected her deeply. He had told her he would give her whatever time she needed. And he would, but he wondered ... *Is it time* *she needs? Or is it something else?*

He ran past the Lincoln Memorial, remembering the first time he laid eyes on Cynthia Madison. It was in medical school and he had fallen for her the minute he had seen her. Which was a problem; he was married at the time, happily, he had thought. He remembered it like it was yesterday; her long blonde hair and the bluest eyes he had ever seen. She smiled and that was it; he was hooked. Maddi had not felt the same, however, and Hank was both disappointed and relieved. He had a beautiful wife and son, and – had Maddi been willing – it was likely he would have sacrificed both to be with her.

Hank had originally been a high school science teacher, but had figured out early on that he wasn't cut out for teaching. He quit after only four years, and immediately applied to medical school. He started at Ohio State soon after his twenty-ninth birthday. He had been married to Jenny, his high school sweetheart, for over ten years when he met Maddi. Hank loved Jenny, but there was something about Maddi he couldn't resist, and Jenny had seen it.

"You're in love with her, Hank."

He couldn't deny it. Though at the time he could honestly tell Jenny they had never slept together, he couldn't say he hadn't wanted to. Jenny had divorced him soon after. But he still loved her. He loved them both. He had tried to explain it to Jenny; she hadn't understood. He couldn't say he blamed her; he didn't understand it himself.

Maddi had come around years later after she and Hank joined forces against a powerful group of trial lawyers. Though they had won the fight, a good friend had lost his life protecting her from a killer, and his death had brought them closer. The relationship had been many things since then: wonderful, tumultuous, and now uncertain. It was the last one, "uncertain," that was draining the life out of him. He loved her, but was no longer sure she loved him back. Though most men would have moved on, Hank couldn't. He felt certain she could love him if she just let herself.

He picked up his pace, struggling to breathe as the cold air mixed with his sudden despair. God, how he missed her. Though he saw her nearly every day, so much had changed. She could have been standing right next to him, but she wouldn't have been close by. He tried to recall the last time the two of them had spent the night together. *Weeks ago ... maybe even months.*

Soon after his move to D.C., he had tried to get Maddi to move in with him. She had refused, without giving him a reason why. Hank knew why. She was in love with someone else. But the object of her affection wasn't a man Hank could compete with; Maddi was in love with a dead man. Martin Henderson had died three-and-a-half years ago, and, though Maddi insisted she had gotten past it, Hank knew she hadn't. *How do you love a dead man?*

He gritted his teeth as he pushed himself even harder. The man's death wasn't the only problem. It was the way he died – the *reason* he died – that kept Hank up at night. What happened in that hotel ballroom three-and-a-half years ago stayed with him as if it had happened only yesterday.

He had been buried under a pillar in a corner of the ballroom, choking on smoke, only minutes from death. From nowhere, he had heard Henderson's voice. *"I'm coming, Hank!"* Henderson had then gone to work removing pieces of the column that had pinned Hank's legs and chest, finally lifting it enough that Maddi could drag him out from underneath.

But what happened next, Hank? What happened after the two of them helped you get out of there? He stopped; he was struggling to breathe. He leaned forward, gulping in air, similar to what he had done right after he was freed from the ballroom. *Say it, Hank. Tell yourself – one more time – what happened after you miraculously escaped the hotel fire.* He took a few more breaths, and then stood and looked up at the sky. Finally, he whispered, "I survived. Maddi and Henderson came in after me, but only Maddi and I came out alive."

He put his head in his hands, ashamed of how things had turned out. How many times had he wished it had been him who had died saving Henderson? *Then maybe Maddi would be in love with me instead of him.*

Suddenly he laughed. "That's ridiculous, Hank."

He resumed his run, slower now, soon rounding the gate to his townhouse apartment. He came to a stop, bending over as he once again waited for his breathing to return to normal. *Henderson died ... saving my life.* It had been unbearable; to think that the man who had trumped him in life had then trumped him in death. He backed against a stone wall, shedding his jacket as he pulled off his cap and ran his hand through his hair. He looked at the Capitol in the distance and sighed. *Maddi is in love with Henderson ... who's dead because he saved my life.*

Chapter 12

WASHINGTON, D.C.

1/5/04

Maddi had left Claire's office and had gone straight to her own office in the Capitol. The sessions with Claire, though draining, were also comforting in an odd sort of way. It felt good to talk to someone who had never known her. Someone who was there for the sole purpose of letting her tell her story. And, though Maddi didn't want to tell her story, she knew she had to. *It's the only way to get rid of this pain.*

She had been seeing the therapist for a month, calling her soon after her friend, Abdulkarim Al-Gharsi, was killed with a bullet to the head ... *while I was sitting right next to him.* The assassination had done her in. She had had a hard time eating, and nightmares had kept her from sleeping for more than one or two hours at a time. It was when she had had to fight tears on the Senate floor that she had decided she needed help. She knew Claire through a colleague and – though it took her nearly a week to make the call – she finally had ... *and it's been one of my better decisions.*

She walked into her office and hung her coat and scarf on a hook by the door. She saw the pile of folders on her desk and sighed. She walked to a credenza and put on a pot of coffee. She went to her desk and stared down at the pile. A calendar sat on the corner of the desk, filled with appointment times and deadlines, a maddening reminder of how over-scheduled her life had become. In bold letters she saw "Senate retreat, Jacksonville," written in the small square for tomorrow's date: Tuesday, January 6th. *Only thirty-six hours.* She had a lot to do. After all, it was her retreat.

She had set it up in order to get the Senate leadership on the same page before going into the election season. Though President Wilcox was a shoe-in for reelection, Maddi felt it was important there were no detractors, at least not among the senate leaders. A few of her colleagues had recently expressed dissatisfaction with the Wilcox foreign policy. They felt he wasn't aggressive enough with their enemies overseas. Maddi couldn't argue the point. After all, diplomacy only got you so far when it came to dealing with crazy dictators. Her job was to somehow appease them – at least until after the election.

The retreat was to last through Friday, and then her weekend was free. *Free for what,* she thought, as she breathed in the rich aroma of the coffee. Maddi rarely did much outside the Senate. Other than the occasional night out for dinner, she barely left her office, except to go home at the end of the day. It had been like that for years. Hank had often tried to get her to go away for a few days, *"...just get out of the Beltway and see how the rest of the world lives."* But she always found a reason to say no. She was far more content to sit in her living room and bury herself in her work. As a matter of fact, weekends felt like the enemy. Too much time to think, to hurt, to miss Henderson.

Once again, she looked at the stack of files. Most of it was from the Senate Arms Committee, a committee she had been assigned to only two weeks ago when a spot became vacant after the junior senator from Arkansas was caught with a prostitute. She had done what she always did when joining a new committee; she had asked for all relevant documents from the past two years. But, as she stared at the large stack of files, she almost regretted being so diligent.

She walked over to the credenza. The well-crafted piece of furniture had been given to her by a dear friend, Sir Arthur Kauffold, who had been the UK's American ambassador for nearly twenty years. He had stepped down six years ago, but the two had stayed in touch. She had met him in England when she was only fifteen. It was he who had encouraged her to stay and attend Oxford, and that decision had dramatically changed her life. Almost overnight, she had gone from a struggling American teenager, to an Oxford scholar with the whole world ahead of her. *Thank God for Kauffold,* she thought as she poured the coffee and threw in a splash of cream.

She carried it to the desk and sat down. She grabbed the first file off the top of the stack and thumbed through it. It was a compilation of every bill that had been passed by the committee since 2002. She read it through quickly; she was familiar with most of the bills through her work as Majority Whip. She grabbed the next file. It consisted of all invoices that had been approved by the committee since January 2002. She was not familiar with these, and began at the top of the stack. There were hundreds of them, and, after an hour of sifting through receipts, she felt like her eyes were starting to cross. She stood and refilled her coffee cup. She carried it to the window and stared out at the brown grass and the gray sky. *Winter in D.C.*

She carried the coffee to her desk and got back to work. As she read through the myriad of invoices, she tried to imagine why the U.S. Army needed so many weapons. After all, there were only so many sorties that could be carried out in a day. She had investigated irregular arms trades about a year ago; large piles of weapons and munitions that had gone to unlikely – even unfriendly – allies. She felt the Pentagon had played a role, and she had gone so far as to subpoena the Joint Chief's aide, Edward Morningstar, to speak before the committee. He had had little to share, however, and she had gotten nowhere. But it was the reason she had been willing – even eager – to join the committee once the Arkansas senator stepped down.

She had nearly reached the end of the folder, when suddenly she stopped. Something wasn't right. She went back to the beginning and sifted through every receipt, rereading each one until she got to the end. She laid several invoices on the desk, separating them by the type of weaponry and the date of sale, and then leaned back and frowned. Silverton Arms, Inc., a weapons manufacturer out of Topeka, Kansas, had been a part of every government arms contract for the past two years.

Maddi chewed on a pencil as she tried to think of a plausible explanation. It wasn't unusual for an arms manufacturer to be granted multiple contracts. What was odd was that no other company had been awarded a contract for at least twenty-four months. A coincidence? Maddi sifted through the receipts. In spite of the fact that the writing was sloppy, and the signatures sloppier still, there was no mistaking it; Silverton had received every single contract. *Why hasn't this triggered any alarms?*

She tried to think of who sat on the Senate Arms Committee. There were twenty-four men and women and, as she went through their names in her mind, she thought about who might be willing to overlook such a thing. Surely all twenty-four of them didn't have a hand in it. They were split nearly evenly by party line, and the chairman – a Texan by the name of Dan Lawford – had never been Maddi's favorite. But she had no reason to think he was corrupt. *Overbearing, a little sleazy, but corrupt?* Same with the others ... some were friends, some merely colleagues, but none of them seemed less than honorable when it came to their senate duties.

Her intercom beeped. "Yes Phil?"

"I have Senator Dan Lawford on the line."

Speak of the devil. "Put him through." She waited. Soon she heard the familiar drawl of the senator from Texas. "Good mornin', Senator Madison."

"Good morning, Dan. What's up?"

"Are you goin' to the committee hearin' this afternoon?"

"Yes, of course I am. I assume you'll be there as well."

There was a chuckle. "Wouldn't miss it."

"So ... what do you need, Dan?"

"I just wanted to make sure you were gonna' be there. I've uncovered some information I think you'll wanna' see."

Maddi frowned. "What sort of information?"

"Just make sure you find me before you head into the chamber." He ended the call and Maddi stared at the phone. She frowned as she hung up the receiver. Yes, Lawford was sleazy; there was no doubt about it. It was hard to believe they were from the same political party. *And now we sit on the same committee ... swell.*

She stared at the paperwork, suddenly fighting a chill as she thought about the call. It wasn't a friendly call from a colleague. No, whatever Dan wanted to show her, it wasn't good. *And he's going to great lengths to make sure I know that.*

Chapter 13
WASHINGTON, D.C.

1/5/04

Morningstar had had the cab driver drop him three blocks from the Pentagon, and he had walked the rest of the way. He reached his office and immediately closed and locked the door. The Madison thing had surprised him. Though he hadn't let on to Chief, he had found it alarming that the senator had requested documents related to Silverton. *What is that bitch looking for?*

He pulled out his laptop and turned it on. He went to the Senate website and plugged in Cynthia Madison. He looked at her picture and leered. *Pretty little thing, aren't you?* He scrolled through her biography and then reviewed some of her recent legislative initiatives. There it was ... just like Lawford had said. She had been put on the Senate Arms Committee two weeks ago. She had clearly decided to dig in. But why? What had made her revisit the arms deals? Was she still obsessed with the investigation a year ago? *It doesn't matter. I need to stop her.*

But how? What form of intimidation could one use against a powerful senator? Scandal? Corruption? He went back through her site. There was nothing juicy there, so he searched through newspapers looking for a scandal or an outrage she might have gotten caught up in. Nothing. He would need to dig deeper ... to look further into Madison's life ... not the public life, but the private one ... *the life no one is aware of.* To do that would require more than computer searches. It would require an actual investigation. But Morningstar couldn't do the digging; he couldn't risk getting caught. And he couldn't use one of his sons. Snooping on a senator could get them in a lot of trouble, which might lead back to him. He would need someone else ... someone dispensable. But whom could he trust to carry out such an investigation?

He chuckled. He knew just the man. He stood from the desk and walked over to a filing cabinet. He knelt down and unlocked the bottom drawer. He rifled through folders until he found what he was looking for. He pulled out a file and grinned. *Herbert Cosgrove.* He carried the file to his desk and sat down. Cosgrove, "Pocks" to those who knew him well, had arrived at the Pentagon only six months earlier. Though the hiring team had believed Cosgrove when he told them he had come from an innocuous military academy in Little Rock, Arkansas, Morningstar, who oversaw the majority of the hirings, had had his doubts. In spite of supporting documents from the academy, there was just something about the man that had made Morningstar feel the need to dig deeper. And he was glad he had. He had learned the truth about Pocks; not the whole truth, but enough to know that the man was hiding a secret. Pocks had not come from Little Rock, but had left a Catholic seminary in upstate New York, and the circumstances surrounding his departure had been questionable, to say the least. He had been found in a compromising position with another seminary student. Morningstar chuckled. *A defrocked priest ... perfect! Not good enough to be a son ... but certainly qualified to take care of a few messy tasks from time to time.*

He looked at a photo of the man and shook his head. There was no way around it; Pocks was ugly. His nose was big, his skin was blotched, and the shirt he was wearing was too tight at his neck, causing the skin to bulge over the collar. *My god, boy, who taught you how to dress?*

It wasn't important. Pocks had other more attractive attributes. He was a demolitions specialist, and could disassemble a bomb quicker than anyone Morningstar had ever seen. *So why the hell had he wanted to be a priest?*

He read the brief biography. Pocks had come to the Pentagon as a part of the new terrorist intervention program, established soon after 9-11. The "Demolitions Identification and Removal Team" – DIRT to insiders – was overseen by General Daniels, which meant that Pocks essentially worked for Morningstar.

It was unclear where or how Pocks had learned his trade, but it didn't matter. The experts felt that the next major terror attack would most likely involve a dirty bomb. They needed men who could not only find the bomb, but could disarm it before it was able to poison an entire city.

He thumbed through a few more pages, stopping when he came to an envelope. He grinned. The return address, "New York Theological Association," was written in the upper left-hand corner. It was addressed to "Edward Morningstar, aide to General Alexander Daniels, The Pentagon," and had been delivered by special courier yesterday. Morningstar had not yet had time to review it. He opened it and pulled out a two-page document. It was handwritten by Bishop Thomas O'Reilly, and it outlined the exact offense that had cost Cosgrove his position at the seminary. Morningstar chuckled as he read it through. The poor boy had been found naked and aroused with one of the other boys on his floor. The two men were engaged in "homosexual behavior," and, though the Bishop had not gone so far as to condemn the act as criminal, he had spelled out in perfect detail, using Scripture and Catholic doctrine, why the behavior had disqualified the boy from becoming a priest. Morningstar laid the papers on the desk and grinned. Cosgrove was his guy.

He lifted the receiver. "Connect me to Herbert Cosgrove in demolitions."

He heard a click, followed by a weak, "Cosgrove here."

"Is this Herbert Cosgrove?"

"Yes."

"This is Edward Morningstar, chief aide to General Alexander Daniels."

There was a pause. "Um, yes sir. What can I do for you, sir?"

"I'd like you to help me out with a problem, Cosgrove."

"Certainly sir."

"The thing is, it's rather delicate. You need to keep it to yourself. Do you understand?"

There was silence.

"I said, do you understand?"

"Um ... yes sir."

"Good. I'll meet you tonight at Kelly's Diner on Wilford Street at 11:30 p.m. Look for me in the back."

He hung up and leaned back in his chair. Herbert Cosgrove – alias Pocks – would be a good addition to the team. The ruined man-of-God with his unique talents would be able to take care of those murky little annoyances that might interfere with Morningstar's plans. *DIRT indeed.* He pulled up the website with Cynthia Madison's picture. He touched her face and grinned. "And I'll start with you, you little bitch."

Chapter 14
WASHINGTON, D.C.

1/5/04

Henderson was cold and his body ached. *What's new?* he thought, as he tightened the scarf around his neck. He had spent most of the last four years chilled and in pain. The scars that covered his forearms and face made even warm spring breezes feel uncomfortable ... let alone the bitter cold of D.C in January. He rubbed his hands and tried to get warm. Suddenly he grinned. *It's nothing I can't handle.*

The phrase was one that Lili had heard him say only once, when she was two or three. From then on, no matter the challenge, she would always find a way to interject it. *"Don't worry about me, Uncle Mart ... it's nothing I can't handle."*

The sky was gray, thick clouds muting what little sun there might have been that time of year. It had left the shed he was hiding in dark and cold. He was huddled in a corner, scrolling through websites, looking for anything he could find on the men who had left the Morgan building at about the same time as Morningstar. Had they been attending a meeting? Or was it just a coincidence that they – and *the Vice-president* – had walked out only minutes before Morningstar? So far, his research had gotten him nowhere. He leaned back and rubbed his eyes.

The shed, about four feet by six, was only two hundred yards from Maddi's house. He had found it the day before, hidden in the backyard brush of an empty Tudor that sat half a block from her home. Henderson had set up shop there, knowing that by being so close he could keep an eye on her. It was something he had forbidden himself from doing until now; as if the hit on Al-Gharsi had somehow opened the door for him to be a part her life. *Funny how a good assassination can pull two people together.*

Earlier that day, he had purchased a pair of blue pants and a dark jacket that resembled the uniform of a city worker, and had then hijacked a vacant city van. He had driven to Maddi's house, pretending he was there to inspect the drainage system beneath the road. He had inconspicuously laid a tripwire in the crease between the sidewalk and the drive, and had then made a show of checking the nearby drain. He had moved on to the next one and, after checking three more drains, he had gotten into the van, returned it to the lot, and had then jogged back to the shed. She had not been home since. The wire would let him know when she came or went, but he had decided he wouldn't spy on her once she was inside her house. There was a line he wouldn't cross ... from surveyor to stalker. But he was tempted ... oh, how he was tempted.

He shivered and reached in his backpack for another scarf. As he was grabbing it, he saw a Christmas card he had gotten from Lili five years ago. He picked it up and held it to the dim light from outside the window. The edges were torn, the writing fading from years of being stashed away, either in his pocket or in the bottom of a backpack. He had saved it because of the poem she had written; a poem far beyond what any four-year-old girl should be capable of...

"'Tis Christmas time, so join me, please
My favored Uncles, Danil and Mart
In lauding o'er our Christmas trees
And sharing in our happy heart
The season brings us hopefulness

And teaches us to look beyond
Future's fears or Past's regrets
And love our lives as He looks on."

Henderson stared at the card. Such a remarkable girl. It had been written soon after her mother had passed; only months before her father would die on the Latvian battlefield. He shook his head and stuffed the card in his bag. She had counted on him ... on him and Danil. *And we failed her.*

He sighed as he rubbed his hands to warm them. He tried to imagine where she might be. *Is she being well cared for? Is she even alive?* He closed his eyes; the very thought of it made him sick. He felt like he would know if she was hurt ... or if she had died. It was another one of her gifts. She had a way of sharing her emotions across space and time ... her boundless joy when she played in the garden beneath his bedroom window ... her endless grief when her mother died.

He rubbed his neck, leaned forward, and got back to work on his research. But, as he stared at the webpages and scrolled through the biographies of the men at the Morgan Building, he couldn't help but think of her. *Are you okay, Lili?* Suddenly a rush of warmth passed through him. It was as if she was whispering past the trees into the cold dark shed, *"I'm okay, Uncle Mart. It's nothing I can't handle."*

Chapter 15
SOMEWHERE IN CHINA'S NORTHERN PROVINCES

1/5/04

"In the depth of winter, I finally learned that within me there lay an invincible summer." Lili thought of the Albert Camus quote and tried to smile. She had never felt so cold. And the thin blanket she had been given was hardly enough. She pulled it even tighter around her, and tucked her head underneath. She had tried to keep track of where she was; it had been impossible. Dark nights mixed with ice-cold days had left her weak and disoriented.

The two men with her had kept a close eye on her, one of them beating her on the shoulder with a long metal pipe whenever she tried to run away ... three times now. She rubbed her shoulder, wincing as she brushed over the bump on the top of her arm.

She lifted her head from the blanket and looked out the window of the rail car. Though it was dark, the moon was bright, and she could see glimmers of the terrain. It looked the same as it had for the past several hours. There were mountains in the distance, with patches of water here and there, along with grasslands that were little more than faded scrub. She searched for a street sign or a building; something that might give her a clue as to where she was. There was nothing.

The man had his hand on the pipe and was patting it in his hand. The other man looked at him and frowned. "Put it away, Chin!" he said in Mandarin. Lili understood him, though she pretended that she didn't. It gave her an advantage.

With dark eyes and thick muscles, Chin reminded her of the Monkey King, the infamous villain from an old Chinese fable. Nothing could hurt the Monkey King, and, as Lili looked at Chin holding the metal pipe, she wondered, *What hurts you, Chin?* He glared at his friend, but finally laid the pipe down beside him.

And he smelled. Not bad, but not good. *Like beef stew.* And, though she was hungry, or maybe because of it, the smell was tough to stomach. All she had had to eat were cups of broth and bologna sandwiches since they had left Latvia. What she wouldn't give for a plate of grey peas with bacon. *Or eggs and toast with Uncle Danil and Aunt Anna.*

Lili's eyes stung as she stared out the window. She longed for Danil and Anna. She hoped they hadn't been hurt when the Chinese men had come for her. She didn't think they had. *It's me they want ... not them.*

She didn't know why she was their target; all she knew was that they wanted her alive. It was confirmed every time Chin beat her with the pipe. *"You're in big trouble if you hurt her, you know,"* the other man would say in harsh Mandarin. Chin would mumble under his breath, but he would stop ... until the next time.

She continued to stare, and soon her eyes glossed over from the passing landscape. She leaned against the wall of the railcar and pulled the blanket to her chin. How many days had she been traveling? She looked down at her boot. She had used a piece of rock to etch a line on the side of it for each day she had been gone, but, after so many, she had resorted to grouping them into weeks. There were five marks for five weeks.

They had stopped from time to time, but never for more than a few hours. It was as if they were being followed, and the slightest delay might get them caught. *By who?* she wondered. *By the people who will save me?* She frowned. If someone was going to save her, they better hurry. She had no idea where she was, but one thing was sure; she was getting farther and farther from Latvia.

She wondered if maybe they were going to be on the run forever, the mighty Chin taunting her endlessly with his long metal pipe. Again, she rubbed her shoulder as she fought a sudden urge to cry. *You will not cry, Lilija Platacis.* Though it hurt her throat and made her eyes burn, she would not give those men the satisfaction of seeing her cry.

Just go to sleep. She closed her eyes, but sleep wouldn't come. She was cold and hungry, and she couldn't get comfortable. So, she did what she had done so many times over the past five weeks; she remembered. And no one could remember quite like Lili. Her eidetic mind allowed her to not only recreate each memory with perfect accuracy, but to recall every page of every book she had ever read. She had gotten through four books already, and was halfway through book number five, "Gulliver's Travels." As she had pictured the stories, page-by-page, she had imagined her mama and papa reading to her in the comfort of her warm, cozy bed. She closed her eyes tighter, squeezing them to hold back the tears. She missed her parents ... and she missed her bed. After a minute, she opened her eyes and sighed. She had gotten past it ... again.

She uncrossed her legs and stretched them in front of her; they had begun to ache. She was still dressed in the clothes she was wearing when she was kidnapped. Her coat was torn, her pants dirty, and her socks inside her boots were stretched and sagging. The blanket pulled away, and the cold air hit her ankles. It made her wince. *How long can I go on like this?*

She had once read an article about a man who had survived six weeks in the bitter cold of northern

Estonia with nothing more than two granola bars and a bottle of water. He had sung aloud whenever he was bored, and had then told stories to the rocks and trees in an effort to stay sane. *Maybe I need to sing aloud.* But she knew it would anger Chin, and she couldn't stand another strike to her arm. Besides, she didn't feel like singing. That was what one did when they were happy...

"Why are you singing, Mama?"
Larissa stopped her rendition of "Teku, Teku Pa Celinu,"(come on, go along the way) and looked down at Lili and grinned. "Because I am happy, Lili. I sing when I am happy."
Lili frowned. "Then why do we sing at funerals?"
Larissa was hanging clothes on the line outside their home in Ventspils. She stopped and turned to Lili. "Because then we are singing for God's happiness."
"How can God be happy when someone dies?"
"Because my dear, he is bringing them home..."

Lili's eyes burned even more and she rubbed them, biting her lip to keep from crying. She was about to delve into another chapter of "Gulliver's Travels," when the train came to a stop. The men stood, and Chin looked at her menacingly as he held the pole in his hand. "Get up!" he said in Chinese. She shrunk against the wall of the train. He raised the pole. "Get up, I say!"

Lili stood, her legs weak from so much time in the train and so little to eat. "Go!" he said again, and then prodded her with his pole. She stumbled to the front of the rail car. Chin looked at his partner and nodded. "It is time." *Time for what?* Lili wondered. She would be so glad to get off the train. *Maybe they're taking me somewhere with a warm bed and a hot shower.*

Chin shoved her and she jumped to the ground.

She fell and was having a hard time getting up. Her legs hurt and she was weak. Chin hopped down and gave her a kick. "Quit faking it!" he said in Chinese. With the help of a pile of cinder blocks, Lili rose to her knees, and then stood, shaking as she tried to stand still. She wrapped her blanket tight around her. Without the protection of the railcar, the frigid air cut right through her. Chin poked her with the pole and she limped forward several steps, following the other man into a big black car. She slid in next to him, and Chin got in on the other side. Though she was afraid, she refused to show it. She looked at Chin and – in perfect Mandarin – she said, "Scoot over." He looked at her and frowned. He raised his arm and she winced, ready for him to hit her. Suddenly he laughed and lowered his arm. He kept laughing, which made her mad, and she crossed her arms and stared straight ahead.

The car pulled away. After several miles, Lili looked up at Chin and said, again in perfect Mandarin, "Where are you taking me?"

Chin looked first at her, and then at his partner. He grinned. After a minute, he bent low to her ear and whispered, "Where no one will ever find you, Lili."

Chapter 16
WASHINGTON, D.C.

1/5/04

Maddi had spent most of the day sifting through the Arms Committee paperwork, but had learned little more than what she had already figured out. Silverton Arms, Inc. had managed to secure every U.S. arms contract for the past two years. And there had been one name on every invoice; Senator Dan Lawford. He was chairman of the committee, so it hadn't seemed like such an odd thing. Until she looked into his rise to the chairmanship. It had taken less than three months from the time he was put on the committee. Maddi tried to recall his selection as committee chairman; she couldn't. Which meant that it had not seemed unusual at the time.

She checked her watch. *Almost five o'clock.* She slid the invoices into the folder, and then carried the stack to the filing cabinet. She knelt down and put the entire stack in the bottom drawer. She locked the cabinet and slid the key in her purse. She needed to get to the senate chamber for a five o'clock vote. It involved a piece of legislation regarding a Yemen arms purchase by a group of separatists. The sale of the arms was a direct violation of a recent embargo, and Lawford had requested that an exemption be given, " *... so we can arm the insurgents as they fight to rid their country of Shiite rebels.*" Maddi was against the exemption; she didn't trust the insurgents. *If only Al-Gharsi was still alive.*

She hurried down the hall to the senate chamber with her secret service agent, Larry Moses following close behind. They reached the chamber, and she smiled at the sergeant-at-arms, a man who had come to the Capitol about the same time she had. "Good afternoon, Tony."

The slight young man in a crisp blue uniform smiled and said, "Good afternoon, Senator. Another late vote?"

Maddi nodded. "Afraid so." She was about to walk into the chamber, when a tall, lanky man positioned himself directly in front of her. *Dan Lawford.*

"Hello, Senator," drawled the Texas senator.

"Hello, Dan. How are you?"

"Just fine. I have something to give you." He grinned, his tobacco-stained teeth uneven, his breath foul. Maddi tried to walk around him. He moved to keep her from entering the chamber. "Dan, we're going to be late for the vote ... for *your* vote. Can we talk afterward?"

"This'll only take a minute." The Texas senator pulled a piece of paper from his jacket pocket. He handed it to Maddi.

"What's this?"

He grinned. "Just a little info that was left out of the file."

Maddi frowned. "What file?"

He moved closer. He smelled as if he had taken a bath in aftershave. Maddi covered her mouth and nose as she took a step back.

He didn't seem to notice. "The file you've been digging through since you joined my committee."

How did he know I requisitioned those files? Maddi glared at him. "I'm sorry ... I have no idea what you're talking about, Dan."

Lawford continued to grin, but his eyes had narrowed. "You know exactly what I'm talking about."

"I assure you, Dan, I have no idea." She forced a

grin. "So ... is this the important information you wanted to share with me?"

Lawton's eye twitched; he looked away. "I just want the file to be complete."

Maddi folded the paper and stuck it in her pocket. "How thoughtful," she said, as she stepped around him. She did her best to stay calm as she marched through the doors of the senate chamber.

Lawford yelled after her, "A word of advice, Senator." Maddi kept walking. "You might want to be careful where you stick that pretty little nose of yours."

Maddi pretended to ignore him as she found her seat. The high-profile bill had pulled in not only those on the Senate Arms Committee, but most of the other senators, as well. The chamber was packed. She saw Lawford walk in just as the gavel hit the lectern. She squeezed the arms of her chair; she was shaking.

The Senate Leader pounded his gavel a second time. His voice boomed from his seat in front of the room. "Is there any further discussion on Senate bill 684?"

Maddi barely heard him. Her thoughts were on Lawford and the piece of paper he had just handed her. Though his words had been vague, his intentions were clear. Maddi had just been threatened.

Chapter 17

WASHINGTON, D.C.

1/5/04

Thirty-six-year-old Simeon – James Roberts not so long ago – stared at his image in the mirror and grinned. He was naked, which is what he preferred, and, as he looked with admiration at the long, lean legs, the narrow hips, and the strong, sinewy arms, he had to marvel at his cleverness. He had been the "Pentagon operative" who had found the elusive Phoenix. *And then I lost him again ... but who's keeping track?*

He had been looking for Phoenix ever since the night of the Al-Gharsi hit, but to no avail. Soon after Christmas, Jacob had told him that if he didn't find Henderson by the first of the year, " ... *don't bother coming back.*" That was when Simeon had pulled out all the stops.

He had reached out to his tight-knit group of former Gulf War buddies for help. He had given them a description of Phoenix, with explicit instructions that they were not to share any of what he was asking them with anyone. *"I don't care if it's your brother, your priest, or even your mamma ... no one can know of this man."*

Through a friend of his stationed in Spain, he had learned that a man fitting Henderson's hard-to-miss description had stowed away on a vessel that had left Spain's Cadiz Harbor on December 25th. It was due to dock nine days later at the North Jersey Pier. Dressed in drag, Simeon had come to the pier – in thirty-degree weather – and had cajoled and flirted and then cajoled some more, until a night watchman had allowed him to stand on the dock while the overseas shipment was unloaded. *"But why you want to do such a thing is beyond me,"* the watchman had said as Simeon had handed him a fifty-dollar-bill. Simeon had smiled coyly. *"I find it exhilarating to watch the big, beefy sailors getting off the ship."*

Wearing a heavy fur coat, he had stationed himself on the dock, and had watched as first the crew, and then the captain left the ship. He had seen no trace of Henderson. He had been about to leave, when all at once he spotted him. Henderson had been lagging back behind a few of the sailors, and, though he had tried to hide his appearance with a scarf, dark glasses, and a stocking cap, Simeon had known it was him. *Who else runs so effortlessly, yet so awkwardly, and grabs his ribs in pain when he takes a deep breath?* No, there had been no doubt about it; it was Henderson.

He had tried to follow him, but was slowed not only by the heavy coat, but by stiletto heels, and had lost him soon after he snuck into a forest that bordered the bay. Simeon had been about to shed the coat and shoes and run after him, but had changed his mind. It would have been impossible to find anybody among those trees, let alone a well-trained assassin. And, though he would never admit it, he was afraid of Henderson. Simeon, too, was highly trained, but he wasn't so sure he would come out ahead – or even alive – in a one-on-one with the man.

So, he had let him go. He had told Jacob that one of the guards had stopped him before he could go after him. *"By the time I got away from the guard, Father, Henderson was long gone."* Simeon could tell that Jacob was upset, but he had not reprimanded him. Which was good; Simon hated to be reprimanded by his father.

But Simeon had spent the last two days trying to

find him ... trying to make it up to Jacob. Fortunately, earlier that day, there had been a breakthrough. Jacob had called him at 8:10 in the morning to let him know that surveillance equipment had identified Henderson as being within a mile of the Pentagon. Simeon had been alarmed. Was Henderson going after Jacob? *What if he tries to kill him?* But he had put it out of his mind once he realized ... Joseph wouldn't hurt Jacob. He, like all of the sons, had way too much to lose.

Over the course of the last three years, Jacob had gone to great lengths to secure his survival. He had learned secrets about every one of the men; things that would crush them – either physically or emotionally – were they to be revealed. On top of it, he had left the information in the hands of six of his closest sons. They had been given keys to safe deposit boxes, and had been told that, if anything happened to him, they were to open the boxes and do whatever was advised. *"For two of you it will be to reveal national secrets that will compromise great men ... for two others it will be to blackmail a straying son ... and for the last two, there will be strategies to ensure that our goals are met, regardless of whether or not I'm here to guide you."* It was brilliant. Henderson wouldn't hurt Jacob ... none of them would. Not only would there be a quick and deadly reprisal, but it would accomplish nothing. Henderson – just like the rest of the sons – needed Jacob far more than Jacob needed any of them.

Once Jacob had alerted Simeon to Henderson's location near the Pentagon, Simeon had made a beeline to the area. He had spent over three hours searching a five-mile radius for the scarred man, knowing he would likely be wearing the same scarf, hat, and sunglasses he had worn on the pier. But he had found no trace of him, and had returned to his apartment to await further instructions.

But he was getting tired of waiting. He angled his legs in front of the mirror and put his arms over his head. He was a remarkable specimen. Lean and shapely like a woman, but strong and clever like a man, he was the greatest of creatures ... he was a chameleon. *I can be whatever I need to be.*

He walked to his closet and pulled out a pair of black pants and a dark turtleneck sweater. Henderson had gone to the Pentagon for a reason ... which meant he probably hadn't left the city. *He's still in D.C. ... and I'm going to find him.*

Simeon put on the clothes and slid into his Burberry shoes. He walked to the mirror and stood in front of it with his hands on his hips. He grinned. He looked good ... *but not nearly as good as I'd look in my black dress and Louboutin boots.* He shook his head. The nightclubs would have to wait. One of the sons had gone astray and – until he was found – all of the 'boys' were in at least a little bit of jeopardy.

He grabbed his coat and put it on. He grinned. *But only I know what all of this is for.* He had been the only son to be let in on the purpose and plans of the family. At least that was what Jacob had told him. *"You need to know what lays ahead, Simeon because you are my most trusted soldier. It is up to you to keep the others in line."* Simeon chuckled as he grabbed his Glock and stuffed it in his pocket. *Believe me, Father ... nothing will please me more.*

Chapter 18
WASHINGTON, D.C.

1/5/04

Once the vote was finished, Maddi could not get out of the senate chamber fast enough. She had not opened the sheet of paper Lawford had given her; she wanted to wait until she got back to her office. Her legs felt weak as she hurried out of the chamber. Her secretary, Phil, was still at his desk, and she nodded as she raced past him and shut the door. She sat at her desk and pulled the sheet of paper from her pocket. As she smoothed it on her desk, she could see that her hands were shaking. *Calm down, Maddi.* It was another receipt, similar to the hundred or so she had already looked at. With one exception: the invoice, requesting arms to aid militants – this time in Iran – had been bid out and then granted to one of Silverton's strongest competitors, Skywalk Weaponry. But the signature was the same as the one she had seen on every other contract ... Dan Lawford.

Maddi leaned back in her chair. *He is 'proving' that Silverton did not get every bid ... which means he knows that it's shady that they got all the rest.* She frowned. And why wasn't this invoice in with all the others? Her eyes widened. *Because this one is a fraud.*

She leaned forward and pushed the intercom. "Phil, contact Skywalk Weaponry and see if they have a copy of an invoice from–" she checked the date "–June 3rd, 2003."

She grabbed her key from her purse, walked over to the filing cabinet, and unlocked it. She sat on the floor, pulled out the stack of files, and placed them beside her. She thumbed through them until she came to a black file that had "Senate Arms Committee members" written across the top. She stood and carried it to her desk. The file contained the biographies of each of the members, and, as she skimmed through the names, she tried to imagine any one of them colluding with Lawford to push arms contracts to Silverton. She could see it with one or two of the members, but there were several on the list she was sure would never compromise their integrity for the sake of an arms manufacturer. *Unless Silverton had financed their campaigns.*

She pushed the intercom again. "And I'll need the names of all major financial backers for each member of the Senate Arms Committee."

She leaned back and stared at the list. She hoped – she *prayed* – she was wrong. The thought that all twenty-four members of the committee had been compromised by campaign contributions was a sickening thought. She thought of her own backers. Had she ever bargained away her integrity to keep the money coming in? She frowned. She couldn't deny it; as long as nobody got hurt, there had likely been a time or two when she had thrown a bone to a wealthy contributor. But this was different. If the entire Senate Arms Committee had been compromised by one single benefactor, and that benefactor had then profited from the committee's decisions, the ramifications would be huge.

She thumbed through the file until she found Lawford's biography. She pulled it out and read it through. Prior to his appointment to the Senate Arms Committee, he had been on the powerful Ways and Means, and his credentials for each were unmatched. He had served in the U.S. Army for eight years, and had been deployed overseas during the first Iraq war. He had earned a medal of valor, and had even been given the Purple Heart after risking his life to save an entire squadron from an attack outside Kuwait. Maddi frowned. It was hard to think of Lawford as a hero. She read on. He had left the army soon after that, and had run for the Texas state senate within a year of his discharge. He had won, and had then been handpicked to fill the role of a U.S. Senator who had been killed in a boating accident outside his home in Crawford. Maddi frowned. *How convenient.*

Lawford's position on the Senate Arms Committee had been approved unanimously by both sides of the aisle. He had been nominated for the role of chairman after only a few months. It normally took years to rise to the chairmanship of a powerful committee. She walked over to the stack of files. She knelt down and dug through the stack for another folder, which would contain the minutes from every Arms Committee meeting since January 2002. She found the file, set it on her lap, and started at the beginning. She was looking for the vote that had made Lawford chairman. Had it been unanimous? Had all twenty-four senators gotten behind the coronation? After twenty minutes of plowing through the notes, she finally found it in the March 4th minutes. His nomination for chairman had come up toward the end of the meeting. He had been nominated by another member of the committee, Francis O'Malley from Connecticut. Maddi hardly knew O'Malley. He was from the opposing party, and had only been a senator for two years. She had actually spoken with him only once, when they were both waiting outside the Oval Office to talk to Wilcox. He had seemed unimposing at the time ... *hardly someone who would conspire with Lawford to divert arms sales to a single manufacturer.*

She walked to her desk and leaned over the

intercom. "Phil. Could you get me whatever you can find on Senator Francis O'Malley from Connecticut?"

She went back to the file and read through the minutes. She reached the end and frowned. Lawford had been voted in as chairman unanimously. *Either no one was paying attention, or every member of this committee is corrupt.* Then again, maybe they didn't share her revulsion of the man. Was it so unusual that a well-regarded senator with a stellar military career had been chosen as chairman? *It is when he had only been on the committee for three months!*

Maddi stood and paced the room. She needed to talk to some of the members, and she would start with O'Malley. Fortunately, he would be at the retreat. But she would need to be discreet. If he had innocently been fooled by the persuasive Dan Lawford that was one thing ... but if he and the others were colluding with the man, well ... that would open a can of worms Maddi didn't even want to think about.

So, let it go. Pretend you don't know any of this. Maddi chuckled. She had never been good at letting things go. She checked the time. 7:30 p.m. Hank was supposed to take her to dinner in an hour, and she hadn't even begun to prepare for the retreat. She needed to get home. She leaned forward and shuffled through the papers until she found the receipt Lawford had given her. Why had he been compelled to "make the record complete?" As she slid it in the file, and then stuffed a few of the folders into her briefcase, she shook her head and frowned. *Because he knows ... if I keep digging ... I'll find something he doesn't want me to see.*

Chapter 19
WASHINGTON, D.C.

1/5/04

The stare from the man standing next to Hank – actually it was more like a scowl – was unnerving. Bill Beaker was his name, and he had not made any effort to hide his resentment of Hank's hiring as the Deputy Director of the Department. The tall, lean Beaker had been with the FBI for ten years, and had been a liaison to the Pentagon for ten more. He had served under Jason Hanover, the Homeland Director, for three years, one of the first hires when the Department was established soon after the 9-11 attacks. Hank was sure Beaker wondered why he had been given a role as Deputy Director with little more than an M.D. after his name. Hank couldn't blame him; he often wondered the same thing. *"You've got a good head on your shoulders,"* Hanover had told him. *"You think before you speak, you use good judgment, and you're not part of the system. These are the things I need ... not more credentials."*

And it didn't hurt that Hank had helped the Illinois Department of Health with the monkey pox outbreak in the spring of 2003. He had done a short stint at a Chicago urgent care, and had been one of the first to identify the strange pattern of symptoms. He had moved aggressively with testing, and had contacted the local health department when he had received the results. The head of Chicago's health department – who just happened to be a friend of Hanover's – had pulled him in to assist with the identification of the virus throughout all of Chicago, and it was through their efforts that the country was able to identify and then contain the virus. Apparently, Hanover was made aware of Hank's efforts, and, because of Hank's ties to Maddi, Hanover hired him only a few weeks later.

Hank raised his pistol, doing his best to ignore Beaker as he sighted the target twenty feet in front of him. He emptied his chamber. Although two of the bullets didn't even hit it, the others were closer than when he started, and he nodded with satisfaction. Beaker didn't bother to hide a smirk. Hank reloaded, aimed, and fired. Closer still. He did the same thing, over and over for the next twenty minutes. He checked his watch. *7:50 p.m.* He was supposed to meet Maddi for dinner at 8:30, so he fired a final round, pleased when every single bullet hit within the vicinity of the heart of the black shadow hanging on a wire. Could he do that when he was in the middle of a real firefight? Probably not. *Hopefully I'll never have to find out.*

He left his ear guards on the counter and holstered his weapon. Beaker had long since left the range, so Hank nodded at the only man still there, the night security guard. "Goodnight Pete."

"Goodnight, Dr. Clarkson."

Pete Morison was one of the few who referred to him as Dr. Clarkson, the others calling him either Hank, Doc, or simply "hey you." They didn't do that in front of Hanover, however; the Director would never permit any form of disrespect to one of his deputies. But Hank got it; he understood why the men resented him. He had gotten the next-to-the-top spot not for years of service, but because Hanover wanted a doctor instead of a military man. After all, bioterror had a lot more to do with medicine than it did with guns or espionage. At least that was what Hanover kept telling him. Regardless, Hank had accepted that he would have to work to earn the respect of the other agents.

He left the range and drove back to his townhouse, where he quickly showered and changed into kakis and a sweater. Just as he was about to leave, his cellphone rang. It was Maddi. He grinned. "You ready?"

There was a pause. "Hank, I have to cancel. I'm so sorry for the late notice." Another pause. "I'm leaving for the retreat tomorrow and I am simply not ready."

Hank frowned. "You gotta' eat, right?"

"Yes. I'll probably just make a TV dinner or something."

Hank sighed. "Tell you what. I'll grab some Chinese and bring it by. I don't even need to stay, unless you want the company."

Another pause. "Hank, I hate for you–"

"I'm on my way."

He ended the call and then pulled a wrinkled "Golden Dragon Buffet" menu from his top drawer. He phoned in an order, and then left his townhouse and walked to his car. He climbed in and pulled out of the lot. As he drove to the Chinese restaurant, he thought back to the last time he and Maddi had had Chinese. The circumstances had been far different. The two of them were actually happy then. Maddi had never been too busy to see him, and her face had lit up whenever he walked into the room. How long ago had it been? *It doesn't matter.* One thing was sure, whenever it was, it had happened before Henderson.

Hank arrived at the restaurant and parked the car. The food wouldn't be ready for another five minutes. He sat there, staring at the steering wheel, thinking about Maddi, Henderson, and how much everything had changed. And now, nearly four years later, there was still nothing he could do about it. No matter how hard he tried to win her back, he failed. Maddi was in love with a dead man ... and, because Henderson would always be dead, there was nothing that was going to change that.

Chapter 20
WASHINGTON, D.C.

1/5/04

Henderson stared down at the wide circular tin on the floor of the shed. Should he risk it? He shivered and watched as his breath crystallized in the air. *I have to.* He had been in the shed for the past five hours, and he was freezing to death. He needed to start a fire, and he wondered if he could do it without being spotted. The shed was hidden by trees on all sides, but it was winter and there were few leaves. And, though the shed was sturdy, there were plenty of gaps between the boards. The smoke would blend with the mist of the cold night, but any hint of a flame would likely be spotted, unless he could keep the flames from rising over the metal rim.

He leaned over, adjusted the small pieces of kindling he had grabbed from outside, and then rolled up balls of newspaper. He struck a match to the side of the rim and lowered it over the kindling. It caught fire and he tamped down the flames with a piece of tile he had found in the shed. He grabbed two logs from a stack of six he had gathered earlier in the day and lowered them into the flames. He had vented the top of the shed, doing his best to steer the smoke toward the trees so it would be harder to see. He had a bucket of water ready to douse the flames if they got too high.

When the fire was under control, he laid next to it to get warm. It felt good to lay by the flames and pretend – for a few seconds anyway – that things were like they used to be. But then he would remember – though Maddi was within a few hundred yards of him

– she was a thousand miles away.

The wire he had laid earlier had been tripped thirty minutes ago, at 7:50 p.m., when Maddi's car had pulled into the drive. He had watched through two slats in the back of the shed as she had walked to the door. Except for the Al-Gharsi hit, he had not been that close to her in four years. And it had nearly dropped him to his knees. But he had refrained from pulling out his binoculars and watching her through the windows of her house. *Don't cross that line, Henderson.*

He sat up and held his hands over the flame. What he wouldn't give to stroll to the house, knock on the door, and stare into the eyes he had never forgotten. He put a hand to the scars over his battered jaw and closed his eyes. *It's not going to happen, Henderson ... let it go.*

His phone vibrated and he held it to his ear. Though he had refused to spy on her, he had tapped her phone, and he felt guilty as he listened to her cancel dinner plans with Hank. He felt even guiltier when he silently cheered. Was she really too busy? Or had something come between them? *Me?* He scoffed. *You're dead, Henderson ... remember?*

He was surprised to hear her say that she was leaving the next day for a retreat. He had been monitoring her senate webpage and had seen no mention of it. When she and Hank ended the call, Henderson opened his computer and, using a hot spot from his phone, logged onto her webpage. He saw it right away; the second item from the top. *"Looking forward to joining my colleagues tomorrow to prepare for the upcoming election."* It gave few details, but, with a little bit of digging, he was able to learn that the retreat was being held at the Grande Dames in downtown Jacksonville. Henderson shivered as he put down the computer and rubbed his hands over the flame. *Florida seems like a pretty good idea right now.*

He had heard Hank say that he was bringing Chinese; it sounded good. He was hungry. He should join them. *The three of us ... and a little egg foo young.* He chuckled and pulled a granola bar and a protein shake from his backpack. He took a bite of the granola as he grabbed his laptop and clicked to the website of the Vice-president, James D. Conner from Pennsylvania. He had yet to find anything that linked Conner to Morningstar, but he felt confident that the two men leaving the Morgan Building at about the same time was no coincidence. He scrolled through the pages, searching for something new; a word or comment he had missed that would tie the two men to one another. He was about to log off, when a statement caught his eye. "The Vice-president has long been an advocate for peace in the Middle East, and is eager to pursue this agenda on behalf of President Wilcox over the course of the next four years." He stared at the words and frowned. *Why would a man advocating for Middle East peace have anything to do with Morningstar?* Then again ... only Henderson knew that Morningstar had been behind the Al-Gharsi hit. Which meant only Henderson knew that Morningstar wanted the exact opposite of peace in the Middle East. *Morningstar has fooled them all.*

He tried to access the site he had hacked into earlier; the one where he had found the reference to the early-morning meeting from a man named Chief. The site had been disabled. Henderson wasn't surprised. He clicked to another website he had visited many times during his days with Morningstar. It was a long shot, but just maybe Morningstar still used the site to communicate with the other men who worked for him. The site was hard to find, buried in a link on an unused Army website from the late 1990's. It required a password to access both the website and the link, which would then take the user to an innocuous memo where Morningstar would cryptically list any action that was to be completed within the next twenty-four hours. It was how Morningstar had told him who to kill; how he had notified him of the time and the target. He went there now, typed in his Phoenix password, and was disappointed to see that there was nothing. *Was I his only stooge?* He went back to the Army website and scoured the page. He was about to log off, when he noticed a new link that had not been there the last time he had looked ... about twenty-four hours ago. He clicked it and was taken to a blank page asking for a user name and password. He stared at it and frowned. Two layers of security just to get to the page, and it was protected with another layer of security. *This site is important.*

He continued to stare at the page, trying to guess what Morningstar might consider a suitable user name. King? God? Masteroftheuniverse? He chuckled. *I know exactly what he would use.* He typed in Jacob. Morningstar had referred to himself as Jacob on more than one occasion. Henderson had assumed it was his middle name, or maybe a nickname his parents had given him. Whenever he said it, he would beam with pride. But what might he use for a password? Henderson sat back and thought about Morningstar's life. There was the world everyone knew; his role as an important Pentagon aide. Would he use a word from that life? *Not likely.* It would be something from his secret world ... the life he shared with his chief assistant, Simeon. Henderson went to the prompt and typed "Simeon." He waited. Nothing. *Dammit!* It was highly probable that the website would lock him out if he got it wrong again. So, who else was in Morningstar's secret world? He frowned. *Me.* Would

Morningstar use his name as a password? And, if so, which one? Henderson? Phoenix? Joseph? He didn't think it would be Henderson; Morningstar had told him on many occasions that Henderson was dead. *"Don't even utter the name, my son."* Which left Phoenix or Joseph. With a shaking finger, he tapped the letter P. He stopped. Morningstar wouldn't use Phoenix. The CIA was aware of Phoenix, and Morningstar couldn't afford to be linked to him under such covert circumstances. He backspaced and started over, his finger still shaking as he typed the six letters for Joseph. He hesitated, and then pushed enter. The page disappeared, and, in its place, were two email exchanges between Jacob and Simeon. His heart was racing. He had done it! The fact that there were only two messages meant that they were likely removed from the site automatically after a certain period of time. He read the first one, which had been sent early that morning. Even with all the security steps, they had stuck to fake names and cryptic phrases. There was mention of an arms shipment going out in a few weeks, and a comment about three ships leaving Africa on January first. *"Make sure they're ready, Simeon."* Henderson frowned. *What are you up to, Morningstar?*

He read the next email. It had been sent soon after the first, and Jacob had referenced two names Henderson didn't recognize. Naphtali and Asher. *What the hell?*

All at once an alert splashed across the screen. "FATAL ERROR. This site has been compromised." Henderson had been detected! He left the site and logged off his computer. He turned off his cellphone. He shoved the laptop in his pack, along with anything else that might identify him. Morningstar's software had detected him, and it was likely – because he had hacked into Morningstar's actual server – it had determined his exact location. He grabbed the water and doused the fire. He was about to grab the detection device for the tripwire in Maddi's driveway when he stopped. The light had come on. Someone was pulling into the drive. He pulled out his binoculars, moved to the back of the shed, and focused the lens through a narrow slat. Hank had arrived. He stepped out of his car carrying a sack full of food; the Chinese dinner. Henderson watched him climb the steps to the porch, and then walk to the front door. He knocked. Henderson waited. Maddi opened the door. She reached up and kissed him on the cheek. Henderson's heart ached. He watched the two of them walk arm in arm into her house. *Get out of here, Henderson! Morningstar knows where you are!*

He disconnected the monitor and shoved it in his pack, along with the binoculars. He walked out of the shed and crept through the trees to a creek about a half-mile away. He followed it for nearly two miles, and then ran through the back door of a department store to the front. He walked onto the sidewalk, blending easily with those who were strolling the mall. He adjusted his scarf, making sure his scars were covered, and pulled his stocking cap lower on his forehead. He had escaped, at least for the time being, but he wouldn't be able to return to the shed ... not any time soon, anyway.

As he walked down the street, he thought of Hank and Maddi. Did she love Hank? He didn't know ... he couldn't tell from the brief conversation he had overheard. He hoped not, but – in a way – he wished she did. Maddi should love and be loved by a good and noble man. *You're crazy, Henderson.*

He continued to walk, looking in every direction for either Morningstar or one of his henchmen. How many did he have? *More than I thought.* Who was

Naphtali? Who was Asher? Suddenly he stopped. *Simeon, Joseph, Naphtali, Asher ... and Jacob!* Morningstar hadn't simply formed an army of men; he had put together a family of sons ... *and I, Joseph, was one of them.*

Chapter 21
WASHINGTON, D.C.

1/5/04

The alert had come across Morningstar's laptop screen like a screeching alarm. Though he couldn't be sure it was Henderson who had hacked into the site, he would bet money on it. He immediately called Simeon. "Where are you?"

"Prowling ... for Joseph."

"I found him. Coordinates 38.8895 N by 77.0353 W. Hurry!"

He then disabled the site, knowing, whoever it was, he would likely try again. *Did the bastard learn anything from the emails?* He thought back. He had been emailing Simeon. They had discussed the arms shipment, though they had been vague about where and when. They had also mentioned the African boats, but, again, they had been vague. He sneered as he closed his computer. *Whoever hacked onto that site learned nothing.*

He stood and walked to his living room bar. He poured a glass of bourbon and drank it in one swallow. *Who was it?* Who had managed to get through not only the army website and the link, but the user name and password, as well? *It had to be Henderson.* Which meant that he was still in D.C. He hoped Simeon would get to him before he got away, but he doubted it. Henderson was the best there was. Morningstar had trained him. *Simeon won't find him.*

He poured another glass of bourbon; his hands were shaking. He grabbed the drink and went to stand by the fire. He stared at the flames, trying to imagine why Henderson was still in D.C. *Is he after me? Has he come back to kill me?*

He took a drink, licking his lips as the bitter whisky calmed him. Of course Henderson hadn't come back to kill him. The man would be a fool to do anything to him. Not only did Morningstar have Lili, but he also knew a secret ... something so ugly about Henderson and his family, it would be like a tidal wave rushing through the international community. Henderson would do whatever it took to keep that secret hidden. *And he knows I've given my other sons access to that secret – and to Lili – should something happen to me.* Morningstar took another sip of whiskey, still uneasy, but calmer than he had been. Henderson hadn't come to kill him ... *he has returned to find a way back into the fold.*

Henderson was probably struggling for a way to apologize. That had to be it. The spying and hacking into Morningstar's email was likely his way of trying to make things right. He was afraid of Morningstar – as they all were – and he was trying to figure out how to come back without losing face. *I must find a way to reach out to him ... to let him know that I forgive him for what he's done to me.*

But Henderson wouldn't stay in D.C. very long, especially now that he knew his position had been compromised. *He will try to run.* Morningstar checked his watch. 8:05 p.m. Simeon was on his way to the coordinates, but Henderson would likely be long gone. Morningstar needed someone else to track him if he left town.

He pulled out his cellphone and dialed. The call was answered and, without waiting for a hello, he said, "Naphtali, it's me. I need you to get a hold of the facial recognition software." He paused. "It's in the warehouse outside town. You have the key."

"Yes sir."

"Then I need you to use that software to monitor every bus station, every Amtrak terminal, and every rest stop within two hundred miles of D.C."

There was silence. "Who am I looking for, Father?"

"I'll send you a photo," he said, and then added, "You're looking for your brother, my son. You're looking for Joseph."

Chapter 22
WASHINGTON, D.C.

1/5/04

Henderson had stayed in the shadows along the mall for another ten minutes, and had then hailed a taxi to take him to a rest stop outside D.C. He needed to get out of town. Maddi was going to Jacksonville ... he would go there, as well. He had reached the stop just before 9:00 p.m., and had then thumbed a ride with a trucker heading south on I-95. They had driven non-stop for the last two hours. Neither one had said a word. Henderson had been glad for the quiet. He needed to think.

Morningstar had put together a family of men ... *of sons.* The man clearly saw himself as the father, Jacob, and – if he stayed true to the Bible – he would have twelve sons to help him carry out his plans. But what were his plans? Henderson had always felt that Morningstar was mentally unstable, but now he wondered how delusional the man had become.

Just outside Jarratt, Virginia, Henderson asked the driver to let him off at the exit to Emporia. It was almost 11:00 and he had a call to make. The driver pulled off the road and Henderson jumped from the cab, thanking the man with a wave and a nod. He checked his watch. *10:59.* He jogged to a phone booth near a strip mall. He sifted through the coins in his pocket, making sure he had four dollars and seventy-five cents. That's how much it cost to call Latvia and talk for less than a minute.

He stepped into the booth, picked up the receiver, and dialed zero. When it was time, he dropped in the coins and waited. It took only one ring for Dain Rozenblats to answer.

"Yes sir?"

"Any luck?"

There was a pause. "No sir. But I've got a lead or two. I hope to have better news by tomorrow's call."

Henderson said goodbye and hung up the phone. It had been the same thing for over a week. Dain was always following "a lead or two." And, though Henderson was beginning to lose hope, he forced himself to believe him ... one more time ...

"Listen, Uncle Mart. Listen to my poem."

Henderson grinned. He loved it when the five-year-old read her poetry. She wasn't like other little girls, and the wisdom of her words often surprised him. "Go ahead, Lili. I'm listening."

She puffed up her shoulders and said aloud,

"I see the storm so far from shore,
Far sooner than occurs to most
I feel the rain, I hear the roar
Long before it hits the coast."

Lili looked at him to make sure he was still listening. She went on ...

"I'm told it is a gift to see
What's up ahead, beyond the plain,
But it's more like a penalty
For still I cannot stop the rain."

Henderson struggled to smile. Lili was remarkable. He wondered if Morningstar knew the truth about her; not only her gifts, but the fact that she was afraid of them. If he did, he would use it against her. Henderson bristled. The very thought of Morningstar not only having Lili, but hurting her, made him so angry he could barely stand it. Had he spoken of Lili's amazing abilities during his drug-induced rants? He hoped not, but he knew he probably had. Why else would the man feel such confidence to use her against him? Then again, if Morningstar thought the girl had something to offer, he might be less inclined to hurt her.

Henderson walked away from the phone booth, appreciating the warmer air of southern Virginia. Though it was a cool fifty degrees, it felt good. He lowered the scarf and pulled his hat from his forehead. He walked up to a group of pedestrians and fell in behind them as they strolled past a row of bars and restaurants. After half a mile or so, he stopped and looked up at the sky. It was a beautiful night, and it made him want to cry. Someone bumped into him and then shied away when they caught sight of his scars. He was used to it. He tightened the scarf over his face and neck, pulled his knit cap lower on his forehead, and walked on ... to the next rest stop, the next highway ramp, and the next trucker.

Chapter 23
WASHINGTON, D.C.

1/5/04

Maddi had spent about twenty minutes with Hank, picking at the Chinese food, making small talk as she tried not to think about Lawford and his threat. She had politely asked Hank to leave just after 9:00, telling him she had a lot to do to get ready for the retreat. But it wasn't the retreat she had worked on after she had given him a quick kiss goodbye. It was the Silverton arms deals. She had sat down with the files and had dug through them, one by one, trying to reconcile the discrepancies in a way that wouldn't imply that the entire Senate Arms Committee was corrupt. By the end of the night, she had failed to do so, and was stunned when she saw that it was after 11:00. She looked at Lawford's invoice a final time, and then shoved it in the folder. She left the entire stack on the coffee table, next to the half-eaten boxes of Chinese. She would go through it all in the morning, before she left for Jacksonville.

Her relief agent, Jeremy Collins, had arrived at 9:05, soon after Hank had left. Maddi had said goodbye to Larry, and had led Collins into the study. Every night was pretty much the same; he would arrive around 9:00, and, after a few hours she would make him tea, put cookies on a tray, and then take it to him, along with a quilt and a pillow. He would then spend the night reading a Patterson novel, listening for the slightest noise to suggest that Maddi wasn't safe. She was grateful for her agents, though she wished they weren't necessary. But the threat from Lawford was just another reminder: Maddi had made some powerful enemies over the years.

She grinned as she stared down at the boxes of Chinese. She had offered Collins some of the leftovers, but he had declined. *"Your tea and cookies will be enough for me."*

She stood from the couch and walked to the kitchen to make the tea. When it was ready, she poured a cup for Collins, and placed three cookies on a plate. She carried the snack into the study. "As requested."

He looked up from his novel and grinned. "Thank you, Senator."

Maddi set the tea and cookies on the table beside him.

He stuffed a cookie in his mouth. "Great ... as usual."

She laughed. Collins wasn't nearly as tall as Larry, and had been harder to get to know, but she liked the man with the freckles and the gentle demeanor. "I'm glad you like it. Do you need anything else?"

He shook his head. "No, thank you. This should do it."

She left the study and walked back to the kitchen. She made a cup of tea for herself and carried it to the living room. She then did what she had done far too often in the last three-and-a-half years; she remembered.

She walked over to the stereo and put in a well-worn CD, and then sat on the sofa, listening to the woeful words of Rickie Lee Jones. She pulled a blanket over her shoulders; not the one she had been given by Henderson's mother. That one, made by the hands of Henderson's nanny, had been too painful to look at night after night, so Maddi had finally tucked it away in an old brown chest that sat just outside her bedroom door. No, this blanket had been given to her by the

President's wife as a thank-you for a fundraiser Maddi had hosted two years ago. *"You have gone above and beyond, dear Cynthia,"* the woman had told her. Maddi sighed as she wrapped the blanket tighter over her shoulders. She grabbed a pillow to her chest, and pretended ... for at least a few minutes anyway ... that things had turned out differently. That her father had never been killed, her mother had never become an alcoholic, and Henderson had never died. The last one was the toughest; she had come to terms with her father's death and her mother's downward spiral into alcoholism. But she couldn't seem to accept the loss of Henderson. There were times when she wished she had never met him, but then she would remember the weekend in Providence and she would know ... being with him had brought her more than happiness ... it had made her sane. The world could have spun off its axis, but she would have been centered in the knowledge of her love for one man...

"I've never really done anything like this, you know."

Henderson looked at her and grinned. "Like what?"

Maddi smiled self-consciously. "Oh ... you know ... asked a man to my room and spent the night with him. It's not really what I do."

Henderson chuckled. They were lying on top of a bearskin rug watching the sun come up over Narragansett Bay. They had been in that spot for the last hour, moving from the couch to the bed to the floor in one fluid motion through the course of the night. And it had felt right. More than anything Maddi had ever done in her life; it was right. Henderson pulled her close. "So, what is it you do?"

Maddi grinned. "I'm industrious. I get things

done. I'm careful, methodical ... never whimsical."

"Do you feel like this is whimsical?"

She laughed. "Of course it is! Look at you, lying there with nothing on, while I drown in your shirt and lean against you as if I've known you forever." She grinned. "What would you call it?"

He turned to face her. "Do you want to know the truth?"

"Of course I do."

"You won't laugh at me?"

Maddi grinned. "I promise ... I won't laugh."

"Well, at the risk of losing my man-card ... I call it love..."

Maddi put her hand to her chest. Remembering Henderson hurt. *So why do I put myself through this?* She knew the answer. Because he had touched her in a place so deep, so real, that to not feel it left her hollow. *So, when does it end?* She sighed as she looked out the window at the black night. *When you make it end.*

She tossed the pillow to the sofa, but kept the blanket over her shoulders. Would she ever be able to leave him behind? She had tried so many times. She leaned forward and sipped her tea. There was no sense in even trying ... she couldn't do it. The pain of not remembering – of losing him completely – was far worse than the hurt she felt every time she thought of him. She once again grabbed the pillow, closed her eyes, and lay against the arm of the sofa. *Maybe someday I will learn how to let him go.*

Chapter 24

WASHINGTON, D.C.

1/5/04

Morningstar checked his watch as he pulled up to the diner where he had agreed to meet Pocks. *11:30 on the dot.* He stopped the car. He looked in the window to see if Pocks was there; no sign of him. Morningstar grabbed his briefcase, stepped out of the car, and locked the door. He walked inside and made his way to the back. He found a table in the corner and sat down.

"Do you want some coffee, sir?"

He nodded.

The waitress brought the coffee; he took a sip and cringed. *No one makes a decent cup of coffee anymore.* Two minutes later, he saw Pocks at the door and waved him over. Pocks walked to the table, his hands in his pockets, an Irish paddy cap sitting awkwardly on his head. Morningstar stared at him over the coffee. "Sit."

The stroppy man took a seat across from him. Pocks was even uglier than he remembered. His nose was not only big, but bulbous, and his forehead was far too wide for the rest of his face. His clothes, not nearly as stylish as Morningstar was used to, did not fit him well, and his hair fell unevenly on his forehead. There were scars on his cheeks and chin that had clearly come from years of untreated acne. *Hence the name Pocks.*

Morningstar looked at him and frowned. "Here's what I want you to do." He set his coffee on the table and reached for his briefcase. He set it in his lap, opened it, and pulled out a folder. There was nothing written on the outside. He handed it to Pocks. "Don't open it here." He lowered his voice. "Inside is

everything you need to know about your assignment."
He paused. "I'm looking for intimidation, Pocks."

The man frowned.

"I want you to scare someone into behaving."

Pocks rolled his tongue against his cheek, still frowning.

Morningstar sighed. "Just read the file. You'll know what to do." He paused. "And then destroy it."

Pocks stuttered. "Do – do I have to ... hurt anyone?"

Morningstar grinned. "No ... not yet, anyway." He offered Pocks a cellphone. "This is how we'll communicate. Don't use it for any other reason."

Pocks stared at the phone without taking it. "I'm ... I'm not sure about this, sir."

Morningstar bristled as he leaned in, crammed the phone into Pocks' chest, and whispered, "You better *get* sure, asshole. I know about the seminary."

Pocks' eyes widened, the expression priceless. He stuffed the phone in his pocket. Never had Morningstar achieved so much with only a few words.

The waitress came by and was about to ask Pocks if he wanted coffee, when Morningstar said, "He's not staying."

She nodded. "Then would you like something to eat, sir?"

Morningstar nodded. "I'll have a piece of cherry pie."

She walked away. Morningstar waved his hand at Pocks. "See ya'."

Pocks stood, carrying the folder awkwardly under one arm as he hurried to the door. Morningstar watched him, amused at how odd and apprehensive the man was. He was perfect. No one would ever suspect him of anything beyond incompetence. *I just hope he's up to the task.*

The pie came and he ate it in four bites. He laid a five-dollar bill on the table and walked out to his car. He had just left the lot when his cellphone rang. "Yes?"

"Father, it's me, Naphtali."

"What's up, son?"

"I found him."

Morningstar grinned. "Excellent! How? Where?"

"I used the facial recognition tracker like you suggested, and I located him just north of the Carolinas."

Morningstar frowned. *Where is he going?*

"What should I do, Father?"

"Just keep an eye on him." He paused. "The guy's clever, so watch him closely, Naphtali ... but don't let him know you're on to him. Got it?"

"Yes Father. I'll be in touch."

Morningstar shoved the phone in his pocket, grinning as he continued his drive. But, instead of going home, he turned left on Pennsylvania Avenue and headed south to Girard Street. It was Monday night, and downtown D.C. was awaiting his arrival. But it wasn't the charmed ballrooms of the privileged and powerful; no, he was headed to a different part of D.C. ... where two-bit whores felt at home, and drug dealers sold their wares openly on the streets.

The ritual on Girard Street had begun years ago, soon after the first Twin Towers bombing in February of 1993. It had been a failure of reconnaissance on Morningstar's part that had allowed the bombing to occur, and, though he didn't care about the loss of life, he did care about the damage to his reputation. So, with clever manipulation of the facts, he had managed to place the blame on a subordinate. He had celebrated his success by hiring a cheap prostitute, who had led him to the hotel on Girard Street and had then introduced him to cocaine. The experience had been magical. The voices he had fought in his head for years had suddenly made sense ... as if the cocaine had become a translator. Then, on his fiftieth birthday in 1999, those voices coalesced into the voice of God. And the two men had spoken as equals, God outlining his hopes and desires, Morningstar vowing to make them come true. Every Monday was the same. He would come to Girard Street, buy his cocaine, and spend the night in the hotel room, communing with God, leader-to-leader, man-to-man.

Morningstar reached Girard at 11:55 p.m. and parked two blocks from the Breezeway Hotel. He knew the place well. The hotel, with its battered neon lights that blinked only some of the letters half of the time, greeted him as he walked up to a man standing half a block away. He handed him a fifty-dollar bill. The man slid a small baggy in his hand, and Morningstar stuffed it in his jacket pocket. He walked to the hotel and went inside. He didn't need to check in; he paid for the room by the month, and carried the key with him. He climbed the stairs to the second floor and walked to the end of the hall, ignoring the smells of weed, decay, and cheap wine. He unlocked the door to his room, and stepped inside. He pulled out the baggy and laid it on a chipped table in the corner. He opened the top drawer and pulled a sheet of paper from a stack that sat about a half inch high. He laid the paper on the table and poured out the contents of the baggy, using a razor blade to form perfect white lines. He took a plastic straw from his pocket, bent over the lines, and inhaled. He grinned as he felt it take hold. Soon he would talk to God. *And I have quite a bit to report.*

Within minutes, he began to dance around the room, slowly at first, and then faster the higher he got. Things were going well. The Middle East was in an uproar and Simeon would soon oversee another arms shipment to the beleaguered region. Reuben, along with two other sailors from different ports in Africa, was navigating his boat – with merchandise – to America's shores. Pocks was about to put a stop to Madison digging into his business, and Naphtali had found Joseph, which meant that Morningstar could eventually bring him home. Yes, things were going well. *God will be pleased.*

He took another hit, and another, and then leapt across the floor, landing on his back with a thud. He laughed as he looked up at the ceiling, the swirls in the paint slowly transforming into God's kind eyes. Morningstar stared at the eyes as he cried out to no one, "It's happening, God ... Your plan ... *our* plan ... is back on track."

TUESDAY, JANUARY 6TH, 2004

"We love to go slow when we're dancing for rain
Dry skin flakes where there's ice in the vein..."

"Start of the Breakdown"
~ Tears for Fears ~

Chapter 25
SAVANNAH, GEORGIA

1/6/04

"Get me out of here!" Henderson sat up, sweat pouring from his forehead as he looked around the hotel room. *Where am I?* He pulled himself to the side of the bed and sat there as he worked to get his breathing under control. After a minute, the scenes from the fiery ballroom faded, and he was able to see the off-white walls of a dingy hotel room. He looked at the clock. *Four a.m.* He had gotten into Savannah, Georgia less than an hour ago and had booked a room in a nondescript hotel at the south end of town. He had lain down to sleep, but, as he stared at the clock, he knew it wasn't going to happen. He stood, walked to the bathroom, and splashed water on his face. He caught a glimpse of himself in the mirror and quickly looked away.

He walked out of the bathroom and threw on his pair of sweatpants, the sweatshirt, and his running shoes. He left the room, careful to lock the door behind him. He placed a nearly invisible strand of hair between the door and the jamb.

The room was on the second floor of a two-story complex on Montgomery Street, a part of town few would enter unarmed in the daytime, let alone in the middle of the night. But Henderson wasn't afraid. He possessed two weapons most men didn't have. One was an ability to kill instantly with a strike of his hand, and the other – far more significant – was an indifference to life ... especially his own.

He walked down the hallway to the stairs, ignoring

the sounds of women pleasing men, or the smells of meth and weed as smoke wafted from under the doorways. He took the stairs two-at-a-time, reached the street, and sidestepped a bum sprawled just outside the door. He jogged through an alley, turned onto a side street, and then ran about a mile to River Street. He could smell the bread baking at a nearby pastry shop and he breathed in, unsettled by the pleasant aroma in such an unpleasant place. He kept running. He turned onto River Street. Though it was after four in the morning, there were college kids huddled at club entrances and stumbling between bars. He watched them, their strong, unscarred bodies tottering down the street. *What a waste.* He ran even harder.

He turned a corner and saw three thugs mulling around a dumpster, two of them keeping watch while one snorted a line of cocaine. When they spied Henderson, the man with the coke shoved the drug case in his back pocket. The other two stepped in front of him, widening their stances and crossing their arms.

"Shit," Henderson muttered. He continued on, avoiding eye contact.

As he got closer, they squared up even more, now totally blocking his path. One of the men pulled a knife, while the other two stepped back to give him room.

Here goes. He ran at the man with the knife. The man stabbed at Henderson's chest, but, before the blade could break the skin, Henderson grabbed the man's wrist and twisted. There was a snap; the man screamed and dropped the knife. Henderson used his other hand to strike his throat. The man choked and dropped to his knees.

The other two looked at one another. In unison, they jumped him. He kicked one of them in the gut with a force that sent the man sprawling into garbage cans, and then punched the other man in the throat, just as he had done to his friend seconds before.

All three lay on the ground gasping and moaning in pain. Henderson picked up the knife and was about to toss it in the trash, when one of the men muttered under his breath, "Fuckin' freak." Henderson stopped. His movements were automatic as he knelt behind the man, reached an arm around his neck, and used his other hand to place the blade of the knife beneath his chin.

"Do you want to see what a *freak* can do?"

The druggy shook his head, his eyes wide with fear.

Henderson hesitated. *Let 'em go … you've scared them … it's enough.* He was about to loosen his grip, when one of the thugs kicked him hard in the shin, forcing him to the ground. Still holding the knife, he jumped to his feet and sliced the man's throat, the other two watching in horror. Blood spattered everywhere. Henderson slid his arm around the neck of the ringleader. "What's wrong? You thought you were the only ones who could cut people up?"

Before the man could react, Henderson slashed his carotid, and then – with the same motion – sliced the third man's throat, as well. He threw the knife to the ground. The three men lay dying in a pool of blood as Henderson stood and, without looking back, resumed his early morning run through the streets of Savannah.

"Assholes," he said aloud. He was only a little troubled by the fact that he felt nothing at all.

Chapter 26
WASHINGTON, D.C.

1/6/04

Hank was tired of reviewing data. Threat after threat; none of them credible, but every one of them requiring an evaluation. Thank god for his team of agents, but he still had to sign off on every one of them. He had been at it since four a.m., and he was spent. Though he had gotten home early from Maddi's, he had had trouble getting to sleep. He had finally resorted to a Benadryl and a beer, and now his head hurt and his eyes felt heavy.

He had awakened early for no good reason, and had immediately gotten to work on the overnight intelligence. It was his routine. Every morning he would get up before sunrise, go to his desk, and read through the data from the night before. He was looking for inconsistencies; pieces that didn't fit. Over the course of his time there, he had noted a few items of interest, but nothing yet that had risen to the level of an alert.

He had found something that had ruined his morning, however...

"Group of senators meeting in Jacksonville, Florida, Grande Dames hotel. Arrival: Tuesday evening, with 9:00 reception. Departure: Friday morning. Attendees: Senators Sanders, Davis, Kitchener, Combs, Holloway, O'Malley, Jefferson, and, Majority Whip, C. Madison. Alert: Madison, targeted twice before, will be accompanied by two bodyguards. The other senators have no such

protection. Spouses/guests have been invited. Status: all members bringing guests except for Madison."

Hank stared at the entry and sighed. Why hadn't Maddi invited him? In the old days – the days before Henderson – she would have. But not anymore. She seemed to prefer her solitude. They could share sweet-and-sour pork, but not much more.

He wasn't sure why the itinerary had been included in the intelligence report. Then again, if a terrorist wanted to make a mark, knocking off twelve senators and their guests would certainly do the trick. He double-checked the event security, happy to see that not only the Secret Service, but the FBI and local law enforcement had been made aware of the retreat. He looked at it one last time, and then clicked to the next report. It contained a compilation of every poison in every lab in nearly every country. The number was staggering. Vials of gases, viruses, injectables ... and those were just the ones that were accounted for. He could only imagine the number of poisons floating around the world that had somehow missed the list.

As he skimmed through the data, he thought about Maddi all alone at the convention. Maybe he would surprise her; just show up whether she wanted him there or not. He could tell her it was part of his job. He leaned back and laughed. *Yeah ... I'm sure she'd buy that one.*

He clicked to the next page, which was a map of flu outbreaks in the U.S. and around the world. As he stared at the page, he wondered how he could justify going down to the retreat. What could he say that would not seem desperate? He laughed. *Nothing ... I am desperate.*

He scrolled past the flu and onto the next page: a summary of recent norovirus outbreaks on several different cruise liners. Coincidence? Likely. He continued to skim through the data, all the while trying to think of a good excuse to fly down to Jacksonville. After about an hour, along with thirty more pages of intelligence, he had all but given up. He turned off his computer and leaned back in his chair. *Maybe I could just pretend there's a threat.*

He got up and walked to the bedroom. He stood in front of the mirror, staring at his thinning hair and the wrinkles around his eyes. He shook his head and frowned. He wasn't getting any younger. *And neither is Maddi.* She was wasting her life longing for a man she would never see again. He sighed. He needed to find an excuse – a bioterror warning or a suspected terrorist – that would give him a reason to fly down to Jacksonville. Suddenly he laughed. *I'm probably the only member of the Homeland Security team who is begging for a threat.*

Chapter 27

WASHINGTON, D.C.

1/6/04

Morningstar stood from the bed, sweaty and satisfied, practically shoving the prostitute away from him. Late last night he had seen her walking the street beneath his hotel window and had lured her upstairs with a fifty-dollar bill. She had strutted upstairs and had helped him finish off the cocaine. They had spent the rest of the night in bed.

He had been tempted to call his girlfriend, Edi, but had decided he wasn't in the mood for her chatter. Besides, Edi didn't know about the cocaine, or the room on Girard Street. If she had, she probably would have disapproved. *And then I'd have to kill her.*

He chuckled as he walked over to the window and opened the dingy curtains. He picked up a half-smoked cigar from a nearby table and lit it, savoring the rich aroma as he watched the sunrise sparkle over the streets and buildings of Washington, D.C. *Morning in America.* He could see the capitol in the distance and he grinned. This was his city; the fact that no one knew it yet meant nothing. *Soon enough, the entire world will know it.*

The whore, whom he had nicknamed Mona for the sounds she made during sex, called for him and he turned to look at her. She was overweight, which had not bothered him in the least last night; but now her pale, chubby thighs showed from under the sheets and it sickened him. In spite of it, however, he licked his lips as he thought about taking her again. *I might as well get my fifty dollars' worth.*

She moaned and turned over, the sheets falling away from her bare belly. It jiggled and a trickle of sweat rolled past her belly button onto the bed. He turned away, disgusted. He raised the window, letting cold air into the room. He breathed it in, clearing his lungs from the dank hotel room air. He liked the cold; it made a man tough. Withstanding the elements, overcoming obstacles, it was how a true soldier was shaped and hardened. And there was no doubt about it; Morningstar was a soldier. Every day he waged war, not only against his enemies, but against his fears.

He breathed in deeper. The air was crisp, cold. He liked the way it stung his cheeks. Though he had never fought in an actual battle, he had engaged in many intellectual ones ... skirmishes fought in a dusky boardroom rather than on a bloodied field ... he was better trained than most for war. Morningstar knew – as sure as sunrise – he was meant to be a soldier.

He had spent most of his childhood dreaming of becoming a Green Beret. He was strong and determined, and had prepared a lifetime for the moment when silver wings would be pinned on his chest; when the world would know he was a member of the esteemed Corp. His father had been a Green Beret, and he and his older brother, Tim, were expected to follow in his footsteps.

Until Texas.

Morningstar sneered as he cracked his knuckles and breathed in the cold, damp air. He had been only eight years old when an ill-fated incident in downtown Laredo had left him with an annoying limp. It was the limp that had brought about his rejection by the Green Berets, and it was the way the limp had occurred that had brought about his rejection by his father. When Morningstar wasn't chosen for the Corp, his father shunned him altogether. *Shows what you know, Dad.*

Morningstar smashed the cigar into the sill of the window. He didn't like to think about his father ... or his brother. *I paid the price for their incompetence.*

He paced the room, the limp more exaggerated when he was angry. Too many people had let him down; his mother, his father, his brother ... all of them, nothing but disappointments. But he had expected more from the Green Berets. The selection committee had been comprised of fools; they had made a huge mistake, and now – nearly thirty years later – their ineptitude still enraged him. How could such a revered organization get it so wrong? *Bureaucratic asses ... they know nothing of greatness.*

He sighed. *"Use it, Morningstar ... use it to keep you angry."* That was what his trainer had told him, and he had followed the advice. He followed it still.

The trainer, former Beret Jake Garret, had been drummed out of the Corp for trash-talking a sergeant. Morningstar had found him by hacking the Corp's database in search of men who had been dishonorably discharged. There were only a few. He had read through their files, looking for that secret ingredient ... that emotional flaw that would make a man indispensable: bitterness. Garret had it in spades.

Morningstar had found him wasting away behind the counter of a dollar store in Culpeper, Virginia, and the man had listened carefully as Morningstar had outlined his disgust with the Green Berets. Garret had eaten it up. He had immediately offered to train him so he could try again. *"And then you can tell them all to go to hell."* Garret had taught him how to shoot, how to use a knife, and how to withstand the harshest interrogation; he had made him into a soldier. Though the limp remained, it was no longer a problem; Garret had trained him to overcome it. Morningstar had then petitioned the committee to let him test again, expecting them to be impressed with his strength of will. They hadn't even considered it. *"A man once rejected can never reapply."*

Morningstar closed his eyes and rubbed his temples. It still made him furious. He had plotted to kill every one of the officers on that committee. He had enlisted Garret's help, along with the few others who had been discharged from the Corp, forming a select group of embittered, yet highly trained soldiers. They were unified by a single goal: to stick it to the Corp.

Morningstar smirked as he recalled the willingness of those men to do whatever he asked; to risk everything to join him in retaliation against a system that had betrayed them all. He had become their commander, and had begun to appreciate his remarkable ability to lead. He had already known he was physically superior to those who had judged him, and intellectually a step ahead, as well. But, after his command of those disgruntled soldiers, he had seen that he was also a far better leader than any of the men who had voted him down. God had made him superior.

Morningstar reached behind him for a half-full glass of cheap wine, and slugged it in one gulp. He stared at the glass and then threw it against the wall. It shattered into pieces. His whore moaned, but said nothing. *Good. I didn't buy you to talk.* He stared out the window, remembering ... *embracing* ... his hatred for the Corp. Though he had planned to kill every one of the officers, he held back, able to see that it would be short-lived gratification compared to what he might accomplish if he could bide his time ... and manage things properly.

And he did. He managed things quite well, as a matter of fact. With a brilliant resume, and perhaps a little bit of guilt on the part of the men who had rejected him, he was able to gain a position as a file clerk within the Corp. He ran errands, delivered messages; whatever was needed. It wasn't long before he was handling minor administrative tasks for some of the officers, and he gradually began to earn their respect. A position became available overseeing paperwork for new recruits, and Morningstar applied.

He was hired and immediately poured himself into the new assignment. Though he hated every one of the recruits for their deficient backgrounds and their less-than-glowing genealogy, he buried his disgust, knowing – in the end – he would rule them all. The new position had given him far more access, and he used it to learn all he could about the men in the outfit, including the commanders. He acquired dirt on every well-placed administrator, and combed through the private worlds of those who could eventually help him. He assisted them in ways they could not overlook, and then undermined them without them ever knowing. He was like a spider, his web entangling every aspect of their lives.

It wasn't long before he met Major General Alexander Daniels, who oversaw all activities of the Green Berets. Daniels was looking for an aide to help with day-to-day operations, and had seen how effectively Morningstar had handled a few of the more delicate tasks. He hired him, and immediately gave him a higher level of security. Morningstar used the access well. He learned even more about the upper echelon of the Corp; their backgrounds, their families, their strengths and weaknesses. Over time he was able to use the information to cement his place at Daniels' side.

Daniels became reliant on Morningstar, entrusting him with more and more responsibility. As Daniels rose through the ranks, he took Morningstar with him, until finally they were both at the Pentagon; Daniels, a four-star general, and Morningstar, his personal aide.

He stared down at a bum stumbling in the street below. The man was clearly drunk, and Morningstar grinned when the lowlife leaned over and retched. *Rough night, buddy?* He opened the window wider, and braced himself as a bitter wind blew into the room. He was invigorated by the ice-cold air against his naked body. *The breath of God.* The mission he had embarked on was his calling; he could no sooner ignore it than he could ignore the lustful moans of his whore in the bed nearby. And, like the whore, he was drawn to it. Born from anger at how weak his country had become, heightened by passion as he saw America's future disappearing before his eyes, his path had been cast in stone by the undisputed message from God, *"Jacob, you will lead your country to greatness once again."*

But it wouldn't stop with America; no, God had chosen him to rule all nations. It would take one man, properly placed, to restore a broken world. Morningstar was that man and, as he breathed in the crisp air and looked out at the Capitol's glistening dome, he smiled at God's words, given to him late last night in the seedy hotel room, *"It is time, dear Jacob. It is time to get it done."*

His cellphone vibrated; it startled him. He checked the time. *5:45 a.m.* He grabbed it from the table. He checked the caller ID. *Pocks.* "Yes."

"It's me, sir. I thought I would update you on what I've learned about the ... uh ... person of interest."

Oh brother. "Go on."

"Yes sir. The uh ... person ... was born and raised in Indiana, and her father died when she was five. The record's sketchy after that, though I show her earning a five-year degree from England's Oxford University at the age of 21." He paused. "That's really impressive, sir." Another pause. "Anyway, she returned to the States and completed medical school at the age of 25.

She did a residency in Ohio, and then opened a practice in her hometown in Indiana. She was only in practice for a few years." Another pause. "I don't know why she left medicine so soon, sir." He cleared his throat. "Anyway, she became a state senator soon after that, and then a U.S. Senator, which she has been now for nearly six years."

Morningstar frowned. That was a lot of life in a short amount of time. And how had she gotten to be Majority Whip after only one term in the Senate? *A remarkable woman, it seems.* "Go on, Pocks."

"The one thing I found that might be useful is that she's apparently really close to her brother." A pause. "I was thinking maybe of using him to ... um ... you know, persuade her."

Morningstar frowned. "Tell me about the brother."

"I won't say his name, sir, because we're on the phone, but he's a doctor in South Carolina. He oversees an inner-city clinic in Columbia. No wife, no kids. There are lots of calls between him and the senator." He paused. "Not much else to tell."

"Doesn't she have a boyfriend?"

"No sir, not from what I could find. She's close to some guy at Homeland, but I don't think it's romantic, sir."

Morningstar nodded. "Sounds like using the brother is your best bet. Do what you have to do, Pocks." He paused. "And make sure she knows you're serious."

"Yes sir."

Morningstar ended the call. He set the phone on the table and checked the time. *Five-fifty-five.* He stared out the window. The bum was now lying in the street, one hand holding an empty bottle of booze, the other holding a brown paper bag. *The man's life's savings.* He chuckled. Pocks had done well. He had

159

clearly understood what was at stake. Did he realize that this assignment served as his rite of passage; his foothold into Morningstar's elite group of men? *From his efforts, it would seem that he does.*

Either way, it was good to know that Madison had someone in her life she cared about. The question now was whether Pocks could use the brother to coerce her to drop her research into Silverton. Could Pocks convince a sitting U.S. Senator to back off for her own good? If not – if Pocks failed – then Morningstar would have to find another way to convince Madison. *And you, Pocks, will pay a dear price.*

He frowned and turned away from the window. No one knew it better than him ... *A man once rejected, can never reapply.*

Chapter 28
SAVANNAH, GEORGIA

1/6/04

Henderson had finished his run, stunned at how quickly – and unabashedly – the Phoenix had taken over and had compelled him to kill three men. *Maybe I'll never get rid of him,* he thought as he stepped into a steaming hot shower in his hotel room. The water felt good ... it numbed him ... to pain ... to murder ... to everything other than shame. Though he hadn't felt it when he sliced their throats, he felt it now. The three men were scum ... *but they were still men.*

After a few minutes, the scars on his hands and forearm turned a fiery red; it was hard to tell which hurt more ... the sting of the water, or the sting of the scars. He welcomed it; the pain that seemed to underscore the path he had traveled. He stood there for nearly an hour ... embracing the hurt, nursing his hatred for the thugs who had brought back so easily the man he was trying to leave behind. But was it them he should hate? Or was it himself ... the assassin who had just killed three men because they called him a freak. *What would Maddi say?* He fell against the wall of the shower. *She would never forgive me ... she will never forgive me.*

After another few minutes he got out of the shower and wrapped a towel around his waist. He walked to the window and stared out at a row of trashcans lining the alley. The sun had come up, but it was hidden by clouds as a gentle rain peppered the alley. It was hardly enough to wash away the filth, however, and he watched, absorbed, as two rats fought over a scrap of garbage. There was someone else who shared the blame for the murder of those men ... Morningstar. He was the one who had saved Henderson, only to change him into someone – *something* – he didn't recognize. Why? What did he want? *And why did he choose me?*

It was a question that had haunted him from the beginning. After all, the only way Morningstar's men were even at the hotel the night of the explosion four years ago was because they had been sent there by Morningstar to keep an eye on him. Why? There had been nothing in Martin Henderson's life to suggest that he would have been willing to join Morningstar's team of sons. Not until he was desperate, drug-dependent, and protective of a little girl he had made vulnerable with his rants, was Morningstar able to mold him into a killer. So, what had been his original plan? *What did he want the accomplished Martin Henderson to do for him?*

He thought of the men leaving the Morgan building twenty-four hours ago. They were certainly accomplished. It was the who's-who of either the political or the industrial bastions of America. Had Morningstar hoped to make him one of them? If so, why? What did those men ... allied with Morningstar so early on a Monday morning ... talk about in that meeting? *If it even was a meeting.* Henderson's research had revealed one thing every one of those men had in common: success ... and power. Was that why Morningstar had been following him? Had he wanted him to join them?

He leaned on the sill, watching as one of the rats scurried into a drainpipe. He didn't know; he might never know ... but it didn't matter. All that mattered was that Morningstar needed to be stopped.

He took a last look, and then walked to the bed. He fell on top of it, reviewing what he knew so far.

Morningstar was a part of at least two groups; the men in the Morgan building, and the soldier sons who did his dirty work. He ruled at least one of those groups, clearly seeing himself as some sort of born-again Jacob. And, from what Henderson could tell, he had at least four sons. Were there eight more out there ... just waiting in the wings? If so, for what? *What are you up to, Morningstar?*

He sat up, opened his laptop, and scrolled through the websites where Morningstar had communicated with him in the past. He was looking for a message to one of the others; a memo that might tell him what the other 'sons' were meant to achieve. Were they, too, assassins ... molded by Morningstar to kill great men? He went from website to website, but found nothing. After twenty minutes, he stood and paced the room, trying to think where else he might look. He stopped at the window. The rats were gone, replaced by a homeless man who was shivering as he dug through the trash in search of a blanket. Henderson watched, thinking he should offer him one of his scarves. What was it the Scriptural Luke had said..."*Whoever has two tunics is to share with him who has none.*"

His eyes widened. *That's it!* He ran to his computer and logged onto a site he had seen only once before. It consisted of an online Bible, which Morningstar had altered to suit his needs. He had shown it to Henderson during his recovery ... when he was still in the Novosibirsk hospital room. Morningstar had used the site to underscore the depth of his control. He wanted Henderson to see that – like God – his power was absolute; that it would be foolish to try to stop him. Henderson had merely smirked at the time. He had nearly forgotten it ... probably on purpose.

But it wasn't Scripture Morningstar had wanted him to focus on. It was Morningstar's interpretation of the truth, typed between the lines, using font, tone, and tenor that would blend with the original. *The man wanted to add his thoughts to the holiest of books ... with some authority.*

The site loaded and he stared at the first page. *"In the beginning God created the heaven and the earth."* He scrolled through a few paragraphs, trying to remember where Morningstar had inserted the changes. Had it been throughout the entire Bible, or only in one place? *Think Henderson.* He went on, searching for added sentences, words from Morningstar, written as if they were gospel. He was halfway through Genesis when he remembered. It was at the end of that book ... when Jacob, on his deathbed, was talking to his sons. Henderson scrolled through the 45th chapter ... the 46th ... stopping at the 47th chapter. There it was; written just before the first paragraph. He stared at the words, still there over three years later, unchanged, from what he could tell. He read them through and began to shake. He remembered them now ... the words of a madman, the delusions of a very sick, very powerful man...

"And let it be known that on this day, December 3rd, of the year 2000, I, Jacob, do declare the following: The year 2000 has been The Year of the Sons."

Henderson stopped. *What the hell?* He read on.

"And their mission is bold, their goals noble. Rulers will fall; kingdoms will crumble. It is the only way to start anew."

Henderson shook his head. *The guy's crazy.* He read more.

"But know this: Regardless of who lives or dies, the journey will go on. Even if it is I, myself who is killed, I will command my sons to follow the path I

have set forth. Nine of the twelve will be given a key; not a single one will possess them all. Keys to the Kingdom ... which will open doors to safe-deposit boxes all over the world. Just as Cain relied on Abel, my sons must rely on one another to fulfill God's Plan. Their actions must be swift, sure, and unrepentant. Every secret shall be revealed, every betrayer crucified, and every piece of God's glorious Plan shall be put into motion ... with or without me. The world will soon know an apocalypse the likes of which has never been imagined."

Henderson stared at the words. He thought he might throw up. Underneath the paragraph, in bold, scripted letters, Morningstar had added ...

"So let it be written ... so let it be done."

Chapter 29
JUST OUTSIDE NORFOLK, VIRGINIA

1/6/04

Naphtali stared at his computer screen. It had been a stroke of luck that the facial recognition software had spotted Joseph in Jarratt. For whatever reason, the man had decided to pull down his scarf and turn his face to the sky, and – voila! – the software had found him and had immediately alerted Naphtali. He grinned. He could hear it in Jacob's voice; he was pleased. Though Naphtali didn't know much about the elusive Joseph, he knew that the man – the *son* – was important to Jacob ... *which means I must do all I can to keep track of him.*

He had taken the first flight he could get into Norfolk, Virginia, and was now holed up in a cheap hotel room staring at screen after screen of live video feed. Though he guessed that Joseph was long gone from Jarratt, he would stay in that hotel room until he got another hit with the recognition software. He could then determine what direction the man was heading.

He leaned back and rubbed his eyes. He had stared at hours of live video feed, and his head was spinning. He stood and walked to the coffee pot. It sat on a notched desk with a drawer that wouldn't open ... the only piece of furniture in the grimy hotel room. He had tried to nap on the twin bed with its lumpy mattress, but had been unable to sleep, even for a few minutes. It was just as well; he needed to find Joseph.

He poured a cup of coffee and carried it to the desk. The software would alert him if an image resembling Joseph's photo was identified, so, while he waited, he learned all he could about the man. Using Joseph's photo to scan the Internet, he was able to learn what the man had done up to that point. And it sent a chill up his spine. Joseph – who the software identified as CIA assassin, the Phoenix – had killed some of the most notorious despots there were ... from North Korea's Minister of Defense, to Uganda's War Secretary, Sanyu Wambuzi. The man had somehow gotten past bodyguards and high-tech security systems to murder some of the most despicable tyrants on the planet. *Good thing I won't ever have to go up against this guy.*

He had just taken a sip of coffee when the alert went off. He magnified the image. It was Joseph, alright; he hadn't changed his appearance. As a matter of fact, he was less disguised than usual. His cap was high on his forehead, and he wasn't wearing a scarf. The scars were prominent. He had a strange gait when he ran ... it was him. Naphtali checked the time stamp. *Four-fifty a.m. About five hours ago.* He watched him running effortlessly in spite of his injuries, and was envious of the man's physique. But not of his face; Joseph was a bona fide freak. He turned a corner and Naphtali checked the location. *Twenty-first and River Street ... Savannah, Georgia.* He leaned over and grabbed his bag. Savannah was about five hours by train. He was about to switch off the laptop when he stopped. He stared at the screen. Joseph was still running, but he had slowed. There were three men in front of him and, from the look of things, they were about to take him on. Naphtali's eyes widened. Was he about to witness Joseph's execution?

He watched as the men squared up in front of Joseph. Naphtali's heart was racing. He grabbed the edges of the desk, waiting to see the three men cut up Joseph and leave him to die. How would he break the news to Jacob? He looked at the screen, nervous, yet excited to watch it go down. But, as he witnessed the battle, it wasn't Joseph who was cut up and left to die. Using nothing more than kicks and hand chops, Joseph had somehow left all three men moaning on the ground. Naphtali watched as Joseph took a step away from them, and then stopped. He saw him turn and pick up the knife that one of the thugs had used. He stared at the screen, speechless, as Joseph – without the slightest hesitation – sliced the throats of the three men who had attacked him. The camera had caught a view of his face ... his eyes, and Naphtali felt sick. The scars repulsed him ... but the eyes terrified him. They were cold, dark ... and empty. Naphtali's palms were sweating as he watched Joseph toss the knife away, and then jog off as though nothing had happened. *Who is this guy?*

His hands were shaking as he turned off the computer. They were still shaking as he stuffed the laptop and a change of clothes into his backpack. Jacob had told him to find Joseph and keep an eye on him. As he ran out the door, he thought of the accounts he had read of the man's hits over the years, and the videotape he had just witnessed. *I sure hope Jacob never asks me to try to bring him in.*

Chapter 30
WASHINGTON, D.C.

1/6/04

Maddi had spent the morning in her office preparing for the retreat. She was the one who had set it up and, as Majority Whip, she would be responsible for the agenda. The focus was the reelection campaign of President Wilcox, so she had spent about two hours reviewing the delegate selection process for each of the fifty states, as well as Puerto Rico and Samoa. She had also gone over the current polling data regarding Wilcox's likeability, as well as his handling of crises overseas. In the first category, Wilcox scored in the 70-plus category. But it was the second category that needed work. He was only polling at 35 percent. That was where she came in. The party – and the Senate – had to turn that number around.

She leaned forward and pushed the intercom. "Good morning, Phil. Do you have the paperwork ready for the retreat?"

"I'll bring it right in."

He walked into her office carrying a large stack of folders. He laid them on the desk. "Everything you asked for, Senator."

"And the items from yesterday?"

"They're on top, Senator."

"Excellent. Thank you, Phil." She paused. "How is Polly doing?"

Polly was Phil's wife, and she had recently lost her mother to cancer. Phil nodded sadly. "She's better, thank you. She really loved the flowers you sent."

Maddi smiled. "Tell her I'm thinking of her."

Phil nodded and left the room. Maddi stared at the stack of folders. Most of them were focused on the upcoming election, but the few that weren't were the ones she was eager to see. She grabbed the top folder. It was titled "Info on financial backers." The next folder had "Francis O'Malley" written along the side. The third one contained a history of Silverton. She thumbed through the rest of the stack, looking for something from Skywalk Weaponry to confirm the bid that Lawford had brought to her attention. There was nothing. She pushed the intercom. "Phil, were you able to speak to someone from Skywalk Weaponry about the receipt from last June?"

"Yes, Senator. They couldn't find it. But they're going to keep looking."

"Thanks, Phil." Maddi leaned back in her chair and frowned. *Lawford's receipt is a fake.*

She opened the first folder. It contained the name of every company that had offered even the slightest financial support for any one of the committee members. There were no surprises. Though Silverton was mentioned in every campaign, they were rarely the major donor, and had given Lawford the least support of all.

The second folder – the one about O'Malley – contained no red flags, either. He had become a senator two years ago, and had immediately been put on the Senate Arms Committee. Prior to that, he had had a stellar military career; he and Lawford had served together during one of Lawford's tours in Iraq. *Which is probably why O'Malley nominated him for chairman.*

Maddi opened the third folder, which summarized the history of Silverton Arms. She skimmed the first page. The company, established in 1992 by J.T. Silverton, had apparently been successful from the start. The CEO had been good friends with the Speaker of the House at the time, the current Vice-president, James Conner. The relationship had instantly put the company at the top of the list when it came to bids. The next two pages outlined every government deal Silverton had been a part of. Maddi saw nothing odd with the bids, but she still couldn't reconcile the fact that – for at least the last two years – they had all gone to Silverton. The only thing that had kept the other two major arms suppliers in business was the work they did for overseas contractors.

At 11:00 a.m., she stood, stretched her arms, and walked to the window. She stared once again at the dormant garden. She put her hand to the glass. It was bullet proof, installed soon after 9-11. She couldn't tell; it didn't look shaded or blurry; it didn't even look thick. She was glad. Though she was thankful for the protection, she hated the thought of being reminded day after day that they were all sitting ducks.

She turned away and walked to the credenza. She poured a third cup of coffee and carried it to her desk. She took a sip as she sat down and got back to work. She was about to revisit the O'Malley file when her intercom buzzed. "Yes, Phil?"

"There's a man on the phone – he won't give his name – but he says he needs to talk to you."

Maddi frowned. "I don't want to talk to someone who won't tell you his name."

There was a pause. "He says it concerns your brother, Andrew."

Maddi tightened her jaw. "Put him through." She tapped the desk with a pencil as she waited.

"Is this Senator Madison?"

"What's happened to Andrew?"

There was a pause. "Nothing ... yet."

Maddi's heart beat faster. The voice was deep; it

almost sounded like someone was trying to disguise it. "Who is this?"

"It's not important."

"What have you done with Andrew?"

"As I said before ... nothing ... yet."

"What do you want?"

"I want you to stop digging into the old business of the Senate Arms Committee."

Maddi frowned. It was the second threat in less than twenty-four hours. "Or what?"

"Or something might happen to him."

The call went dead. Maddi slammed down the receiver and stared at the phone. She stood and walked to the door. She opened it and said, "Phil, have the FBI trace that call."

He nodded and picked up his phone. She motioned to her Secret Service agent, Larry. "Could you come into my office please?"

He walked in and took a seat in front of the desk. Tall and thin, he seemed too long for the chair. He was sitting stone-faced, his short dark hair reminding her of his military background. Maddi was grateful for it as she looked at him and frowned.

"What's wrong, Senator?"

"Someone has just threatened my brother, Andrew."

His eyes narrowed. "Do you know who it was? Or why?"

She stared at him. Should she tell him about Silverton? Or Lawford's threat the day before? *Not yet ... not before I know what I've found that has gotten their attention.* "No. Is there any way we can put an agent with Andrew?"

Larry shook his head. "Probably not, Senator. Idle threats are made all the time." He paused. "Where is Andrew?"

"South Carolina. Columbia." She frowned. "So, what can I do?"

He leaned forward. "Call him. Warn him. And if he sees anything that doesn't look right, have him call the police." He paused. "Tell him to call you if that happens. And then let me know. If the slightest thing seems out of whack, I can contact local law enforcement and get them to assign someone to keep an eye on him."

Maddi nodded. "Okay. Thanks Larry."

He stood to go but stopped at the door. "I overheard you ask Phil to have the FBI trace the call. I'll make my boss aware." He paused. "Are you okay, Senator?"

Maddi was staring at the phone. She looked up and forced a smile. "Yes, I'm fine, Larry. Thank you." But she wasn't fine ... she wasn't fine at all. Her favorite person in the world had just been threatened ... *and all because I decided to look into a few arms contracts.* Should she stop? Heed the threat from the mystery caller? She frowned. As much as she didn't want to quit, she knew she had to. She couldn't risk her brother's life just to expose political corruption. But it left her uneasy. Clearly, she was on to something, and – once she found a way to keep Andrew safe – she would most certainly pursue it.

Chapter 31
WASHINGTON, D.C.

1/6/04

Morningstar had left the Breezeway Hotel, had gone home to shower, and had gotten to the Pentagon by eight a.m. Except for a slight hangover, he had felt rested and ready to go. That had been nearly four hours ago, and, in that time, he had completed three military assessments for General Daniels, had fired two insubordinate clerks that manned the demolitions unit at the Pentagon, and had drunk four cups of coffee. *Now it's time for the work I really want to do.* He chuckled. He was about to oversee the first steps of what would be one of the greatest takeovers in the history of the world.

He checked his calendar. It was Tuesday, the sixth of January. By February 1st, he should have things well underway. He thought of Joseph and smiled wistfully. His favored son would admire the intricacy of his plan ... the genius of each move on an imaginary chessboard. How many times had the two of them battled over a real chessboard? Mahogany and pearl, with solid gold pieces ... checks that soon became checkmates. Back and forth ... ruthless and unforgiving ... Morningstar on top, and then Henderson ... hours of battling until finally, one of them gave in. It was how he had gotten Henderson through those first couple of weeks after the explosion. *Refocus your mind, my son ... your body will follow suit.*

Morningstar stood and walked to a filing cabinet. He unlocked the top drawer and pulled out a photo. It was of him and Henderson in the hospital room in

Novosibirsk. Though Morningstar had been careful to avoid photos – especially with his sons – he had permitted this one. It had been the nurse's idea, *"… you two have become so close."* Henderson had objected, but she had insisted. It was as if she was blind to the monster he had become. It was clear she had become fond of him. Though Morningstar had been surprised at her ability to feel affection for such a scarred and broken man, he understood. He felt the same.

Suddenly he threw the photo back into the drawer. He slammed it shut and locked it. "To hell with you, Henderson!"

He cracked his knuckles as he walked to the window. It had started to rain. *I don't need Henderson; I don't need anybody.* He combed his hands through his hair, staring through the glass at the rain. No, he didn't need Henderson … but Henderson needed him. The man was not equipped to be on his own … not anymore. He was disfigured, and in constant pain. He had no one in his life … *except me.*

Morningstar felt a sudden pang of grief. He *did* need Henderson … or at least he wanted him at his side as he carried out his plans. Yes, the boy had strayed, but Morningstar would forgive him. *It is what fathers do.*

He walked to his desk and pulled out his cellphone. He dialed and, after only one ring, a deep voice said, "Yes, Father?"

"Where are you, Naphtali?"

"On my way to Georgia."

"Georgia?"

"Yes, Father. I used the recognition software and was able to spot him in Savannah."

"Good. Get him for me."

There was a pause. "Get him, sir?"

"Yes. I want you to bring him in."

Naphtali stuttered. "There's ... there's something you need to know about ... about this guy, sir."

Morningstar frowned. "What is it, Naphtali?"

There was a pause. "Only ... a ... few hours ago, I saw him ... slice the throats of three street thugs, simply because they ... got in his way."

Morningstar's eyes widened. He laughed. "Tell me about it, Naphtali."

"Tell you about it?"

"Yes. How did he do it? How did he kill the three men?"

Another pause. "Uh ... with his bare hands, sir. And then he used their own knife to cut all three of their throats."

Magnificent! "Bring him in, son."

Silence. "But sir, I—"

Morningstar narrowed his eyes. "Are you *afraid* of him, Naphtali?"

"Well, no sir, I guess not. But he seems ... a bit deranged, Father."

"All the more reason you should bring him in, Naphtali."

"But how, Father?"

"You figure it out. Now get to it!"

Morningstar ended the call. He leaned back and grinned. Henderson had honed his skills, and was now using them for matters no longer dictated by an overseer.

He stood and walked back to the filing cabinet. Again, he unlocked the top drawer and pulled out the photo. He stared at the scarred man wrapped in bandages, and felt an ache in his heart. He had created a masterpiece. Henderson had become a perfect killing machine, and, from what Naphtali was telling him, it appeared that he was still on top of his game. No, Morningstar hadn't lost him ... *but it seems, my son, you may have lost yourself.*

179

Chapter 32
JACKSONVILLE, FLORIDA

1/6/04

Henderson had been shaken up by the 'Morningstar Doctrine' buried in the online Bible. There was something so utterly disturbed about it ... and so diabolical. It was a bad combination. He had packed his bag and had left the Savannah hotel room by 7:30 a.m. He had taken a cab to the nearest truck stop, and had been picked up five minutes later by a trucker heading south on I-95. The driver had wanted to chat, but it hadn't taken long for him to see that Henderson was in no mood for talking. Henderson needed to think. Could Morningstar do it? Did he possess the cruelty and the credentials to carry it off? The answer was yes.

The driver had dropped Henderson just outside Jacksonville at 9:55 a.m. Henderson had immediately gone to a department store and had purchased a pair of clippers, a change of clothes, and a new pair of glasses. He had then gone to a bathroom and had cut his hair short, mourning the loss of his wild blonde hair nearly as much as he had mourned the loss of his old life. It was the only part of him that had not been destroyed ... either by the fire or by Morningstar. But the haircut felt good. It was time for a change.

He had checked into a cheap hotel about four blocks from where Maddi would be staying. Using the alias Sam Dawson, he had kept on the sunglasses and the scarf, and had paid for the room with cash. The clerk hadn't questioned it; he hadn't even asked for ID. It was clear from the surroundings, he had checked in sketchier guests.

The hotel room was bleak, but the bed was comfortable, and Henderson had managed to sleep a solid two hours. When he awoke, it was almost noon. He sat up and stared at the faded wallpaper, its formal pattern barely visible. There was crown molding throughout the room and, though it was now chipped and pulling free of the walls, it was clear that at one time the room, the hotel, had been fashionable; maybe even chic. Henderson could afford to stay anywhere he wanted, but it was this type of room he always chose. Why? He wasn't sure. Less attention? Perhaps. Or maybe he was just better suited to tarnished rooms that had once known better days. *Like me.*

He stood and walked to the window. The sun was shining and he could feel its warmth through the glass. He opened the window and listened for the ocean. Though he wasn't on the beach, he could hear it in the distance ... the rhythmic roar of waves against the sand, the splintered cry of seagulls. It reminded him of Boston. He closed the window.

He walked to the bed and sat down, absently turning and patting the pillow. It was what Morningstar used to do when he came into his hospital room during those early days after the fire. He would pat the pillow and say, *"Is everything okay, son?"* Henderson would usually respond with a grunt or a moan, and Morningstar would pull out a vial of painkiller. With a flourish, he would insert a syringe into the vial, fill it, and put it in Henderson's IV. The effect was almost instantaneous.

Morningstar had been like a savior in those early days. Henderson had come to look forward to his visits. He flinched. The very thought of it made him sick. But it hadn't taken him long to understand what Morningstar was really up to...

~ ~ ~

He awoke, groggy, confused. His body ached, his skin burned as if it was still on fire. He needed more medicine. He looked around. Where was he? Where was the man with the syringe? The only light came from a table lamp in the corner. It cast a glow on pocked and peeling walls. There were two narrow windows covered by blinds which let in hints of daylight around the edges. The linoleum was cracked and had pulled away from the floor. He watched as a cockroach escaped underneath it.

He remembered. He was in a hospital room in Novosibirsk, Russia. He had been there for a month, recovering from burns that covered his face, his neck, and his left arm, along with fractures in both of his legs. The pain had been unbearable. But one man had helped him through it. One man had given him the drug that had allowed him to escape the pain, at least for small bits of time, so he could sleep, or dream, or renew his desire to live. He spotted him. Edward Morningstar was sitting across from him on the other side of the bed. The small man with the gray eyes had his legs crossed and his head down as he wrote fervently in a journal, turning on and off a recorder, replaying a stranger's words and then jotting them down. Henderson listened as the voice was quiet, even wistful, and then, suddenly became loud and angry. "I'll watch over her, friend," it said. And then, after a minute, it cried out, "I don't know him ... we're not related!" Morningstar grinned and wrote in his book.

Henderson watched him, trying to understand. He thought about the words, listening closer as Morningstar played them back one more time. Suddenly, he gasped. He covered his mouth; he felt like he was going to be sick. He recognized the voice on the recorder. It was his. It was Henderson who was spitting out those words, those memories ... some he couldn't recall, others he had tried to forget. It was Henderson who was revealing to the man across the bed his deepest thoughts, his greatest fears. Morningstar had used the painkiller Dilaudid to unlock Henderson's mind. 'Dear god, what have I told that man?' He tried to think what he might have said, what trusts he might have betrayed. Who had he jeopardized by his need for the drug? He looked at the IV in his arm and began to cry, not even bothering to hide it. If Dilaudid was responsible for the sacrifice of his secrets, so be it; he couldn't live without the drug...

~ ~ ~

Henderson pushed hard against his temples. *It's ancient history.* But it had changed everything. The secrets he had given Morningstar had given the man power over him, and now, as he tried to take that power back, he cursed the drug and his weakness for it. *If only I had been stronger.*

He stood and walked to the bathroom. Leaving the light off, he stared in the mirror. It was better that way. In the shadows of darkness, the scars faded and the fractured jaw all but disappeared. The only thing he could see was an outline. But, as his eyes adjusted to the darkness, the scars became clearer. He could see the gaping skin beneath the left eyelid, and the tightly drawn membrane that covered his left cheek and ran all the way to his collarbone. How many times had he tried to get rid of those scars? Six, seven, maybe eight times? Morningstar had recruited a renowned Russian surgeon to try to surgically remove them. Trained in America, the man now did plastics repairs and identity changes for the well-to-do from around the world. But the surgeries had failed. And the last two had made things even worse.

Henderson leaned forward, resting his hands on the sink. He could see the scars clearly now, and he stared at them, suddenly curious why Morningstar had worked so hard to get rid of them. Henderson had assumed it was an act of compassion, but as he thought about it now, he knew that couldn't be the case. Morningstar didn't possess compassion. So why had he done it?

He combed a hand through his hair and took a step back. He stood there, suddenly curious about something he had never given a thought to until now. He left the bathroom and sat on the bed. What had Morningstar hoped to achieve with the surgeries? Why go to the trouble and expense of banishing scars that had nothing to do with him or his empire? He stood and paced the room. Could it be that Morningstar had not been trying to fix him, but had been trying to *change* him ... to make him into someone completely different ... *to change my face, along with the rest of me, into an image that suited him?*

Suddenly he stopped. He was shaking. The very thought of it was abhorrent. But, as he stood in the dank hotel room and looked around at faded walls, he knew it was true. *Morningstar tried to have me re-made ... in his image ... so I would become a true son.*

Chapter 33

WASHINGTON, D.C.

1/6/04

Maddi wasn't sure why she had put off calling Andrew. She had pulled out her phone, and had even dialed the numbers, but had not yet pushed send. She had eaten a light lunch, and had taken a quick walk to the Capitol library; it was as if she was doing all she could to avoid calling him. *I call Andrew all the time ... why not now?* She leaned back and sighed. She knew why. Because she didn't want to believe it. She didn't want to think the threat was legitimate. It seemed ridiculous. Why go after Andrew over trivial arms deals, many of which were years old? She stared at her phone. She was about to shove it in her pocket one more time, when she thought of Larry's advice. *"Call him. Warn him. And if he sees anything that doesn't look right, have him call the police."* Finally, after staring at it for another two minutes, she pushed send. It was answered right away. "This is Doctor Madison."

Maddi grinned. "Hello, Doctor Madison. It's your little sister."

"Maddi! How're things in the center of the universe?"

She laughed. "Overrated and corrupt. How about you?"

"Things are good. What's up?"

She sighed. "I hate to do this, Andrew, but I don't have a choice."

There was a pause. "What's going on, Maddi?"

"A few hours ago, I got a call from some guy who wouldn't tell me his name."

"Why'd you take the call?"

She hesitated. "Because he told Phil that he had information concerning you."

There was silence. "So, what did he say?"

She sighed. "He threatened you."

More silence. "I see. Any idea why?"

"No ... well, maybe." She paused. "I've just become a member of the Senate Arms Committee. As a result, I've been looking into arms deals completed over the last two years. I think I'm making a few folks nervous."

"It's your gift."

Maddi chuckled. "Yes, but I can't be putting you at risk just because I'm curious."

Andrew laughed. "It goes far beyond curious, I'm afraid, Sis. You're unrelenting."

Her eyes burned. It was confirmed; she couldn't do it. As much as she wanted to find whatever was lurking in the Senate Arms records, she couldn't put Andrew's life at risk. "I'm going to stop. But stay on your toes, in case the nut follows through."

"You're not going to stop, Maddi. I'm a big boy. I can take care of myself."

"Yes, but what about Amanda? It's not worth it." She paused. "Don't worry, Andrew. I'll find another way to look into this ... without putting you or your family at risk."

There was a pause. "I'll be ready just in case."

She sighed. "Okay. Promise me you'll let me know immediately if anything weird happens. Larry can call the local police and get someone to keep an eye on you."

"Will do." He paused. "How about you? Are you okay? Are you safe?"

"Absolutely. I have the FBI tracing the call, and Larry and Collins are two of the best secret service agents in the business. I'll be fine."

"I've heard that before."

"I'll call you tomorrow from Jacksonville. I'm heading there tonight for a Senate retreat."

"Got it." There was a pause. "Watch your back, Maddi."

Maddi closed her eyes. She felt like she was going to cry. She cleared her throat. "You too."

They ended the call and Maddi tucked the phone in her pocket. She pulled the stack of files in front of her and got back to work. But her mind kept drifting to the call from the stranger. *"... quit digging ... or something might happen to him."* She tightened her jaw as she pulled another Silverton contract in front of her. *I'll quit digging ... for now. But, once I find a way to keep Andrew and Amanda safe, I will figure out who is behind this.*

Chapter 34
JACKSONVILLE, FLORIDA

1/6/04

Henderson had fallen asleep. When he awoke, it took him a minute to remember where he was ... who he was. Those were the moments he cherished; those first few seconds when he would forget that he was a killer, and would feel the way he used to ... hopeful ... alive. He had been a good man then ... a fervent man with plans to make the world a better place.

He sat up and rubbed his eyes. *And I have done just the opposite.*

He was coming to terms with all he had learned in the last twenty-four hours, and it was taking its toll. Morningstar had developed a plan to bring about chaos, and, though Henderson had no idea what that might look like, he sensed that, whatever Morningstar was up to, it would involve a major disruption to the world as it was.

Not only that; by some terrible quirk of fate, he had ended up beholden to the man, and that man had molded him into a killer. He had tried to mold him into a son, as well, but, fortunately, he had failed. The irony was that if Morningstar's sons hadn't been there in the first place, Henderson would have died in the hotel fire. *Which would have been a far better outcome.*

Henderson had contemplated suicide many times over the last three years. *Better to kill myself than to kill others.* But then he would remember Lili. Morningstar had told him he would have Lili kidnapped and killed if Henderson ever left him ... even if it was by his own hand. *"You can't kill me, and you can't kill yourself. You have to get the job done, son."* But still it haunted him ... the ever-present urge to put a bullet through his brain. It was there when he blasted Bilczor in Kiev ... and when he stabbed Okeke on the beach in northern Africa ... *and when I shot Al-Gharsi in the forehead while he was sharing a bottle of wine with Maddi.*

He leaned back and stared at the ceiling. It was faded white, with a stain next to the bathroom door. He could see cobwebs in the corners. *Another five-star hotel.* He thought of Maddi sitting next to Al-Gharsi, her incredible smile easing into a laugh as he said something funny. How did she know him? Had they been friends for long? Or had it been more superficial ... maybe a political friendship? He hoped that was the case, though Maddi rarely had superficial friendships. It was the one thing he had learned about her almost from the start...

"I'm going to tell you something that is going to sound strange."

He grinned. "I like strange."

She laughed. "Of course you do." She cleared her throat. "You ready?"

He nodded.

"Okay. This night ... this incredible time that we have spent together is not binding."

He frowned. "Not binding. I wouldn't even—"

"Let me finish. It's not binding, but, no matter what happens ... you are now a part of my inner circle."

Henderson grinned. "Your inner circle? What's that?" He pulled her closer. Never had he felt so much for another human being.

She smiled. "We are now connected ... lifelong friends. Not to be discarded."

He frowned. "What an odd thing to say."

She pulled away. "Yeah, well, I told you it would sound strange. But I like to put it out there from the start. It makes things more comfortable. No strings ... just friends for life."

He grinned. "What if, after a few days, you decide you don't like me?"

She leaned into him. "I already know I like you ... and I will tomorrow ... and the day after ... and the day after that."

"How can you be so sure?"

"Because I already like you more than most ... and with me, things like that don't change."

"Okay ... friends for life. Part of your inner circle."
He paused. "So, do we have a pledge or a secret handshake?"

She reached up and kissed him. "Yes," and then pulled him to her...

~ ~ ~

Henderson closed his eyes. His entire body was shaking. *God, how I miss you, Maddi.* He sat up and opened his laptop. He typed in Al-Gharsi's name. His hands were sweating. He wiped them on his shirt. He had never allowed himself to look back at the lives of the people he killed ... the children who no longer had a father ... the wife without a husband. But he had to do it. He had to know how Maddi and Al-Gharsi were connected.

He clicked the first article he came to, "A celebration of a great man." He winced as he skimmed the piece. Al-Gharsi had been revered. At one point, he had even been referred to as " ... the last hope for the Middle East." *If you're going to kill someone, Henderson, make it someone revered.* He felt sick. He made himself go on, clicking the next article, and then the next. All of them were the same: full of praise for

Al-Gharsi's nobility, followed by a grief-laden lament for the wife and child he had left behind. Henderson closed his eyes. He didn't want to read any more. *Keep going, Henderson.* He massaged his temples as he clicked on the next article. He skimmed the first few paragraphs. He stopped. He had found it. The article was documenting the Senate hearings that had taken place in October of 2000. He read it closer and cringed.

"Because of those hearings, Al-Gharsi established a close relationship with the Chairman of the Senate Foreign Relations Committee, Cynthia Madison from Indiana. She eventually became his 'partner in peace,' and this relationship, fostered over the last three years, is what set the table for the Yemen-Omani talks that were to be held in New York on November 30th, 2003. Because of Al-Gharsi's assassination by the Omani leader, those talks were derailed, and renewed violence has devastated the region... "

Partners in Peace ... holy shit, Henderson. What did you do? He closed the laptop and fell back on the bed, trying to come to terms with it ... the pain he had caused, not just to Maddi or to Middle East peace, but to all the families that had lost loved ones whenever he had pulled the trigger for Morningstar. Though most of his hits had been third-world dictators, even they had someone who had mourned them. But Al-Gharsi's murder was clearly the most egregious. It had transformed an entire region from hopeful peace to utter destruction. How many people had died or been displaced, all because of Henderson's single bullet on a cold night in November 2003?

He grabbed his journal from his backpack, opened it, and wrote...

Tuesday, January 6th, 2004

My dear Maddi ... I'm guilty. I've done a terrible thing. I'm so very sorry. I know these words carry little comfort to those I've hurt. And there are so many ... so many people whose lives were changed in a terrible way by what I've done. So, I want to at least tell you why I did it. What it was that compelled me to steal and lie and kill...

He stopped. He put down the pen and laid the journal on the bed. He couldn't do it. He had tried so many times to write about Lili. But he couldn't. Why? Guilt?

Yes.

He closed his eyes, suddenly hit with the realization that all the killing had been for nothing. After all of Morningstar's threats, and the wrangling that followed as Henderson struggled with his soul and lost the fight, Morningstar took Lili anyway...

"It's time you face the truth, Henderson."

Henderson looked at him and frowned. "What are you talking about?"

The two men were sitting at the breakfast table in the cold, sterile kitchen of his apartment in Novosibirsk. They had had breakfast in the kitchen every morning for the past two months. Henderson was getting better. He had somehow weaned himself off the painkiller, and he was able to walk nearly a mile with the help of a cane. He had almost forgotten the incident with the Dilaudid and his memories. Almost.

Morningstar smirked. "Surely you know that I own you. Not quite the same as one owns a car or a house, but every bit as real."

*Henderson could feel his blood pressure rising.
"How's that?"*

*Morningstar grinned. "Your father is Walter
Henderson. He lives on King's Drive in Boston. Your
mother, Dora, is a dutiful wife who has – shall we say
– tolerated your father's exploits over the past three
decades."*

*Henderson tightened his jaw. He saw
Morningstar grin with satisfaction. "Shall I go on?"*

Henderson frowned. "Sure."

*"The outcome of your father's dalliance is quite
intriguing," he chuckled, " ... but I won't go into it
now." He paused. "Your good friend, Albins, died in
battle a few months back, and he entrusted you with
the care of his little girl." Another pause. "How's that
going, I wonder?"*

*Henderson glared at the man. "Leave Lili out of
it!"*

*Morningstar laughed. "Ah, but I can't. Lili is
everything. She is the reason you will follow through
with this training, along with anything else I ask of
you." He leaned closer. "She is the reason you will lie,
steal, and even kill for me, Henderson ..."*

She was ... and he did. Fourteen times. And each
time, he swore it would be his last. But it took the
murder of Maddi's friend to make him stop. And Lili
was the final victim. *Al-Gharsi is dead ... the Middle
East is on fire ... and Lili is gone.* The reason he
couldn't talk about Lili in his journal was because he
had failed her. He had failed everybody. *While Maddi
was forging friendships and partners in peace ... I was
making the world a terrible place to be.*

He leaned against the pillow. He couldn't live with
it. Not only had he done the unthinkable ... *fourteen
times* ... but, in the end, he had lost Lili anyway. And

not only Lili. He had lost Maddi, too. Whether or not she ever learned the truth, he would always know what he had done, not only on that cold night in November, but thirteen other times. And it didn't matter that he had been trying to protect a little girl. He had stolen more than a dozen lives, and the death of at least one of them had impacted the world in such a way that hundreds, maybe thousands would eventually suffer. No, he couldn't live with it. But he would have to ... at least for now. Until Lili was found, and Morningstar and his soldiers were stopped in their crazed pursuit of Armageddon, he would hold off doing what he should have done three years ago. In the words of Camus, *"But in the end ... one needs more courage to live than to kill himself."*

Chapter 35
WASHINGTON, D.C.

1/6/04

Maddi was on her fourth cup of coffee, and she felt like her eyes were crossing. She laid down the file she was reading and stood and stretched her arms. She walked over to the stereo and turned it on. As a Mozart piano concerto filled the room, she strolled to the window and once again stared out at the faded grass. She hated to think that her efforts to get at the truth had put her brother in danger. After all, their job had always been to protect one another.

She frowned, once again curious about what had pushed someone to make such a threat. *Just because I've decided to curb my investigation, doesn't mean I can't dissect what I already have.* She walked back to her desk and sat down. She thumbed through the documents for what felt like the hundredth time. What had she missed? She stopped. She reread a passage on one of the pages. How had she not seen it?

"The increased tension in the Middle East, brought about by the untimely death of Abdulkarim Al-Gharsi, has resulted in a sudden need for weapons in the region. Though there is an ongoing debate over who should receive those arms, it is incumbent upon the Pentagon to prepare a shipment for delivery within the next forty-five days. An order will be created and the bidding process can begin."

She checked the date. Monday, December 1st. *Only two days after Al-Gharsi was killed!* She pushed her intercom. "Phil, contact the Pentagon. Get me anything you can find on the recent build-up in tensions between Yemen and Oman." She paused. "Tell them it's a routine inquiry before my trip overseas next month."

She sat back in her seat. Her hands were shaking. She felt sick to her stomach. She stood and walked to the bathroom. She splashed water on her face, staring in the mirror as the water dripped from her chin. Just thinking about Al-Gharsi – and how he died – could still unhinge her.

She dried her face and walked back to the desk. She was about to pick up the file, when Phil walked in carrying two sheets of paper. "They sent these over by fax."

"That was quick."

"Yes, they had it ready for a committee briefing." He paused. "They said it's all they have."

Maddi frowned. *Only two pieces of paper?* "Thanks Phil."

She sat down and read through the pages. They were prepared statements, likely designed as press releases. There was nothing new. They concluded with what she already knew: "The path to peace had rested on the relationship between Al-Gharsi and the leader from Oman, which means we will soon see renewed war break out in the Middle East." *What's new?* she thought, as she leaned back and sighed.

Peace wasn't between nations ... it was between men, between leaders ... *and, in this case, both leaders are dead.* She had never understood why the Omani had killed Al-Gharsi. They had spent nearly a year working on the peace plan. Maybe that was why it had been so hard for the world to accept Al-Gharsi's assassination. There was no logic to it. He hadn't been murdered by some crazed killer; he had been killed by a friend ... a man who had wanted peace every bit as much as he had.

Maddi rested her head on the desk, exhausted from thinking about it. She was startled when she heard the clock strike a single chime. *1:00 p.m.* She was scheduled to fly out of Dulles at 4:45, and she still had to pack. She grabbed the documents from the Pentagon, and the folders from the Senate Arms Committee, and stuffed them in her briefcase. She turned off the stereo and grabbed her coat. She was about to put on her scarf, when she stopped. She held it in her hands, staring at the bold red silk. It had been a gift from Andrew several Christmases ago. He had given it to her *"...so I can find you in a crowd."* Maddi clutched the scarf. *Andrew is in danger ... because of me.* She thought about Al-Gharsi. She had to learn more. But how could she keep looking without letting anyone know? *I'll go through back channels instead of my usual routes.* But she would have to be careful. She couldn't give whoever had threatened her a reason to go after Andrew.

Suddenly she wondered ... *am I safe?* Had the threat against Andrew simply been a precursor for someone to come after her? She threw the scarf around her neck, brushing off any concerns as she walked out of the office. Larry fell in behind her. He would keep her safe; he and Collins.

They left the Capitol and climbed into the back of a black sedan that had been sitting there all morning, ready whenever she was. This was her life. Protected and important; involved in some of the most significant matters of the day. As she leaned back, she looked out the tinted glass at the gray sky and wondered, *If I am so protected, then why do I suddenly feel so vulnerable?*

Chapter 36
JACKSONVILLE, FLORIDA

1/6/04

Henderson had spent nearly an hour lying on the bed, and he finally forced himself to get up. He had work to do. Morningstar and his soldiers were plotting Armageddon. It was up to Henderson to stop them. But he couldn't do it until he knew exactly how they intended on pulling it off. Simeon's email had mentioned an arms shipment, as well as the arrival of three boats from Africa. *How would that spark Armageddon?* Were the two events connected? Part of the same sinister plot? Henderson needed to get a look at more of those emails.

But he had already been compromised in the effort. Morningstar's software had detected him, and he was certain the madman had then deleted the entire string of emails. Fortunately, for Henderson, he had one more option ... one final way to figure out what Morningstar and his men were up to. But first he needed an identity ... something legitimate. The cheap hotel hadn't required ID, but where he was about to go most certainly would.

He brushed his teeth and ran a comb through his hair. He would stay with the name he had used to check in, Sam Dawson. Short hair, glasses ... was it enough? The scars from the fire had made it impossible to grow a beard. And, though he could purchase one, the thought of the scratchy thing on his blemished cheeks for longer than an hour or two made him grimace. No beard. He would use makeup to cover the worst of his scars.

But he would need money to obtain the proper ID. Fortunately, he had plenty. Morningstar had paid him well through the years. He kept the cash in safe-deposit boxes up and down the eastern seaboard. But it would take more than money ... it would also take connections. He had made a few friends through the years; men who would help him whenever he needed it, no questions asked. He had one such friend not far from Jacksonville, in a quiet little town known as Cedar Key. That would be his next stop.

He shoved his laptop into his backpack and put on a hooded sweatshirt. It was too hot for a scarf, but the kids wore hoodies regardless of the temperature. It would cover the back and sides of his neck, and he could use his hand to cover his chin. He put on his sunglasses and threw his backpack over his shoulder. He left the hotel, squinting in spite of the sunglasses. It was 79 degrees and the sweatshirt made him hot. He didn't care. It was necessary.

It was a twenty-minute cab ride to downtown Cedar Key. He paid the fare, and then walked four blocks to a small body shop on the north end of town. He strolled in and looked around. It was a nondescript garage with tools on the walls and oil stains on the floor. The odor of grease mixed with the smell of fried chicken; leftovers were lying in a red and white box on the counter. There was a man behind a cash register, absorbed in a *Sports Illustrated* magazine. Henderson could hear two men talking in the back. He walked up to the man with the magazine. "I'm looking for Danny."

The man looked up, not even trying to hide his revulsion when he saw Henderson's scars. Without saying a word, he laid his magazine on the counter and walked to the back. A minute later, he returned with a second man. It was Danny. Henderson hadn't seen him in over two years, but he had hardly changed. He was as big as an ox, with thick hands and an oversized gut. He grinned when he saw Henderson. He motioned for him to follow him to the back. He waved off the other mechanic, and then looked at Henderson. "It's good to see you."

"You too, Danny." He paused. "How's Stella?"

Stella was Danny's common law wife. She had been raped two years ago, and it was Henderson who had found her rapist, and had then hung him by his ankles from the limb of a tree, strung up like a side of beef for the authorities to find.

Danny smiled. "She's good." He paused. "How are you?"

Henderson frowned. "Livin' the dream, Danny."

The two men had met during one of Henderson's excursions on behalf of Morningstar. He had needed help finding a drop for a delivery, and had run into Danny on the side of the road, doing his best to change a tire without a jack. Henderson had stopped to help him and, when he had learned that Danny was an auto mechanic, it had made him laugh for the first time in years. *"You're a mechanic who doesn't even carry a jack in your car?"* To thank him, the man had invited him back to his house for dinner, and had then given him a place to stay for the night. The two men had talked until the sun came up, and that was when Danny had shared what he did on the side. *"I get fake ID's. It's a way to make extra cash so Stella and I can retire someday."* It wasn't much, but the fact that Danny was a good man who broke the law from time to time had allowed for a bond between the two men.

Danny grinned. "What can I do for you?"

"I need a driver's license and a credit card ... for Sam Dawson."

"How soon?"

Henderson sighed. "Asap."

Danny nodded. "Let me see what I can do."

Henderson pulled out his wallet. He counted out five one-hundred-dollar bills and handed them to Danny.

Danny shoved the money away. "This one's on me." He smiled. "Give me an hour."

Henderson nodded and walked out the back of the shop. His stomach growled and he walked to a diner, two doors down. He found a table in the back, and ordered coffee and a sandwich. He pulled out his laptop and plugged it in. There was an arms shipment to investigate, along with three boats coming in from Africa. He would start with the arms shipment.

The waitress brought the coffee. He took a sip and waited for her to leave. He then clicked to the website where he had uncovered the exchange between Jacob and Simeon. The website was gone. Henderson wasn't surprised. He took another sip of coffee, and then clicked to a Pentagon website, and then to two or three Army sites, looking for anything that might indicate the date or place of a shipment. There was nothing.

He sat back and frowned. He needed to know where and when the shipment was being sent. He thought back to his experience with arms shipments in the past. His job had been to carry the weapons from the warehouse to a drop point, and then load them into the shipping vans. He sat up. *That's it!* Silverton didn't use their own vans to move the weapons; they accepted bids from various shipping companies. He pulled up one of the companies from a past shipment. He hacked the site, hoping he might get lucky and see information about the shipment. There was nothing. He then hacked any other shipping companies he had known Silverton to use. Again, there was nothing. That information was probably not released until the bid had been granted. He frowned. If he wanted the information, he would need to place a bid on the shipment ... and win.

He pulled up Silverton's website to see if they provided a link for companies to place a bid. He scrolled through the site, stopping when he came to the tab that said "Contact us." He opened the tab and read through the information. At the very end, he saw it. *"Contact information for anyone interested in securing a bid to ship our goods."* He clicked the link and read through the information. All they needed was the name of the company, an address, and an email where they could send a formal application. He typed in the name of a fake company, Global Industries, Inc., and supplied the number of a post office box in Camden, Maine, that he had used several times in the past. He plugged in one of several untraceable email addresses, and clicked 'submit.'

The waitress was back. He clicked off the Silverton website and held out his cup. She filled it and walked away.

He was hoping the request for an application was routed automatically. If so, he should have an application in his email within the next minute or two. He had barely even stirred the second cup of coffee, when he received a message. He didn't open it. Before he could fill out the bid application, he would need more information. Who else was bidding? How much were their bids? He had to make sure he came in the lowest. The only way he was going to learn the time and location of the shipment was if he was granted the bid.

But it wasn't that simple. Before Silverton would grant him the bid, they would need verification that his company had done something like this in the past. He would have to somehow convey that Global Industries had transported shipments for other arms manufacturers. The Silverton representative was likely to call the references personally.

Henderson logged off the site and laid a ten-dollar bill on the table. He slid the laptop into his backpack and threw it over his shoulder. He left the diner and walked back to the garage. The same man was at the counter, and – without saying a word – he stood and walked to the back. Danny walked out and frowned. "You're early."

Henderson reached in his pocket and, making sure the man at the counter couldn't see, he pulled the same five bills from his wallet and held them out. "I need a second ID ... for Carter Hoffman." He paused. "And I want you to take the cash this time, Danny. I'm asking a lot." He paused. "Hell ... give it to Stella and tell her to buy a new outfit or something." He waited for Danny to take the money.

Danny finally took the bills and shoved them in his pocket. "For Stella."

Henderson nodded. "For the second ID, I only need evidence that the guy exists. A computer presence with an unflappable history." He paused. "As I said, his name is Carter Hoffman, and he's a longshoreman who started his own company four years ago. Call it Global Industries, Inc." He looked at Danny. "It needs to appear to be a reputable company that has shipped arms for some of the bigger dealers. Calls will be made to confirm. Can you handle it?"

Danny rubbed his chin and then nodded. "I'll take care of it. Give me thirty minutes."

Henderson thanked him and left the shop. He walked to a nearby minimart and bought a track phone, along with granola bars and two bottles of water. He walked back to the garage, prepared to wait in the lobby with fried chicken man while Danny finished up his request. As he walked to the door, he saw Danny standing there with a brown paper bag in his hand.

Henderson grinned. "That was quick."

Danny handed him the bag. "It's easy when you don't need any plastic."

"Thanks Danny." Henderson put out his hand to shake, and then immediately pulled his sleeve over the scars.

Danny shook his hand, not even noticing. "Any time, pal." He paused. "Do you need a place to stay? Stella and I have fixed up that back room you stayed in last time. It's got a wide screen TV ... it's pretty nice back there."

Henderson grinned. "No thanks. Another time, perhaps." He turned and walked out the door. He carried the bag a few blocks away to a park. He sat on a secluded bench and opened it. Everything was there: The Sam Dawson ID and a credit card, along with the data for Carter Hoffman. It included his background information, as well as several references for his company, Global Industries, Inc. Henderson knew that if Silverton called the references, they would get Danny or one of his pals. And any one of them would vouch for Carter Hoffman.

Henderson walked back to the diner. This time he ordered a piece of pie and a pot of tea. He pulled out his laptop and plugged it in to charge. He would need a website. That one was easy. Henderson had built lots of websites over the years, usually as a way to lure in a prospective target. Using a site he had accessed many times, he threw together a webpage, complete with the owner's name and the name of the company. He added a photo from a defunct shipping company in California which showed several large vans sitting in front of a warehouse. He pasted it into the site. He then found a picture of a man from Canada who was wearing overalls and a cap, and inserted it beside his name, Carter Hoffman. He placed the number for his track phone next to his name. He sat back and looked at the site. *Not bad ... not bad at all.*

The waitress brought the pie and the pot of tea. Now it was time to figure out who else had bid on the shipment and how much. He poured a cup of tea, and then clicked to Silverton to see if he could find the information. He clicked a tab for prospective bidders, and saw a banner across the top that showed the deadline for applications: midnight Tuesday, January 6th. He grinned. *Tonight.* His would likely be the final bid before they closed applications.

He hacked the site, hoping information about potential bidders was on their internal server. The waitress walked past his table and smiled; he closed the laptop. Once she was gone, he opened it and looked at the screen. There were bids from two shipping companies, neither of which he had heard of. The first company had put in a bid of $4,000; the second had come in at $3750. He would need to not only beat those amounts, but convince Silverton to take a chance on a company they had never used before. *Not an easy task.* He could only hope that Danny had done a good job making the company seem respectable.

He leaned back and sipped the tea. Simeon's email to Jacob had said that the shipment was going out "soon." That could mean tomorrow, or six weeks from now. Once he placed his bid, he would need at least a few days to put things in place. He clicked back to the email he had gotten from Silverton. It was a form letter thanking him for his interest in offering shipping services for Silverton, and it had an attachment. Henderson opened it. It was the bid application. He filled it out, using the information from Danny, along with the information he had injected into his website. At the end of the document, he inserted his bid. $3500. *That should do it.* He pushed send. An automatic reply thanked him and said that it would take at least two business days for Silverton to respond.

He turned off his computer, unplugged it, and shoved it in his bag. He had done it. If all went well, he would secure the contract by the end of the week. He would then learn not only the details concerning the time and place of the arms shipment, but he could even arrange to transport the weapons if he so desired. *Or destroy them ... so they can't kill the people of Yemen ... the people my assassination of Al-Gharsi has put in harm's way.*

Chapter 37

WASHINGTON, D.C.

1/6/04

Morningstar pounded his desk. He was pissed. He had just been informed by his boss, General Daniels, that a member of the Senate Arms Committee had requested information related to the recent build-up in tensions between Yemen and Oman. *"What do you suppose that's all about, Morningstar?"*

"I don't know, sir. I'll look into it."

He had looked into it and what he had found had made him angry. The request had come from Phil Jenkins, the personal secretary to one Cynthia Madison, senator from Indiana, and newly chosen member of the Senate Arms Committee. *Nosy bitch!*

And it had come through only minutes ago. Fortunately, Morningstar – with the help of Sam Lawford – had already prepared a set of talking points for the press. There was little on those two pieces of paper that would alter Madison's thinking.

Morningstar had also learned that Madison was sponsoring a retreat in Jacksonville, Florida. Had she requested the information on Yemen to discuss at the retreat? *I need to stop her!* But that had been what he had asked Pocks to take care of. Clearly he had failed. *What's my ex-priest been doing? Masturbating?*

He grabbed his cellphone from the top drawer and dialed. Not waiting for a hello, he shouted, "A lot of good you did, Pocks!"

"What ... what do you mean, sir?"

"Not only has the bitch not stopped her investigation; she has heightened it!"

There was a pause. "Um ... well, sir..."

"Well sir, what? You better fix this, Pocks! Or trust me, you'll wish you had!"

Another pause. "I'll handle it, sir. I'll go after the brother."

"No, forget the brother." He paused. "There's a Senate retreat about to take place in Jacksonville. I'm sending you down there on behalf of the Pentagon."

Silence.

"Pocks, are you there?"

"Um, yes sir. What do I do once I get there, sir?"

Morningstar was about to tell him to kill Madison when he stopped himself. He couldn't be connected to such a thing, and he wasn't sure Pocks could stand up to questioning. *But Simeon could ... especially if he had someone to take the fall.* He grinned. "Get a room in a nearby hotel and sit tight. You're there as liaison between the Pentagon and the Senate leaders. Stay out of the way." He paused. "A man named Simeon will contact you when the time is right." Another pause. "And then, Pocks, you will do whatever he tells you. Understand?"

"Um, yes sir. Sure, sir."

"Good." He ended the call. He stood and stared at a picture on his wall. It was of the communist leader, Stalin, and beneath it, it said, *"Death is the solution to all problems. No man – no problem."* Morningstar grinned. Stalin had been ruthless and evil ... *and right.*

Chapter 38
CEDAR KEY, FLORIDA

1/6/04

Henderson checked his watch. *3:15.* Maddi was due in less than five hours. He was still in Cedar Key; he needed to get to Gainesville, and then back to Jacksonville by eight p.m. Now that he had put together a plan to learn about the arms shipment, it was time to figure out what Simeon had been referring to when he had mentioned the three boats from Africa. And there was only one way to do that. He needed to find a way to look back at the emails between Jacob and Simeon over the last several months. Surely one of them had elaborated on the boats. If Henderson could figure out what they were bringing, or when they were expected to arrive, it was possible he could put a stop to it.

He walked to the corner and waved down a cab. "The nearest truck stop," he said as he climbed in back. There was only one device capable of giving him access to deleted emails. The device, known as an SSHD, was a satellite surveillance hacking device created by the U.S. Army in the early nineties to keep track of the military maneuvers of China and Russia. The device had had several upgrades, but Henderson preferred the original design. He had confiscated the equipment from the Pentagon's storage facility during an early morning rendezvous with Morningstar two years ago. The outdated device had been relegated to a shelf in the back and, when his mentor wasn't looking, Henderson had grabbed it and had stuffed it under his jacket. He had taken it to Gainesville, where he had set up a storage cache deep in the Waccasassa Forest. He had picked the area not only because of its thick vegetation, but also because it was right next to a college town. It was easy to hide among the many oddballs who inhabited a town like Gainesville.

It took about fifteen minutes to get to a truck stop north of town. He paid the fare and walked to the exit, where the trucks were about to leave for the highway. He waited, thumbing down the first one to hit the ramp. The guy stopped and rolled down his window. "Where ya' headed?"

"Gainesville."

The man nodded. "I'm going down to Tampa ... I'll drop you on the way."

Henderson nodded and climbed in the cab. The driver tried to make small talk, but Henderson shut him down as best he could. Not only did it hurt for him to talk for any length of time, but there was little he could say – to anyone – that didn't risk giving him away.

Then again, it wasn't like anyone really knew of him. The Phoenix had been one of the Pentagon's best kept secrets. Morningstar had run him through as CIA, designating him a "handled operative," which meant that only one or two officers even knew of his existence.

The driver switched on the radio. Henderson leaned back and listened as the Dixie Chicks sang "Landslide." *Stevie Nicks did it better*. He checked his watch. 4:00 p.m. He should be in Gainesville by five. He could hopefully accomplish what he needed by 5:30 ... 5:45 at the latest, and then get another trucker to bring him back to Jacksonville by 7:30. Which would give him about an hour before Maddi was scheduled to arrive. He shook his head. *Why does it matter?* It wasn't like he could buy her a drink or meet her for dinner. He grinned. *But wouldn't it be nice...*

"I recommend the filet."

Maddi grinned. "I'm not much of a meat-eater. How about the salmon?"

Henderson nodded. "Anything Marco DaSilva serves is excellent."

The waiter came and Henderson ordered a bottle of wine and an appetizer. Though he had been starving only minutes ago, he had suddenly lost his appetite. It surprised him. Yes, Cynthia Madison was a beautiful woman, but he had been with many beautiful women. So, what was it? For some reason, she had gotten under his skin, and he felt like a high school boy as he tried to think of something clever to say.

She looked at him and grinned. "What are you thinking about?"

He laughed. "I'm trying to think of an adroit comment that will knock you off your feet."

She was in the middle of a sip of wine and she nearly choked. She set the glass on the table and grinned. "I see. And have you?"

He laughed. "Obviously not."

She leaned closer. "Don't worry ... I'm knocked off my feet already..."

Henderson tightened his jaw as he stared out at the highway. After a minute, he closed his eyes and tried to nap. As the truck rolled south on route 10, he imagined Maddi with him as he drifted to sleep, her arms wrapped around him instead of the sticky sweatshirt. No, he would never know that again, but he would do his best to remember it ... every chance he got. It was what he had done for the past four years ... *and it is what I will do for the next forty.*

Chapter 39
WASHINGTON, D.C.

1/6/04

Morningstar had not spoken to Simeon since the night before, when he had called him to let him know that he had put Naphtali on the hunt for Henderson. He had heard the disappointment in Simeon's voice, but had reassured him that the only reason he had given the task to Naphtali was because he needed Simeon in D.C. *"You're too important to send away just now."* It had worked. His son had instantly calmed down. But now Morningstar needed Simeon to go to Florida to stop Madison. Simeon would wonder why it was suddenly okay for him to leave town when it hadn't been before. Morningstar smirked. He didn't owe Simeon an explanation ... he didn't owe any of them an explanation. *They owe me ... their purpose, their livelihoods ... their very lives!* He picked up his phone and dialed. Again, he didn't wait for a hello. "Simeon, I have a mission for you ... a big one. In Jacksonville."

"As in Florida?" There was a pause. "I thought you needed me here."

"I do, but I need you down there even more."

Another pause. "Okay. What do you need me to do?"

"There's a Senate retreat set to begin tomorrow."

"A retreat?"

"Yes, and I need you to be there."

"Why, Father?"

"The details will be on the website. You'll have 60,000 dollars to work with. You can access it through the bank we always use. There's a branch at Dulles."

"That's a lot of money. What do you want me to do, Father?"

"As I said, Simeon … I'll put it on the website." He paused. "And I've got a guy down there to help you. His name is Pocks."

This time the pause was longer. When Simeon finally spoke, his tone had changed. "I don't need help, Father."

"I think with this situation you might."

"Why? What's so special about this situation?"

Morningstar grinned. "Let's just say that something is going to disrupt that retreat."

"Disrupt it, sir?"

Morningstar lowered his voice. "Yes. And there will be no survivors."

Chapter 40

JUST OUTSIDE NORFOLK, VIRGINIA

1/6/04

Naphtali had thrown up twice and was hanging his head out the hotel window breathing in the air. He was trying to clear his head so he could figure out his next move. He looked over his shoulder at the clock. *4:10*. He combed a strand of black stringy hair from his forehead, wiped away the sweat, and massaged his neck. He had barely moved since the call from Jacob ... over four hours ago. He had not gone on to Savannah; he had not even left Norfolk, immobilized but what was being asked of him. *"Bring in Joseph, my son."* Naphtali knew he couldn't do it ... Joseph, the skilled and measured assassin, had clearly come unhinged. Every time Naphtali thought about the video of the attack on the three men, he would find himself once again in the bathroom, leaning over the toilet, doing his best not to vomit.

But what do I do? He had been instructed to get Joseph ... to fail was not an option. He knew what happened to the sons that botched an order from Jacob; he had seen it with Issachar in December of 2000. The man had completely screwed up his mission, had gone on a drinking binge in a Cleveland bar, and had gotten into a brawl with two of the locals. He had run away like a coward, and, with little compunction, Jacob had had him killed. *And I was the one who did it.* Naphtali knew the same would happen to him ... he would be murdered ... or, at the very least, beaten to a pulp and then humiliated.

He stared out at the gray afternoon, watching as an

old man walked a huge St. Bernard along the canal. It was more like the dog was walking him. Naphtali winced as he thought of what would happen if he tried to 'bring in' Joseph. *It would be like that dog ... he would bring me in, instead of the other way around.*

Perhaps Naphtali could come up with a way to lure him back ... make him *want* to come home. But how? What could he do to make the errant Joseph return? *"Bring him in, Naphtali."*

Again, he ran to the bathroom. This time he stopped at the sink and splashed water on his face. *You have to do it, Naphtali.* He gritted his teeth and nodded, and then immediately leaned over and wretched. It was decided. He couldn't do it.

But he also couldn't disappoint Jacob. *So, what do I do?* He rinsed his mouth and stared in the mirror. His eyes were a deep gray ... like Jacob's. But, unlike Jacob's, they held none of the wisdom ... and none of the cold-hearted control that had intimidated Naphtali since the moment they met. How long had it been? He thought back ... it was June of 2000, and Naphtali – Leroy Cooper at the time – had been brought before Morningstar as a Pentagon spy. But, rather than force him to endure the humiliation of a court-marshal, Morningstar had orchestrated his escape, and had then made him one of his own ... a soldier, a warrior, a son of Jacob. *And this is how I repay him?*

He took a last look in the mirror and then ran to the bed. He grabbed his computer and the few items he had brought with him and threw them in his backpack. He needed to get away – far away – from Joseph ... and from Jacob. Though he knew the consequences would be significant, they weren't half as significant as lying dead on the ground in a pool of blood. *Or facing Jacob's wrath when I fail.*

But running away would have its own set of

consequences. Naphtali was making a decision that would change his life forever. He would be forced to live on the run; always looking over his shoulder, forever hiding not only from the Pentagon, but from the man who had created him ... the father who had taken him in when no one else would have him.

He stopped. He couldn't do it. He couldn't leave Jacob. *But I sure as hell can't confront Joseph.* He grabbed his bag, ran out of the hotel room, and down the hall. He reached the stairwell and took the steps two-at-a-time to the first floor. He ran through the lobby to the street. There was a bus station two blocks away. He sprinted to the station and went inside. He bought a ticket for the next bus heading west. It was about to leave, and he ran out and climbed aboard. He gave the driver his ticket.

The man took it and nodded. "Where're ya headed, bud?"

Naphtali frowned. "As far away from here as this bus will take me."

Leroy Cooper, *Naphtali*, was in the wind.

Chapter 41

WASHINGTON, D.C.

1/6/04

Simeon stared at his cellphone. Jacob had given him an assistant. Why? *And who the hell is Pocks?* He frowned as he pulled himself to the side of the bed. Though it was after four in the afternoon, he had only just awakened. Once the assignment to find Henderson had been handed off to another son, Simeon had decided to have a night on the town. And it had been a rough one – the part he remembered, anyway.

He grabbed his computer from the nightstand and pulled it to his lap. He needed to check the website and learn what Morningstar had in mind for him. Sixty-thousand dollars was a lot of money. Then again, offing a bunch of senators at a retreat wasn't going to be easy. He logged onto the site, clicked the link, and read through the details. There wasn't a lot more than Jacob had given him on the phone. Twelve senators were staying at the Grande Dames Hotel in Jacksonville from tonight through Friday. In the last line, Morningstar had made a point of mentioning the Majority Whip. Simeon nodded. *She's the target.*

He went to the senate website to see what he could learn about the retreat. There was a short paragraph near the bottom of the page that stated that twelve senators – along with their spouses – were to attend an opening reception in the Seminole Room of the Grand Dames Hotel at 9:00 p.m. that evening. That was it. No itinerary ... no explanation for the retreat ... no names.

Simeon rubbed his eyes. Though the reception was that night, the senators were scheduled to be in

Jacksonville through the 9th. That gave him plenty of time. He was hung over and would need a day or two to plan the hit. He would fly down tomorrow. He shoved his computer onto the bed and leaned against the headboard. His temples were pounding. *Tequila ... it does it every time.*

After a minute, he stumbled into the bathroom. He had just splashed water on his face, when he thought again about the assignment. Why would Jacob send someone down there to help him? And why not one of the other sons? Suddenly he grinned. *Jacob wants a patsy ... in case something goes wrong.*

He wiped his face and walked back to the bed. He lay across the covers as he thought through the assignment. There were only twelve senators attending the retreat. Why? And why didn't the senate website mention their names? Or give an itinerary? Jacob had indicated that the retreat was to last through Friday, but the senate website had said no such thing. He sat up. What if Jacob had gotten it wrong? *Jacob never gets anything wrong.* But what if this time he did? Simeon needed to call the hotel and confirm that the senators were staying through Friday. Then again, it was doubtful the hotel staff would release that information. *I'll just hack the hotel website and find out for myself.*

He sat up and pulled the computer onto his lap. He opened it and typed in the Grande Dames Hotel. He used a Pentagon hacking device to get into reservations. He scrolled through the list, looking for a familiar name. The Majority Whip, Cynthia Madison was supposed to be coming, but he didn't see her name. He did see a name he recognized, however: Francis O'Malley from Connecticut. Simeon had delivered a package to the man not long ago. O'Malley had booked the room through Friday. *Bingo!* Suddenly he frowned.

That didn't mean anything. It was January in D.C. O'Malley might have simply extended his trip in order to get some sun. He looked for another familiar name. He saw none he knew. *Why isn't Madison's name listed?* He frowned. *Because she's the Majority Whip, you dumbass.* She would have bodyguards; the room had probably been booked in one of their names. That had to be it. Unless Jacob was wrong about that, as well. *Jacob is never wrong!*

He went to the banquets section of the website to look for special events tagged to the retreat. There was only one and it was taking place that night in the Seminole Room. *Only one event for a three-day Senate retreat?* Either Jacob was wrong and the retreat was lasting only a day, or the senators were planning to leave the hotel for the rest of the functions. Regardless, Simeon's only sure shot at offing all twelve senators would be tonight in the Seminole Room.

He groaned. He was in no condition to fly. He stood and walked into the kitchen. *Coffee ... that's what I need.* He put on a pot, and then walked back to his bedroom. He had to book a flight ... pronto. He checked the clock by the bed. *4:15.* He got online and logged into a reservation site. Using the name Don Walton, he booked the 5:40 flight to Jacksonville. It would be tight but he could make it if he hurried. As he stood and walked into the kitchen, he thought about Morningstar's words: *"...there will be no survivors."* He frowned as he poured a cup of coffee. How was he supposed to kill twelve senators ... *by tonight?* He carried the coffee into the bathroom and turned on the shower. Maybe he should just bomb the entire hotel; he could have a bomb ready within the hour. Though the thought was appealing, Simeon knew it wouldn't be that easy. Ever since 9-11, the security surrounding big events, especially those involving twelve high-ranking senators, made it nearly impossible to get anywhere close to such a gathering. *I'd have to bomb the entire block.*

He had slept naked so there was nothing to take off as he stepped into the shower and turned it as hot as it would go. The steam filled his lungs, making him cough. It felt good. He had smoked several packs of cigarettes at the nightclub, and the coughing helped to clear out at least some of the tar. He stood there for about five minutes, going over in his mind various ways to kill twelve senators. He could create a special delivery with a bomb in a gift box, but he doubted it would even make it past the door. Or, he could poison their food using Middle Eastern peppers. He had done it once before with a group of men at a poker party. He grinned. *It had been fun to watch.* The more he thought about it, the more he liked it. He could sprinkle in a little resiniferatoxin, a pepper more toxic than capsaicin, and then watch from the wings as they all clutched their throats and fell over dead. But how would he gain access to the food? And what was to say the senators would eat the dish with the pepper? He turned his face to the stream of water. He had just about resigned himself to finding some lackey ... *Pocks* ... and strapping a bomb to his chest, when a coughing spasm nearly brought him to his knees. Then it hit him. *Poison gas!*

He turned off the water and stepped out of the shower. He wrapped himself in a towel and walked to the closet. He slid on a pair of dark pants and a turtleneck. He put on horn-rimmed glasses, and etched a scar over his right eyebrow for the Walton disguise. He put on a red wig with a matching mustache, and packed a bag. He threw in his computer, and ran out the door of his first-floor flat. He jogged to the corner and flagged down a cab. "Dulles."

He leaned back for the twenty-minute ride to the airport. He thought about how he could use poison gas to kill the senators. First, he would have to choose the gas. He pulled his laptop from his bag, created a hot spot with his phone, and entered "poisonous gases" in his search engine. He waited and then scrolled through the list. There was Prussic acid, a derivative of cyanide. He grinned as he read about the tasteless, odorless gas that would disperse with only a little heat. He could place it in containers sitting on tables in the reception hall, and allow it to fill the room as the temperature rose. The senators would never know what hit them. He read a bit more and frowned. It was too combustible. There would likely be candles on the tables. The gas could ignite and disperse too rapidly, too unevenly, and too unpredictably. Morningstar had said to kill them all. They might escape before all twelve had died. He read on. He came to boron dichloride and stopped. That could work. Again, it was tasteless and odorless, and again, he could set it out in containers on the tables. *But what if the senators take their time getting there?* The gas was highly decomposable. It might dissipate before they even entered the room. He scrolled through the list impatiently. He stopped again. *"Sarin gas ... tasteless and odorless, it maintains its stability when kept in an enclosed container."* His eyes widened. He could disperse it over several hours. Even if a few of the senators were late to the reception, they would still be exposed to the gas.

He had used Sarin gas once before ... overseas for a hit on a small village in northern Africa. It had worked well. *It will kill them before anyone knows it's there.* He nodded. *And I can blame it on Al-Qaida.*

The cabby turned onto Virginia Avenue, merged onto highway I-66, and drove west. They were about ten minutes away. Simeon had to come up with a delivery system. A sprayer? A fan? He shivered; it was freezing in the back of the cab. He tapped the partition. "Hey, could you maybe throw some heat back here?"

The man nodded and turned up the heat. Simeon's eyes widened. *The ventilation system.* He could use the hotel's ventilation system to disperse the Sarin gas into the conference room.

Now that he had a method and a means, he had to get a hold of some sarin gas ... quickly. But it wouldn't be easy. There was an international monitoring system for chemical weapons; Sarin gas was on the list. He wondered if his contact from his last experience with the gas was still in business. If he was, would he be able to deliver it in time? He checked his watch. *4:45.* He needed the gas by 7:45. *Three hours.* He would have to call the contact right away if he wanted to have it in time. He'd be too rushed at the airport, and he couldn't make a call like that on the plane.

He looked at the partition that separated him from the driver. It looked solid, and there was a microphone between them. It was turned off; he could tell by the red light. If he kept his voice low, the driver wouldn't be able to hear him. *And I'll speak in Arabic ... just in case.* Simeon pulled out his phone, searched his contact list, and dialed. It was answered by a deep voice with a Middle Eastern accent. "نعـم، هو من هذا؟" *"Yes, who is this?"*

Simeon whispered, "يعقـــوب ابـن." *"A son of Jacob."*

There was a pause. Staying with the Arabic, the man said, "I see. Code phrase?"

Simeon replied in Arabic. "Muhammad sees all."

Another pause. "What do you need?"

Simeon lowered his voice. "Gas. Sarin." He paused. "And a canister of DIC."

"Of course. Where to?"

"Jacksonville. The downtown YMCA. Locker

number 417."

"How soon?"

"Tonight. By 7:45."

Another pause. "That is very soon."

"I know. Jacob said to get it done."

"It will take extra."

Simeon paused. Morningstar had allotted 60,000 to complete the job. "How much?"

"Fifty thousand."

Holy shit! That only leaves me ten! "That's a lot of money."

"It is a lot you ask for ... so quickly."

Simeon frowned. What else would he need to buy ... other than clothes for a disguise and a room for the night. He did the math in his head. He could still pocket about $9,500. *Not bad for one night's work.* He nodded. "Okay ... it's a deal."

"Wire it to the same bank. I'll take care of things at my end."

The caller hung up. Simeon grinned. The man – an unnamed friend of Jacob – would get him the gas. *He always comes through.*

The cab rounded the bend that would take them to the airport. Simeon was eager to get there. He needed to transfer the money before he boarded the plane. If all went well, the Sarin gas would be waiting for him at the Jacksonville YMCA. Simeon had rented lockers in several YMCA's along the eastern seaboard, always under a different name; it was the best way to exchange goods without leaving a trail.

The only thing that remained was to find a way to get the gas into the Grande Dames' ventilation system. The A/C would be on; he had seen on the news that northern Florida was having a hotter-than-normal January. *So how is A/C provided?* He typed the question into his search engine and read the first entry.

"The conditioner has three main parts: a compressor, a condenser, and an evaporator. The condenser contains chemicals that can convert from a gas to a liquid and back to a gas. The chemical allows for the transfer of heat from the air inside to the outside..."

The cab pulled up to the departure gate and came to a stop. Simeon sent a quick email to Morningstar to let him know what he was about to do, and then closed his laptop and shoved it in his bag. He paid the cabby and got out of the car. He ran through the terminal doors, grinning as he reached the security checkpoint. *Air conditioning maintenance, here I come.*

...of the woods, a D-cell battery in his lap and
...x on the ground next to him. He had two
...ither try to come up with a plausible
..., or scare the tar out of the boy and his

...ked at the boy and — with the greatest regret
...ed into the light, revealing deep scars on his
...as well as a slight divot in his scalp, where a
...the hotel blast had dented his skull. At the
..., he jutted out his disfigured jaw and, with
...ly voice he had grown to hate, he growled,
...worst nightmare. Now get the hell away from

...boy's eyes were as wide as quarters. "O-Okay,
...He turned and ran, yelling at his friend,
...a monster in that cave, Johnny! Run! Run for
..."

...Henderson put the battery in his pack, he
...a glimpse of his scarred forearms, and was
...y angry when he saw a few sparse tears spill
...s hands. He wiped them away. The boy was
...e was a monster. He pulled the hood over his
...d grabbed his backpack. He dragged the metal
...ts hiding place, buried it, and then covered it
...rt, followed by the boulder. As he stood and
...d pine needles from his pants, he threw the
...ck over his shoulder and frowned. *And this
...r needs to hurry back to Jacksonville ... Maddi
...nger.*

Chapter 42
GAINESVILLE, FLORIDA

1/6/04

It was just after 5:00 when the trucker dropped
Henderson at a rest stop just outside Gainesville. He
jogged to the Waccasassa Forest about a mile away, and
then strolled the paths, pretending to take interest in
the sinkholes that often stretched a half-mile beneath
the earth's surface. When he was certain no one was
watching, he stepped off the path and followed
predetermined landmarks through the brush to an area
deep in the forest. After about 200 yards, he stopped.
He had marked the site with a large boulder. Staying
low behind the trees, he shoved the boulder out of the
way and began to dig. After about two feet, he came to
the top of the container that held his equipment. The
container was about the size of a footlocker, and was
made of stainless steel. He dug some more, and then
lifted it out of the hole. He covered the hole with the
boulder, and dragged the locker to a nearby cave. He
did a quick check for wildcats or snakes, and then
pulled the locker inside. He checked his watch. 5:25.
He plugged in the code to a padlock on the lid, touched
his thumb to a receptacle, and opened it. He took
inventory. It was all there ... a satellite tracking device,
a spare laptop with an untraceable IP address, and a
battery-powered generator with digital hot-spot
capability. He took a D-cell battery from his backpack
and slid it into the generator. He pulled out the
tracking device, plugged it into the generator, and
turned it on. It barely made a sound, the quiet hum
mixing easily with the sounds of the forest.

He pulled away his hood and set the computer on his lap. He typed in Morningstar's email address. He angled the tracking device so it could pick up a satellite beam, and then waited to see if it could crack not only Morningstar's password, but the encryption code Henderson was sure he and his sons had added to hide their communications. Again, he checked his watch. 5:32. He needed to hurry. While the laptop worked on breaking the code, Henderson leaned out just beyond the opening of the cave to make sure no one was nearby. He heard a ping from his computer and checked the screen. *I'm in!* Deleted emails from Morningstar's private account were staring back at him. There were hundreds of them. Though he would have loved to have read every one, there wasn't time. Not only did he want to get back to Jacksonville before Maddi arrived, but there was always a chance that Morningstar had rigged this account like he had the others, and that Henderson's location would soon be compromised. He scrolled to the last several entries, stopping at the most recent. It had been sent only minutes ago from an unidentified source. It was encrypted. He turned a dial to heighten the satellite signal, and then used a digital interceptor to try to break the code. He froze. He had heard laughter. He stuck out his head. He spotted two boys running through the woods. *Shit!*

He looked at the computer screen. A rapid series of combinations was trying to break the encryption code. He could hear the boys; they were less than thirty feet away. He waited. Twenty feet ... now ten. A light blinked, he looked at the screen. He was in. He stared at the memo. It was from Simeon. But it wasn't discussing arms shipments or boats from Africa. *"I have a plan for the retreat, Father. It will take care of the dirty dozen ... and will take her breath away."*

The two boys w
He needed to hurr
stunned by the mem

He still knew no
it would have to wait
everything. How m
dozen?' Could he hav
else? Maybe a group o
were meeting somew
reason, Morningstar n
had said that he was ab
frowned. *He is focused*

There was only one ؟
might interest Mornin؟
twelve people, where at le
Morningstar and Simeo
and it isn't good.

He shut off the satel
metal lockbox. He logged
top. He pulled the battery f
the ground, and then set t؟
next to the computer. He lo
to return his battery to his ؟
the boys say, "Hey Mister, w

Henderson looked up. T؟
entrance. He couldn't be an؟
hijacked a piece of timber fr؟
using it as a walking stick. ؟
hair stuck out from undernea
rows of freckles covered his n
wearing a backpack, and H
pocketknife sticking out of
adventurer out for a day in the
The fading sunlight was about ؟
cave, but Henderson lowered h
What else could he do? Here he ؟

the middle
a metal bo
choices. ؟
explanatio؟
friend.

He loo؟
– he scoot
forehead,
beam fror
same tim؟
the grave؟
"I'm your؟
here!"

The ؟
Mister!"
"There's
your life؟

As ؟
caught ؟
instantl؟
onto hi؟
right. H؟
head ar؟
box to ؟
with di؟
brushe؟
backpa؟
monst؟
is in d؟

Chapter 42
GAINESVILLE, FLORIDA

1/6/04

It was just after 5:00 when the trucker dropped Henderson at a rest stop just outside Gainesville. He jogged to the Waccasassa Forest about a mile away, and then strolled the paths, pretending to take interest in the sinkholes that often stretched a half-mile beneath the earth's surface. When he was certain no one was watching, he stepped off the path and followed predetermined landmarks through the brush to an area deep in the forest. After about 200 yards, he stopped. He had marked the site with a large boulder. Staying low behind the trees, he shoved the boulder out of the way and began to dig. After about two feet, he came to the top of the container that held his equipment. The container was about the size of a footlocker, and was made of stainless steel. He dug some more, and then lifted it out of the hole. He covered the hole with the boulder, and dragged the locker to a nearby cave. He did a quick check for wildcats or snakes, and then pulled the locker inside. He checked his watch. 5:25. He plugged in the code to a padlock on the lid, touched his thumb to a receptacle, and opened it. He took inventory. It was all there ... a satellite tracking device, a spare laptop with an untraceable IP address, and a battery-powered generator with digital hot-spot capability. He took a D-cell battery from his backpack and slid it into the generator. He pulled out the tracking device, plugged it into the generator, and turned it on. It barely made a sound, the quiet hum mixing easily with the sounds of the forest.

He pulled away his hood and set the computer on his lap. He typed in Morningstar's email address. He angled the tracking device so it could pick up a satellite beam, and then waited to see if it could crack not only Morningstar's password, but the encryption code Henderson was sure he and his sons had added to hide their communications. Again, he checked his watch. 5:32. He needed to hurry. While the laptop worked on breaking the code, Henderson leaned out just beyond the opening of the cave to make sure no one was nearby. He heard a ping from his computer and checked the screen. *I'm in!* Deleted emails from Morningstar's private account were staring back at him. There were hundreds of them. Though he would have loved to have read every one, there wasn't time. Not only did he want to get back to Jacksonville before Maddi arrived, but there was always a chance that Morningstar had rigged this account like he had the others, and that Henderson's location would soon be compromised. He scrolled to the last several entries, stopping at the most recent. It had been sent only minutes ago from an unidentified source. It was encrypted. He turned a dial to heighten the satellite signal, and then used a digital interceptor to try to break the code. He froze. He had heard laughter. He stuck out his head. He spotted two boys running through the woods. *Shit!*

He looked at the computer screen. A rapid series of combinations was trying to break the encryption code. He could hear the boys; they were less than thirty feet away. He waited. Twenty feet ... now ten. A light blinked, he looked at the screen. He was in. He stared at the memo. It was from Simeon. But it wasn't discussing arms shipments or boats from Africa. *"I have a plan for the retreat, Father. It will take care of the dirty dozen ... and will take her breath away."*

The two boys were only a few feet from the cave. He needed to hurry, but he couldn't move. He was stunned by the memo. *Get out of here, Henderson!*

He still knew nothing about the African boats, but it would have to wait. Simeon's message had changed everything. How many retreats involved a 'dirty dozen?' Could he have been talking about something else? Maybe a group of leaders – twelve of them – who were meeting somewhere else, and, for whatever reason, Morningstar needed them gone? But Simeon had said that he was about to take *her* breath away. He frowned. *He is focused on a woman ... at a retreat!*

There was only one gathering he could think of that might interest Morningstar; only one retreat with twelve people, where at least one of them was a woman. *Morningstar and Simeon are planning something ... and it isn't good.*

He shut off the satellite device and put it in the metal lockbox. He logged off the laptop and set it on top. He pulled the battery from the generator, laid it on the ground, and then set the generator in the lockbox next to the computer. He locked the box and was about to return his battery to his pack, when he heard one of the boys say, "Hey Mister, who are you?"

Henderson looked up. The boy was standing at the entrance. He couldn't be any older than ten. He had hijacked a piece of timber from a fallen tree and was using it as a walking stick. Strands of straw-colored hair stuck out from underneath a Gator ball cap, and rows of freckles covered his nose and cheeks. He was wearing a backpack, and Henderson could see a pocketknife sticking out of his pants pocket. *An adventurer out for a day in the woods with his friend.* The fading sunlight was about to find its way into the cave, but Henderson lowered his hood in spite of it. What else could he do? Here he sat, hiding in a cave in the middle of the woods, a D-cell battery in his lap and a metal box on the ground next to him. He had two choices. Either try to come up with a plausible explanation, or scare the tar out of the boy and his friend.

He looked at the boy and – with the greatest regret – he scooted into the light, revealing deep scars on his forehead, as well as a slight divot in his scalp, where a beam from the hotel blast had dented his skull. At the same time, he jutted out his disfigured jaw and, with the gravelly voice he had grown to hate, he growled, "I'm your worst nightmare. Now get the hell away from here!"

The boy's eyes were as wide as quarters. "O-Okay, Mister!" He turned and ran, yelling at his friend, "There's a monster in that cave, Johnny! Run! Run for your life!"

As Henderson put the battery in his pack, he caught a glimpse of his scarred forearms, and was instantly angry when he saw a few sparse tears spill onto his hands. He wiped them away. The boy was right. He was a monster. He pulled the hood over his head and grabbed his backpack. He dragged the metal box to its hiding place, buried it, and then covered it with dirt, followed by the boulder. As he stood and brushed pine needles from his pants, he threw the backpack over his shoulder and frowned. *And this monster needs to hurry back to Jacksonville ... Maddi is in danger.*

Chapter 43
WASHINGTON, D.C.

1/6/04

Hank had had enough of bioterrorism threats. He had spent the afternoon reviewing everything from Rocky Mountain spotted fever to Legionnaires Disease. He laid down the file he had been working on and sighed. He checked the clock. 6:00 p.m. Maddi was on her way to the conference. *Without me.*

He turned to his laptop and pulled up the itinerary for the retreat. It had been sent to him as a matter of course; Homeland was informed about any gathering involving members of Congress. He read it through and frowned. Tonight, they were holding a welcoming ceremony. "Senators and guests to attend a reception at 9:00 p.m. in the Seminole Conference Room located on the second floor of the hotel." *Senators and guests.*

He logged off and closed his laptop. He rubbed his eyes, and then pulled the stack of files in front of him. *I might as well get something done for the good of the country ... it's not like I have anything else to do.* He stared at the files. They were tedious. Each one contained a potential bacterial or viral threat that had come in from the night before. They had been assessed and summarized by his team, and now needed his review. There were over thirty of them. He began to sift through each one, carefully discerning those that seemed benign – nearly all of them – and the few that would require further investigation. There were only two of those; he pulled them from the stack and set them aside. He put the others in a pile on the floor, and looked at the first potential threat, trying to stay focused as he imagined Maddi at the reception with no one at her side. *She'd rather go alone than take me with her?*

He read through the threat. "There have been a cluster of infections with what appears to be an unidentified virus. It has infected four members of a tribal community in southwest Arizona." He read his agent's summary, and then looked closer at the symptoms. After several minutes he was able to dismiss the illness as the stomach flu. *Norovirus ... nothing more.* He wrote up a quick memo to have the area health department culture the stool to confirm.

He went on to the next folder. "The CDC has been made aware of a sudden increase in the number of flu victims that have been hospitalized, many of them ending up on a ventilator. The greatest numbers appear to be coming from the upper Midwest." He looked at the type of illness, the reason for the hospitalizations, and the incidence of flu around the country. It had been a tough year, and the flu vaccine had been a poor match. *No wonder so many ended up sicker than usual.* Though the distribution was a bit out of the norm, he set it aside, deciding he would contact the epidemiologist at Wisconsin's Green County Health Department tomorrow morning.

He was about to shove the file into his bottom drawer, when his secretary walked in with a folder. "These just came in, Doctor."

He took the folder and laid it on his desk. "Thanks, Jana." He knew what it was. He received the same file at the end of each work day. It contained a summary of lab viruses and poisonous gases that had been transported in the past twenty-four hours. The paperwork was the only way to track them. Claiming their use for research, developed countries often swapped the substances back and forth. The tracking sheets more or less guaranteed that a missing viral culture or vial of gas would be quickly identified.

Hank sighed as he opened the file. There were about ten photocopied invoices paper-clipped to the inside flap, and on the other side was a paper with the heading, "Ongoing monitoring of viruses/poisonous gases/chemical weapons." It was stamped "6:00 p.m. EST, January 5th through January 6th, 2004." The first line read, "We have noted a recent uptick in the number of vials without a corresponding tracking slip. This raises the specter of a possible attack." Hank frowned as he thumbed through the invoices. They showed all exchanges, domestic and abroad, in the last twenty-four hours. The most recent was a canister of sarin gas that had been shipped from Saudi Arabia the day before. It was highlighted in red with a note that said, "was due to arrive at the CDC lab in Atlanta at 5:00 p.m. EST ... it was a no-show." He frowned. Though that happened from time to time ... a mistaken destination ticket or a mistyped invoice, it still raised a flag. He went back to the cover document. "Though we've intercepted no chatter, and have seen no evidence to suggest a pending assault, all agencies are advised to review the invoices and be watchful for any sign that one of these substances has been released within U.S. borders." Hank read through the symptoms that might accompany an assault from Sarin gas and frowned. *I think it would be pretty clear if someone used this stuff in America.* But by then it would be too late. How did they expect him to stop something like that? He flagged it and laid the file on his desk. *I'll look into it in the morning.*

He stood and slid his laptop into his briefcase. It was 6:15 and he was eager to get home. He didn't know why, however. It wasn't like he had any plans. *I'll order pizza, drink a beer, and watch some hockey.* Sounded like a great night. He walked to the door and, as he was about to open it, he glanced back at the file on his desk. He frowned. *Meanwhile, some nut job could be plotting to kill American citizens with a canister of poisonous gas.* He walked back and grabbed the file. He would review the invoices between halves.

Chapter 44
WASHINGTON, D.C.

1/6/04

Morningstar stared at his computer screen, reading again the email he had gotten just over an hour ago.

"I have a plan for the retreat, Father. It will take care of the dirty dozen ... and will take her breath away."

He grinned. Simeon had clearly come up with a plan. But Morningstar was still antsy. The retreat was to begin soon, and he had yet to hear exactly *how* Simeon was going to "...take her breath away." And when was it going to happen? Tonight? Tomorrow? He had told Simeon to stay with secure email; a phone call at this point would be too risky. So, he was sitting at his desk in his living room, his computer on, a glass of brandy in one hand and a cigar in the other. He had been there for over an hour now, and was beginning to wonder if Simeon was going to give him any more details. *Maybe he wants to surprise me.*

He checked his watch. *6:20 p.m.* He had hijacked a retreat itinerary from the domestic terror unit just before he left his office. It listed a nine o'clock reception, to be held that night in the Seminole Room at the Grande Dames Hotel. Would Simeon try to do something tonight? Or would he wait until tomorrow, or maybe even the day after, when he would have time to put a little more detail into the plan? He grinned. It was hard to tell about Simeon.

He needed another drink. He stood and walked to the bar. What Simeon was about to do was big. It was one thing to kill a senator, but to kill twelve of them, well ... that was huge. He poured a glass of brandy – his third – and carried it to his desk. Killing all twelve was essential; it would divert suspicion. A terrorist's motives were obvious, and therefore rarely explored. A simple "Allah Akbar!" and any question as to why the attack had occurred was quickly dismissed. An assassination on the other hand, prompted an investigation into all possible motives.

He pulled up a cable news website and saw a comment about the Majority Whip and her friendship with the President. There was a picture of the two of them arm in arm. He stared at it and frowned. *Well-connected ... aren't we?* He couldn't wait for her to be taken out. Had Simeon understood that she was the main target? Morningstar went back to the email. *"... it will take her breath away."* He grinned. *He understood.*

He polished off the brandy, smacked his lips, and slammed the glass on the desk. He laughed. "By the end of the week, well-connected bitch, you'll be dead."

Chapter 45
JACKSONVILLE, FLORIDA

1/6/04

Maddi hated to fly domestic. But she had been forced to; the military transport plane she often used was unavailable. And all first-class tickets were taken, so she and her bodyguards sat in economy class as the 747 jetted to Jacksonville. The flight was expected to land at 6:55 p.m., which should have her at the Grande Dames Hotel by 7:30. There was a reception scheduled for nine; plenty of time to freshen up.

As they flew along the coast, she looked out and saw daylight fading, the sun's reflection lighting up the Atlantic Ocean as if it was on fire. She stared at the water, watching as, within seconds, day turned to night, and the sky was suddenly awash in darkness. She sat back and looked around the cabin, wondering if there were other senators on the plane. It was doubtful. Most of them had access to private jets through wealthy donors or powerful lobbyists. It wasn't that Maddi didn't have similar connections; she just made a point of not using them if she didn't have to. No sense giving the media something to talk about ... or her constituents a reason to vote her out at the next election.

And there was always a 'next election.' It sometimes felt like all she did was run for reelection. It was amazing that any of them had time to actually govern. And when they weren't running for reelection, the special-interest groups monopolized their time and energy. Maddi hated that part of the job. She often had to remind herself why she had come to D.C. in the first place.

She closed her eyes. *And why was that, Senator Madison?* She grinned. *To make America – and the world – better and safer.* It was President Wilcox's reelection slogan. "Give me another four years ... so we can continue to make America better and safer."

It was why she had planned the retreat in the first place. Though Wilcox, like many politicians, sometimes got caught up in the hype, she believed in him. He had done what he had set out to do, and the country was on a better track economically than it had been in decades. Foreign Policy was always a struggle, and the advent of Al-Qaida had made it all the more difficult. Though many of her fellow senators doubted Wilcox's resolve, she knew that his measured approach in the Middle East would be better in the long run. *Now I just have to convince the others.*

And she would do her best to make the retreat as pleasant as possible. Her hope was that by inviting spouses, the senators would be more apt to loosen up ... to be receptive to the notion that a cautious approach to the Middle East would bear fruit in the long run. Did she believe it? Not entirely ... but she would pretend that she did, at least until Wilcox was reelected.

She had thought about inviting Hank, and wasn't quite sure why she hadn't. She knew he was busy; his job was nonstop. But he would have enjoyed the break. *So, why didn't I ask him?* For one thing, Hank despised small talk. But he had mastered the art, mostly for her. Her senate colleagues were fond of him, and he had found a way to fit into a world he didn't really enjoy. All of sudden, she missed him. She tried to imagine what he was doing. He had likely gone home for the night, and was about to order pizza and watch hockey. She grinned. She wished she had invited him. *Maybe I'll call him and see if he can fly in tomorrow afternoon.*

She felt the plane begin its descent. Within minutes they were on the ground, and she waited as the passengers lined the aisle and then stepped off the plane. She followed the last of them, her bodyguards behind her. When they were inside the terminal, she turned to Larry. "Do we have a car?"

He nodded. "Waiting out front once we've picked up our luggage."

They retrieved their bags, and walked outside. The warm air was refreshing. Maddi turned her face to the sky. The moon was covered by clouds, and she could smell rain in the air. There would be a shower before the night was over.

Larry spotted the sedan. They walked over and Larry verified the driver's ID. When he was satisfied, he and Maddi slid in back, while Collins sat up front. "The Grande Dames," Larry said. "And we'll need to keep the car."

The driver nodded and drove away from the terminal. They eased onto the highway and, fifteen minutes later, pulled up to the entrance of the Grande Dames Hotel. Larry arranged for the valet – who had been vetted prior to their arrival – to park the car. He then ordered a cab to deliver the driver back to the agency.

They checked into the hotel, and Larry and Collins did a quick inspection of Maddi's suite. The bellman delivered their bags, and Larry carried Maddi's bag into the master bedroom. He put his things in the room next to hers, while Collins checked into the suite next door. The retreat was scheduled through Friday; he and Larry would work twelve-hour shifts throughout their stay.

Maddi walked into her bedroom and unpacked her bag. The reception wasn't to start for another hour-and-a-half. She laid out a dress and was about to take a shower, when she stopped. She stared at the dress. It was the same dress she had worn in Providence ... the night that had ended with Henderson in her room ... the only night the two of them had ever spent together. Her legs felt weak and she sat on the bed. *Come on, Maddi, you have got to quit doing this to yourself ...*

"So how did you get the name Maddi?"

Maddi scooted closer to him. "I'm only Maddi to my closest friends."

He nodded. "I see."

She grinned. "It's a long story."

Henderson smiled and she felt her heart skip a beat. "I've got nothing but time." He put his arm around her. They were seated on the sofa in front of the bay window. It was nearly one a.m., and they had not moved since they walked into her hotel room three hours ago.

Maddi smiled. "It started when I was at Oxford. They like to call you by your last name over there."

"I see"

Maddi nodded. "Yes. I was Madison, one of my friends was Williamson ... you get it."

Henderson grinned. "I get it."

"Anyway, I decided that Williamson took too long to say, so I just called him Willy."

Henderson nodded. "And then, of course, he called you Maddi, and it stuck."

She nodded. "Pretty much."

He smiled. "So, do I get to call you Maddi?"

She grinned, looked up at him, and pulled him close. "Are you one of my closest friends?"

He kissed her and said "I hope so..."

Maddi lifted the dress from the bed and pulled it to her chest. She was shaking. She had to stop thinking about him. It was only getting worse. It seemed like she couldn't go for more than a few hours without a Henderson memory disrupting her day and throwing her completely off balance.

And it hurt. Not just emotionally, but physically. Her temples would pound, her legs would ache ... as if she had a fever. *Henderson fever ... I've found a new bug.*

She chuckled wryly and laid the dress on the bed. She stepped out of her clothes, grabbed a robe and slippers supplied by the hotel, and walked into the bathroom. She took a shower, and then put on the robe and walked over to the desk. She checked her watch. *8:05.* There was time to get a little work done before the reception. She grabbed her briefcase and pulled out the folders concerning the Silverton arms deals. She needed to be ready to discuss it if the chance presented itself. She skimmed the files for what seemed like the hundredth time, stopping when she got to the part about Yemen and Al-Gharsi. She laid the folder on the desk. It hurt to remember his murder, but it hurt even more to think of all that had come about because of it ... the demise of a peace process that had seemed more hopeful than any that had come before it. And now the region had fallen into turmoil once again.

Suddenly she could see him ... Al-Gharsi ... his bloodied head face down on the tablecloth next to her. She rubbed her eyes as she stood and walked to the patio's sliding doors. The hotel sat right on the beach, and she had an oceanfront view. She stepped onto the terrace and let the breeze blow back her hair. It felt good ... the wind in her face, the mist from the sea dousing her cheeks with salty brine. She looked out at the water. The moon had snuck through the clouds and was glistening on the waves. It brought tears to her eyes. Again, she thought of Henderson and the night in

Providence. But it wasn't an ocean they had looked at; it was a bay. As silent tears made their way down her cheeks, she stared at the water and whispered, "I miss you, Martin Henderson, more than you will ever know."

~~~

Henderson had gotten back to Jacksonville just before eight. He had immediately made his way to the Grande Dames. But not through the lobby with its elegantly framed artwork or its oversized fountain; no, he had stationed himself a half mile from the complex, on the beach, hidden among a thick hedge of bushes that abutted a ramp to the highway. It was close enough. He had hacked into the hotel the night before, and had seen a room listed under her agent's name, Larry Moses. He had then accessed a hotel blueprint, and was able to aim his binoculars directly at the terrace of her room. Was it stalking? Yes. Did he care? *Not anymore.*

He knelt in the brush and stared at her room through binoculars. He didn't expect to actually see her ... he was hoping to catch her silhouette in the window to confirm that she was okay. But suddenly, there she was ... *in nothing but a robe*. His heart raced as he watched her walk onto the terrace. Tightening the lens, he was able to see the lines on her face, the fine hairs around her forehead; even the fading mascara that lined her lashes. He saw the wind blow her hair and he pretended it was his hand that had brushed the bangs from her face. It was hard to see her so close; he wanted to turn away, but he couldn't. The robe was tied at the waist, but hung loose on her shoulders, hugging her much like he wished he was doing. His hands were shaking; he held the lens tighter ... he didn't want to miss a single minute. He trained it on her eyes, surprised when he saw her start to cry. He increased

248

the magnification, and watched as she mouthed the words. *"I miss you, Martin Henderson..."*

He threw the binoculars to the ground. He couldn't stand it. Never had he hurt so bad ... he had burned alive, his legs had been broken, and he had been shot in the chest more than once; but none of it hurt as much as he hurt right then. He felt like a knife was cutting his heart; like a bomb had exploded in his brain. Until that moment, he had not realized how much he loved her, and, until that moment, he had not been sure she loved him back. But now he knew ... he had seen her say it. She *missed* him, to the point of tears. It didn't comfort him ... it only made it worse. Not only could he never have her ... but now he knew, she wanted him, too. And the knowledge of it made him want her even more. *We are both miserable ... and we are both alone.*

A tower in the distance rang out a single chime, he checked his watch. *8:15 ... I need to get busy.* Maddi was about to attend a reception and, though he couldn't be sure what Simeon was up to, something told him that – for whatever reason – Morningstar's son was about to do all he could to disrupt it. *"... it will take her breath away."* What had Simeon meant by it? Was he even talking about Maddi? It didn't matter; Henderson couldn't take the chance.

He picked up the binoculars and took a final look, watching as she wiped tears from her cheeks and then turned and walked inside. He shoved the binoculars in his pack and stood from his hiding place. He stared at the terrace and whispered, "I miss you, too, Cynthia Madison."

Chapter 46
JACKSONVILLE, FLORIDA

1/6/04

Simeon's plane had landed at the Jacksonville airport at 7:25 p.m., and he had immediately taken a taxi downtown. Before he left D.C., he had used a bank in the Dulles terminal to wire 200,000 in Saudi Riyals, the equivalent of about 50,000 dollars, to a bank in Saudi Arabia. He had done the same thing many times over the last four years; no one had even batted an eye. If all went well, there should be a canister of sarin gas waiting for him in a locker in the Jacksonville YMCA.

He was basically killing twelve senators in order to take out just one. Wouldn't it be a shame if he killed nearly all of them, but Madison somehow escaped? More than a shame; it would likely be the end of him. Jacob had given him a task; it was imperative he complete it. He knew what happened to those who failed.

So, he had come up with a backup plan. It would require help from his new accomplice, Pocks, however. He would call him once he got settled.

He arrived downtown, paid the fare, and walked three blocks to a local department store. He bought a pair of overalls, a white ball cap, and a black wig and mustache left over from Halloween. At the last minute, he threw in an eyebrow pencil, and a bottle of makeup two shades lighter than his own skin. He walked another two blocks to the YMCA and was pleased to see a package waiting for him in locker 417. He was careful as he took the cardboard box from the locker. He tucked it under his arm and walked down Beach

Boulevard to find a hotel. It was 8:20 ... he needed to hurry.

His biggest challenge was to figure out a way for the gas to be introduced into the Grande Dames' ventilation system. Security would be more than tight; it would be unbeatable. Thanks to 9-11, all major hotels were carefully monitored, and packages and deliveries were inspected prior to being brought into the hotel. No one could get past reception without proper credentials. Simeon – regardless of who he pretended to be –would likely not get past the lobby. *But gas is invisible; it doesn't need ID.*

He turned the corner, walked into a cheap hotel, and arranged for a room, using the same alias, Don Walton. He had used the name several times in the past, and had a driver's license and a credit card. He paid for the room and then climbed the stairs to a suite at the end of the hall. He walked in and locked the door. He set the box on the bed. He dropped his carryon on the floor, and tossed his sack with the overalls on the chair. He sat on a faded footstool, pulled out his phone, and dialed the number Morningstar had given him for the mysterious Pocks. He waited through one, two, three rings, and was about to hang up, when a tentative voice said "Hel – hello?"

Simeon rolled his eyes. "Pocks?"

"Yes."

"This is Simeon."

There was a pause. "Um, yeah, I was told you would call."

"You're going to be a valet."

Another pause. "A valet?"

"Yeah. But not until I tell you to."

"Okay. Just tell me what you want me to do."

Simeon went over the plan, and made Pocks go through it several times. When he felt confident that

Pocks understood his role, he said, "Any questions?"

"Only one."

"What's that?"

"How are you going to let me know it's time?"

Simeon grinned. "You'll hear a gunshot, Pocks. That's when you'll know."

"What if something goes wrong?"

"It won't." He paused. "But if it does, just hightail it out of there. Got it?"

"Yeah, I guess so."

"Good. Nine o'clock. Don't be late."

"Got it."

Simeon ended the call. He opened his laptop and clicked to Cynthia Madison's senate webpage. He stared at her picture and licked his lips. *Quite the looker, aren't you.* He almost hoped the sarin gas attack failed. His backup plan was not only clever, but it would give him time alone with her ... *an opportunity to enjoy that bitch ... up close and personal.*

He set the laptop on the bed and stared down at the box he had picked up at the YMCA. He opened the lid. Inside was a cloth satchel, and he could see bulges from two separate canisters. He knew what they were. The first contained the Sarin gas; the second held an agent known as DIC, which would activate the poison. Splitting the two agents allowed him to transport the gas with less risk. The plan was simple. The Grande Dames was an older hotel and had not been updated for several years; it still used an antiquated air conditioning system. A renovation was underway, but had not yet been completed. As a result, the hotel still relied on canisters of Freon gas to cool the hotel. With just a little research, Simeon had managed to learn the name of the supplier: *Climate Control, Inc.* If he could gain access to the canisters, he could swap two of theirs for his two containers. But he couldn't just waltz into the hotel and ask to replace two canisters. He needed a reason.

He grabbed his computer, set it on his lap, and did a quick search of *Climate Control, Inc.* It was a small operation located in downtown Jacksonville, and had been in business since 1956. Its reputation was impeccable. It had served the needs of some of the larger area hotels for decades. Though Simeon's overalls were not likely to match the uniform of the company, he could say he had been called in from the warehouse to help with a problem concerning the delivery of Freon into the hotel's ventilation system. He feigned a southern accent. "I been around a long time ... I know how these older systems work," he stuck out his chest, " ... and you can't just slide 'em in, boys ... it takes a man to get it right!" He laughed. All he needed was his well-planned disguise, and a warm, reassuring manner. *Piece of cake.*

His plan was to show up at the hotel at 8:55. He would tell the clerk that he had been called in to fix the air-conditioning. If he was persuasive, he would be taken to the utility room that housed the AC. He would have about two minutes to replace the existing canisters with his canisters of Sarin gas and DIC. Once he was certain the Sarin gas cylinder was stationary inside the unit, he would pull away the barrier that separated the two gases, allowing them to mix. The now-volatile Sarin gas wouldn't enter the hotel right away, however; not until the canister in front of it was empty. He had done his research. The canisters were cycled over a two-hour span, and the last batch had been cycled through at 7:15 ... which meant the next cycle would begin at around nine-fifteen. *Right after the senators arrive at their little soirée.* He would have the new valet, Pocks, barricade the front door, and then wait while the Sarin gas entered the ventilation system and spread throughout the hotel. *Voila!* By 9:20, everyone would be dead. *It's so simple.*

He checked his watch. *8:40.* It was time to go. He took out an ID he had used in the past; he needed to do his best to look like the man in the photo. He frowned as he looked at the wig he had gotten at the department store. Though it was the same color, it wasn't cut nearly the same as the picture. *I can hide most of it under the hat.* He pulled the overalls overtop his clothes, put on the black wig, and then tucked nearly all of it under the cap. He used the makeup to change his skin tone, and etched lines next to his eyes and along his cheeks with the eyebrow pencil. He pasted the mustache over his lip, and then looked from the photo ID to the mirror. *Perfect.* "Mort Meyers, inspector." He shoved the ID in his wallet and slid his laptop into his bag. He checked the room. He wouldn't be back. He slid the bag with the gas over one shoulder, his carryon over the other. He crept out of the room, careful to keep his face hidden from cameras as he left the hotel out a back door. He walked calmly to the sidewalk. *Showtime.*

Ten minutes later, he reached the Grande Dames and stood outside. It was a balmy night. The moon was covered by clouds, but the streetlights were bright and welcoming. He saw two young boys walk by carrying skateboards. He stopped them. "Hey fellas ... ya' wanna' earn some quick cash?"

Their eyes widened. The taller of the two nodded. "Sure. What do we gotta do?"

Simeon grinned and pulled out his wallet. "I want you to walk into the Grande Dames and go to the back of the lobby. Don't try to go any further; they won't let you." He paused. "After a minute or two, you'll see me come through the door and walk to the counter. Count to sixty, and then walk past me to the door. On the way, one of you needs to say – loud enough for the clerk to hear – 'Mom says she isn't going to stay here again if they don't fix the air-conditioning.' The other one will nod and say, 'Yeah, my dad said the same thing.'"

The boys looked at him and frowned. The taller one said, "Is that it? The AC's broken and our folks are pissed?"

Simeon laughed. "Yep ... that's all you have to do." He pulled two twenty-dollar bills from his wallet and held them in front of the boys.

They exchanged glances. The taller one said, "Let's do it, Bobby." He grabbed both bills and handed one to the smaller boy.

Simeon nodded. "Go on in. Wait for me to walk up to the desk. Give it a minute or two, and then make your move." He paused. "Do you remember what you're supposed to say?"

The boys nodded and the taller one recited the lines for both of them. Simeon grinned. "Excellent."

The boys ran off, hiding their skateboards in the bushes a few yards from the hotel entrance. They walked inside and disappeared. Simeon waited thirty seconds, and then sauntered through the door into the lobby. He went up to the desk and set his bag on the counter. He smiled warmly at a clerk. "Good evening, Ma'am. I'm here about the air-conditioning."

The girl, she looked like she was only nineteen or twenty, frowned and turned to an older clerk standing next to her. "Do you know anything about the AC, Mel?"

The older clerk frowned and shook his head. "No. Let me get the manager."

Simeon swallowed. *Keep your cool.* The manager, a middle-aged man who was about twenty pounds overweight, walked out to the counter. "Do you have ID?"

Simeon pulled out his fake ID and handed it to the

manager. "Mort Meyers at your service, sir."

The manager looked at the ID, and then at Simeon. "I don't show that we called for service on the AC."

Simeon forced himself to stay calm. "Beats me. I was just told to come here and fix the AC." He paused. "They sent me in special from Mississippi. No skin off my back, though. I could use a night on the beach." He gathered his bag and was about to walk away, when the taller boy strutted past the desk and muttered the comment about the AC. The smaller one echoed the complaint, loud enough for the manager – and anyone else in the lobby – to hear. Simeon stopped. He looked over his shoulder at the manager and shrugged. "Maybe you just haven't been told yet."

The manager hesitated. Simeon smiled. "It's your call. It'll prob'ly only take about a minute to fix." He leaned in closer. "Happens all the time with these older units."

The manager rubbed his chin, and then shook his head and sighed. "Let me make a call."

Simeon tightened his jaw, but nodded affably. The manager walked into the back room. Simeon gripped his bags tighter, ready to run if things didn't go well.

A minute later, the manager walked out frowning. "No one's answering at Home Office." He mumbled something about the bigwigs having banker's hours, and then motioned to Simeon to follow him as he stepped from behind the counter. "Let's go. But I'm going to have to watch you the entire time."

Simeon exhaled. "Okay by me."

The manager led Simeon out of the hotel through a side door, and walked him into a large room that abutted the back of the building. "Like I said, buddy, I got my eyes on you."

Simeon nodded. *Whatever, asshole.* He walked up to the unit and quickly located the canisters that were being used to provide the Freon gas. He lifted his bags to a shelf beside him, and then focused on the unit. "Ah, I already see the problem. There's a defective canister." He made a show of looking in one of his bags. "Good thing I brought a replacement." He removed the canister from the AC unit and set it on the floor. As slowly as he could without it seeming strange, he pulled the canister of Sarin gas from his bag. He put it exactly where the other canister had been, connecting it to a compressor inside the unit. He slid the DIC canister next to it, and opened the valve that would allow the two gases to mix. When the DIC canister was empty, he pulled it away and slid it in his bag. The entire process had taken him less than sixty seconds, and he smiled with satisfaction. He picked up the old Freon gas canister and threw it in his bag next to the DIC container. He grabbed his bags, throwing one over each shoulder. "That should do it." He turned and walked to the door, the manager right behind him. "It should take only a few minutes to regulate," he grinned, "...and then you'll be as cool as a cucumber."

The manager smiled. "Thank you, Mr. Myers." He reached out his hand.

Simeon had to grit his teeth to keep from laughing as he stopped and shook the man's hand. "No problem. I'll send the bill to your home office."

He walked away, forcing himself to maintain a casual gait until he was well out of sight of the manager, as well as any cameras that might be monitoring the area. He needed to get away from there as fast as he could. Once the gas was released, it would go first to the lobby, and then filter out to the guest rooms and the reception halls. The guests would start dropping like flies. That manager – if he survived – would remember him. Within minutes, Mort Myers' description would be flashed on every TV station within a fifty-mile radius. Though Simeon would have removed his disguise by then, there was no need to tempt fate.

When he was far enough away, he slipped into an alley and pulled off the wig and mustache. He took off the hat, and used a handkerchief to wipe away the make-up. He slid out of the overalls and rolled all of it into a ball. He buried it in an over-filled dumpster and lit a match. He checked his watch. *9:07*. The Sarin gas would be released soon. *Which gives me just enough time to find a spot nearby so I can watch.*

Chapter 47
WASHINGTON, D.C.

1/6/04

Morningstar had not left his living room and was finishing off his fourth brandy of the night. The fact that Simeon had given him no specifics was weighing on him. *Does that asshole think he's too good to check in?* Morningstar didn't know when or how or even where Simeon was going to take out the senators. Morningstar assumed it would be at the hotel, and he hoped it would happen that night. *The sooner the better,* he thought as he stood to go for a fifth drink.

But the longer he waited, the more he needed to know. He couldn't call Simeon; it could put both of them at risk ... *but I can call Pocks.* After all, Pocks had been sent to Jacksonville on behalf of General Daniels. He was there to serve as liaison between the senators and the Pentagon. *Nothing fishy about that.* Morningstar had given him a private cellphone. He dialed the number and waited.

Pocks answered on the fourth ring. "Hello?"

"It's me. Have you heard from Simeon?"

"Y – yes sir. My ... my instructions are clear, sir."

"Good. Do you know when he plans to carry out his task?"

"I'm assuming any minute sir, because I just barricaded the front door of the hotel."

Morningstar frowned. *Barricaded a door?* "Do you know anything about what he's planning, Pocks?"

"No sir."

Morningstar ended the call without a comment. *Pocks has barricaded a door ... which means it's happening tonight!* He raised his fist in triumph, and knocked over a half-full carafe of wine. He grabbed a towel, deciding his next drink should maybe be a coke instead of another glass of brandy. He needed to stay alert. He didn't want to miss one second of the TV coverage. He cleaned up the wine and then poured himself a coke. He walked to the sofa and switched on the TV. He leaned back and threw a comforter over his lap. He was ready. He had a front row seat to the destruction not only of the bitch who had become a thorn in his side, but of an entire cadre of bureaucrats. He laughed as he clicked to a 24-hour news station. *The world would thank me if they knew.*

Chapter 48
JACKSONVILLE, FLORIDA

1/6/04

Henderson had gotten back to his hotel room at 8:30, and had spent the next half-hour staring at his computer, looking through any site he could think of to try to figure out not only why Simeon might want to kill twelve U.S. Senators, but how and when. He had referenced a retreat, and the 'dirty dozen.' Was it the same retreat where Maddi was about to meet with eleven other senators and their spouses? *It has to be.* How was Simeon going to "take her breath away?" *And who has the balls to kill twelve U.S. Senators?* He frowned. He knew the answer to that one: Morningstar.

He leaned back in his chair. Though he couldn't be one-hundred percent certain that Simeon was targeting Maddi's retreat, he felt like it was a strong possibility. But when? Tonight? Tomorrow?

He leaned forward and pulled up the same site he had accessed twenty-four hours ago, where Morningstar used to send him the specifics for his assassinations. It was possible he also used the site with Simeon. It had been a foolproof communication device ... able to tell him the when, the where, and the who of a hit, without arousing suspicion in anyone who might stumble on the site. He logged onto the rarely used army website, using a password he had used as the Phoenix. Because he had been discovered – twice now – he made sure to route his connection through three separate servers in various parts of the country. It would take someone at least twenty-four hours to find him. *By then I'll be gone.* He waited for the site to load, and then clicked on a link buried in a disclaimer at the bottom of the page. The link took him to a different site. He plugged in a second password and waited.

The screen changed to show an outline; an itinerary of sorts; it was the same format he had seen many times in the past. He read the information, and his palms began to sweat.

Date: Tuesday, January 6th, through Friday, January 9th, 2004

Meeting goal: Exchange of info between the Pentagon and Congress

Those present: Pentagon officials, members of the House and Senate

Those absent: Twelve Senators on retreat, including Majority Whip.

Henderson's legs felt like they were going to give out. He stared at the data. Though he still didn't know the why, there was no doubt about it: Maddi was in danger. And it might take place as early as *that night.*

He checked his watch. It was ten after nine; the reception had already begun. He had to act quickly. Should he call the police? He frowned. *And tell them what? That a man named Simeon might be trying to kill the senators?* They would laugh in his face.

He stared at the computer screen. *So how do I stop this?* He tried to think who might be in a position to help him. He clicked to a cloaked email account he had used in the past and typed a message. He read it through, and then read it again. It needed to be convincing. He saved it and went to a government website that listed the names and numbers of the various departments. There was only one other man who cared enough about Maddi to act impulsively in the face of a possible threat against her. He found the number and dialed.

"Department of Homeland Security. May I help you?"

He cleared his throat. "Yes, may I speak to Dr. Hank Clarkson, please?"

Chapter 49
WASHINGTON, D.C.

1/6/04

Hank had gotten home just after seven. The minute he had opened the door to his townhouse apartment, he had felt lonely. Maddi had chosen to not invite him to Jacksonville, in spite of the fact that every other senator had brought someone. Why? He had no idea. The only comfort was that she hadn't taken anyone else ... at least as far as he knew. *What if she's meeting someone?* He shook his head. *She's not meeting anyone ... the man she loves is dead.*

He had decided to go for a run, and had followed his same path that took him past the Capitol, down Pennsylvania Avenue, and then back home. The entire run took about an hour. He got back to his apartment just before nine, took a quick shower, and then threw on a pair of sweats and a t-shirt. He passed on the pizza, fixed a TV dinner instead, and poured himself a beer. He carried the meal to his coffee table, along with the folder he had brought home with the chemical weapons invoices. He would look through the invoices while he watched the hockey game. He had just turned on the TV when his phone rang. "Hello?"

"It's Jana, sir. I have a man on the line who insists he needs to talk to you."

"Who is it?"

"He wouldn't give me his name, sir, but he says you'll want to talk to him."

"Jana, I don't normally talk to anonymous–"

"He said it had something to do with Senator Madison, sir."

Hank frowned. "Okay, put him through."

He waited. Within seconds he heard a deep, raspy voice. "Dr. Clarkson?"

"Yes. Who is this?"

There was a pause. "Just call me a friend."

Hank frowned. "Okay *friend* ... how do you know Senator Madison?"

Another pause, this one longer. "I'm about to send you an email. It's imperative that you do everything it says." He cleared his throat. "Please. We share a common interest."

The line went dead. Hank stared at the phone. He made a quick call to Homeland, and asked Jana to have the call traced. She had beaten him to it. "They're working on it, Doctor, but they're not having any luck."

He hung up the phone and opened his laptop. He clicked onto his department email site. He waited. Within seconds he heard the ding of an arriving email. He opened it and read it through. He sat back, stunned.

"You know me, but you don't. It's not important. The senators at the retreat are about to be attacked. I don't know how or why; I only know that it could happen tonight ... within the next few minutes. I beg of you ... stop it!"

Hank stared at email. He checked the time. 9:15. The opening reception had already begun. "*... it could happen tonight."* How soon? Was there time to stop it? How could he stop it? He grabbed his phone and dialed Hanover's private cellphone.

Hanover answered after the first ring. "Yeah, Hank, what do you need?"

"I need you to call down to the Grande Dames Hotel in Jacksonville, Florida, and get the senators who are there on that retreat out of that hotel ... now!"

There was a pause. "With all due respect, Hank, I don't–"

"Hanover, we can talk about the particulars later. Just stop the damn thing ... now!"

Another pause. "Hank, I'm going to do this, but if you're wrong–"

"Then I'm wrong. I'm an idiot and you can fire me. Please, sir. Just do it."

"Okay."

The line went dead. Hank tried to call Maddi. She didn't answer her cell. He looked up the number for the hotel. He dialed and, without waiting for a hello, he said, "This is Dr. Hank Clarkson with the Department of Homeland Security. I need to speak to Senator Cynthia Madison ... now. It's an emergency!"

"I'm sorry, sir, but I was instructed to not interrupt the conference."

I'm with the damned Department of Homeland Security, Moron! Hank cleared his throat. "Yes, but I'm guessing that doesn't include a call from the Deputy Director of Homeland Security."

There was a pause. All of sudden there were screams in the background. Hank heard the clerk say, "Oh dear god!" and then the line went dead.

Chapter 50

JACKSONVILLE, FLORIDA

1/6/04

Maddi walked into the Seminole Meeting Room of the Grand Dames Hotel, and instantly felt lonely ... which surprised her. She had chosen to come to the retreat by herself for a reason; she was in charge of the event, and the last thing she needed was someone to worry about. But, as she looked across the meeting hall, and saw the couples drinking wine or sipping cocktails, she wished she had brought someone. *Hank.* He would have been perfect for that sort of thing. He asked so little of her, especially when she was busy ... which was most of the time. So why hadn't she asked him? She sighed. The answer to that question would take far longer for her to figure out than the few minutes she had before the reception got underway.

She grabbed a glass of wine from a steward who had just walked by, and made her way to a couple on the other side of the room. It was Senator O'Malley from Texas, and his outspoken wife, Nancy. Though the thin woman with big hair was considered garish by most of the bigwigs in the Beltway, Maddi liked her. She was honest and direct; qualities Maddi admired ... even if she did come off a bit insolent from time to time. *Maybe she can give me the real scoop on Lawford.*

She had nearly reached them, when a staff member from the hotel burst into the conference room and ran over to her. His breaths were quick as he pulled her aside and whispered, "I'm ... I'm sorry to bother you, Senator Madison, but we've just received a call ... from the Director of Homeland Security. He said we need to evacuate the hotel ... right away!"

Maddi frowned. Keeping her voice low, she said, "The Director himself called?"

The man nodded. He was shaking. "Yes ... yes Ma'am. And he said to waste no time."

Maddi narrowed her eyes. Was this for real? What on earth would have compelled Jason Hanover to make such a call? *Something serious.* She nodded. "Okay. But we need to do it in a way that won't cause a panic."

The man frowned. "I don't know if there's time, Ma'am. Some of the guests have already–"

Maddi stared at the man. "Have what?"

"There's ... there's something terrible happening, Senator."

Maddi's Secret Service agent, Larry, walked up to her. "Is everything okay, Senator?"

Maddi whispered, "No. Jason Hanover just called the hotel and told the manager that all guests need to evacuate the premises immediately."

Larry's phone rang and he took the call. He looked at Maddi and frowned. "That was my boss. He confirms the order."

Just then, screams could be heard from the lobby. Larry grabbed her arm. "Let's go, Senator."

The manager's eyes widened and he looked around the room. "This way!"

He pointed to an exit and Larry more or less dragged Maddi in the direction of the door. She stopped him. "Wait! Get the others first!"

The senators and their spouses had heard the screams, and had begun to panic. They were all talking at once, and Maddi had to yell to be heard. "We need to leave the hotel, but we need to do it in an orderly fashion." She pointed to the exit. "We're going through that door and down the back stairs. Don't run. Once everyone's outside, we'll take it from there."

Nobody moved. Maddi turned to the O'Malley's. "Let's go, Nancy. Come on, Francis."

The senator looked at her and nodded. He took his wife by the elbow, and they hurried to the door. Maddi urged another couple to follow them, and then did the same with the others until everybody was heading out the door, two by two, to the staircase. She fell in behind them with Larry at her side. The minute they entered the staircase, they heard more screams somewhere in the hotel, and they picked up their pace, taking the stairs as fast as they could. The women were slowed by their heels, and finally Maddi yelled, "Take off your shoes! Let's go!"

They reached the first floor and the hotel manager threw open the door. An alarm sounded, and the manager ushered the guests out the door. He steered them away from the hotel, ignoring the light rain that had begun to fall. He directed them to a patch of grass at the side of the hotel. The women did their best to cover their hair, while some of the men took off their jackets and held them over their wives' heads. The manager leaned closer to Maddi and whispered, "We have to keep going, Senator. The Director said to get everyone at least two hundred feet away."

Maddi could feel herself starting to shake. *A bomb ... why else would he want to get us so far away?* She did her best to keep her cool, as she and Larry ushered the senators, their spouses, and now several other hotel guests across the parking lot to a grassy berm abutting Beach Boulevard. They were forced to stop there. Maddi tried to guess whether they had gone two hundred feet. It didn't look like it. "This is as far as we can go," she said to the manager.

He nodded. "I'm sure it's enough."

He turned and was about to run back to the hotel when Maddi grabbed him by the arm. "Where are you going?"

He swallowed. Maddi could see that he was scared. "I – I have to help get the others out of there."

All at once, a horde of guests ran out a side door, some of them shoving, a few of them yelling and screaming. They were all running toward the parking lot. What was happening? And why had Jason Hanover made the call himself ... *at 9:20 at night?* She frowned. *Because there was no time to go through proper channels.* She reached for her phone to call Hank, and then realized she had left it in the room. Those had been her instructions for all conference attendees. *"No cellphones, no computers." Way to go, Maddi.* She turned to ask Larry for his phone. He was using it.

Guests continued to pour out of the building. *They're evacuating the entire hotel!* Which meant that the threat was not only against the senators. Or maybe it was, but it had put the entire hotel at risk.

The sidewalk was quickly filled not only with hotel guests, but with onlookers who had seen the commotion. There were more screams from inside the hotel, louder, more frantic than before. About ten people ran out covering their mouths. They fell to the ground, writhing, clutching their throats. *Poison! Dear god, someone has poisoned the guests!* All at once, a gunshot splintered the air, and a strident "Allah Akbar!" could be heard about a hundred feet away. Maddi turned in the direction of the cry, but could see nothing through the rain. She grabbed Larry's arm. "We need to get these people away from here!"

She was about to try to force the crowd from the sidewalk onto the busy thoroughfare, when Larry pulled out his phone. "Bring me Senator Cynthia Madison's car ... now!"

He motioned to a few of the senators. "Get your cars, or wave down a cab, a bus, whatever you can find."

He paused. "Everybody needs to get away from here!"

Maddi's second agent, Collins, ran up to them, his gun raised and ready. Just then, their black town car pulled up. Larry turned to Collins. "I'm getting–"

Collins nodded. "I heard you. Go … get out of here!"

Maddi slid into the back seat. "Just drive," Larry said, as he slid in beside her.

The driver pulled away. Maddi frowned. "What's going on, Larry?"

He was on his phone. "I don't know, but I'm about to find out."

~~~

The valet driver looked in his rearview mirror. It was the senator alright. He had never seen her up close; only in the newspapers or on TV. She was even prettier in person. He focused on the road, hoping the Secret Service agent couldn't see his face. Things had gone better than expected; the look of relief might give him away.

He had heard Simeon's gunshot, which was followed by the call from the senator's bodyguard, and he had done exactly what he was supposed to. But he was nervous. He had never done anything like this. It was one thing to get caught with your pants down in front of the Bishop at First Blood Seminary; it was quite another to kidnap a U.S. Senator. *I'm just driving her car,* he tried to tell himself. And, though the mysterious Simeon had told him he would be saving her life, somehow it didn't feel like it. *Why was I told to wear a disguise if I'm saving her life?* He tugged at his fake beard. He didn't like it, but what choice did he have? He couldn't risk being identified, and he couldn't risk defying Morningstar, who had told him to do whatever Simeon said. As long as he wasn't asked to break any laws, he would follow Simeon's instructions. *I'm just driving her car.*

He drove along Beach Boulevard, rubbing his forehead as he thought through Simeon's instructions. Simeon's first question had been whether he knew Senator Madison. He had scoffed. Of course he knew her. Everybody knew her. Simeon had added, *"Well, you're about to save her life, my friend. But no one can know about this."* Pocks had frowned. *"Why? I mean if we're saving her, why can't anyone know?"* Simeon had blurted out, *"Because I said so, you dumb shit!"* When he had spoken again, it had been with the same calm voice he had used in the beginning. *"What we're doing isn't sanctioned, Pocks. But trust me; it's the right thing to do."*

Pocks had wanted to say no ... to turn down the assignment, but he couldn't. Morningstar had ordered him to do whatever Simeon said.

Simeon had added, *"You need to become a hotel valet. Find a guy and steal his uniform and badge."*

Pocks had stopped him. *"Won't the other guys know that I'm not who I say?"*

There had been a pause. *"You need to be creative, Pocks. Wear a disguise ... wait until the last minute ... and stay out of their way."*

Pocks had nodded. *"Okay ... then what?"*

Simeon had continued. *"At nine-fifteen on the dot, I want you to block anyone from using the front doors."*

Pocks had frowned. *"How do I do that?"*

He had heard the frustration in Simeon's voice. *"I don't know ... maybe throw a stick in the two door handles."*

"Got it. What do I do after that?"

Another pause. *"If the original plan fails, you'll hear me fire a shot. Then, you need to grab the senator's town car, and wait for her bodyguard to call you."*

"Why will he call me?"

A sigh. *"Because he's going to want to get out of there."* Another pause. *"Make sure you disable the GPS. Do you know how to do that?"*

Pocks had been insulted. *"Better than most,"* he had said, with more confidence than he had displayed since the phone call began.

"Good. Then you need to pick her up and take her away from there."

"Why?

"I'm not sure. Just a feeling. All I know is it will be up to us – to you – to save that lady if something goes wrong."

Pocks had wondered why they were only saving one of the senators. He had been about to ask, when Simeon had added, *"I'll find other drivers to do the same for the rest of them, but I wanted you to have the privilege of saving the Majority Whip. Are you up to it, Pocks?"*

Pocks had nodded, though he wasn't up to it at all. As he looked at her in the rearview mirror, he grinned in spite of his shaking hands. He had done it. He had fulfilled his obligation to Morningstar. But there was one more step ... one final duty to complete. Simeon had told it to him just before he had ended the call. *"Once you have her, Pocks, take her to the Pier. I'll look after her from there."*

Chapter 51

JACKSONVILLE, FLORIDA

1/6/04

Once Henderson had finished sending the email to Hank, he had grabbed his backpack and had sprinted to Maddi's hotel. He was hiding among a grove of trees near the front of the building, oblivious to the rain. He pulled out his binoculars just in time to see Maddi run from the side of the hotel holding her Secret Service agent's arm. She was following the other senators, who had run out in what looked like a controlled panic, and now the entire group was standing in a tuft of grass that lined Beach Boulevard. He gripped the binoculars, stunned as he saw about ten guests run out of the hotel, followed by several more that fell to the ground writhing, clutching their throats. *He's poisoned them!* Henderson thought of Simeon's comment. *"It'll take her breath away."* He bristled. *Damn you, Simeon!* But the majority of the guests appeared to have made it out okay. Maddi was one of them. *Way to go, Hank.*

He watched as Maddi and the others huddled in the grass. Had they been the target ... the dirty dozen, with Maddi being the one whose breath Simeon had hoped to take away? Most likely. Either way, from what Henderson could tell, the ruse had failed. Yes, Simeon had managed to poison a few of the guests, but the senators – the dirty dozen – had been spared. *Simeon must be off his game.* Henderson frowned. Simeon was never off his game.

He heard a gunshot and instantly grabbed his Glock. Was it the police, or an assassin? He heard a loud "Allah Akbar!" from somewhere behind the hotel. *Al-Qaida?* He was about to run from his hiding place and ignore the fact that he was a scarred freak with a gun, when he saw a town car pull up, and then watched as Maddi and her agent slid into the back. Henderson sighed, relieved. Her agent had found a way to get her away from there. Suddenly he frowned. *Who's driving?* Whoever it was had likely not been vetted ... her agent was taking a huge risk.

Was an Al-Qaida operative responsible for the gunshot? Or was it Simeon? *It had to be Simeon.* If so, why hadn't he killed her? Even with her agents standing next to her, Simeon was good enough to take her out with a single shot. But he hadn't even tried. Why? *Because he needed it to look like an attack on all of them, not just her.* Henderson frowned. So why the gunshot in the first place? He shoved his gun in his belt and started running. *Because ... for whatever reason ... he wanted Maddi to get into that car.*

Chapter 52
WASHINGTON, D.C.

1/6/04

Morningstar was on his third coke, and had sobered up considerably. He was glued to his TV set, waiting impatiently for news of the 'dreadful attack at the Grande Dames Hotel.' He was halfway through a sip of cola when a "breaking news" banner appeared at the top of the screen.

"Guests at Jacksonville's Grande Dames Hotel evacuated. Unknown substance said to have been released."

"Way to go, Simeon!" He stood and was on his way to the bar for a celebratory beverage, when he stopped. An announcer had come on.

"Following the evacuation of the Grande Dames Hotel in Jacksonville, Florida, there are now reports of a gunshot in the vicinity of the hotel. "Allah Akbar" was shouted, but the terror group has not yet claimed responsibility There are at least ten fatalities from an unknown poison; the other guests have either escaped exposure, or will recover. The FBI and Homeland Security have been called in to assist with the investigation."

The announcer paused, and put his hand to his earpiece.

"I have just been informed that a number of U.S.

senators were staying at the hotel. None of them appear to have been injured or–"

Morningstar grabbed his remote and threw it at the TV. It missed the screen, but knocked over a replica of the statue of liberty that had been given to him by General Daniels. The statue broke into pieces. Morningstar yelled, "Jesus, Simeon, can't you do a goddamned thing right!"

He pulled out his phone and dialed Simeon's number. "What the hell are you doing?"

There was a pause. Simeon's voice was nearly a whisper. "Don't worry, Father. I have a backup plan."

Morningstar frowned. "Is Pocks involved?"

"Yes. He has been a part of both plans."

"Well, the first one clearly didn't work."

"Don't worry, Father. I've made it look like terror, and I've dispersed the senators. I'm ready to follow through on the original goal, but with a twist."

"With a twist?" Morningstar rubbed the back of his neck. "What are you about to do, Simeon?"

Morningstar heard a chuckle. "As we speak, Father, that bitch is on her way to the pier, where she's about to have a meeting with the Atlantic Ocean, a semi-automatic, and me."

~~~

Maddi and Larry had been in the town car for about five minutes. It felt like an hour. Larry had been on the phone the entire time, but knew little more than he had when they left the hotel. He had learned one thing, however; Homeland Security had taken charge of the situation. The guests were being taken to a nearby Marriott that was scheduled to open in two weeks. He looked at Maddi and frowned. "I'm not taking you to another hotel ... not yet, anyway." He leaned forward and tapped the divider that separated the front seat from the back. "Drop us at the police station."

The driver seemed to hesitate, but then nodded. Larry looked at Maddi. "Are you okay?"

She sighed. "I'm fine, Larry. Why the police station?"

"Because I can't think of anyplace else where I'll be sure that you're safe."

The car turned right, and Larry frowned.

Maddi looked at him. "What's wrong?"

He pulled out his weapon and tapped it against the glass. "I said to take us to the police station, driver."

The man nodded. "I'm using evasive maneuvers, sir ... in case anyone's following us." He grinned into the rearview mirror. "Something I learned in the military."

Larry narrowed his eyes. "What branch, soldier?"

"The marines," the driver said proudly, "Semper Fi."

Larry nodded. "Semper Fi."

But Maddi wasn't convinced. As they drove on, she found herself wondering about the valet driver's 'evasive maneuvers.' She looked at Larry, who had not yet put his gun away. Clearly, he was wondering about them as well.

~~~

Pocks' hands were shaking, so he grabbed the wheel tighter. *Semper Fi? Oh brother.* He hoped he had been convincing. He looked in his mirror at the agent. The man's expression was hard to read.

Simeon's instructions had been clear. *"Take her to the pier, Pocks."* But a Secret Service agent had just ordered him to drive them to the police station. Who was in charge? Who should he listen to?

He decided to stay with Morningstar and Simeon; after all, they were the ones who could do him the most damage. *"Stay with the one who brung ya', Herbie."* He grinned. It was an old expression his grandmother had once told him. *"Never leave a girl stranded at a dance ... you stay with the one who brung ya..."* And he would. But he was glad for the disguise ... a dark wig, a pair of tinted glasses, and a heavy beard. It wasn't much, but it would keep the agent from identifying him if things went south.

He continued the drive to the pier. The rain was falling harder now, and he was having trouble seeing the road. He clutched the wheel tighter. He would deliver Madison, and then drive away before he could be implicated in the crime ... *if it is a crime.* He shivered. What if he was arrested? What if something happened to her once he dropped her at the pier? His hands began to shake even more. It was a federal crime to kidnap a U.S. senator. *No one will recognize you, Pocks ... it's why you're wearing the beard.* He stroked it again to make sure it was still in place. He adjusted his glasses and lowered his head so his face no longer showed in the rearview mirror.

Simeon had assured him that dropping Madison at the pier was for her own safety. Did Simeon know something the Secret Service agent didn't? *Not likely.* But what if he did? What if someone in the Secret Service was dirty? Maybe Simeon – working through the Pentagon – had learned the truth, and an FBI boat was waiting off shore to whisk the senator to safety. And then, once she was safe, they would take her agent into custody. *Which is why we couldn't tell anyone what we were up to!*

He hoped that was the case. The senator was a good woman and had done good work, not only for her state of Indiana, but for the nation as a whole. She had tackled the Trial Lawyers ... that alone was enough to grant her sainthood. Yes, he hoped – he *prayed* – that

Simeon's plan would ensure her safety. Pocks was a good Catholic boy, in spite of what the priests at the seminary had said. He believed in the sanctity of life, and didn't want to be a part of anything that undermined that belief.

He flinched. What did it matter? Morningstar had him by the balls. He needed the job at the Pentagon; if he was let go, he would never be hired again. Not by anyone reputable, anyway. Not only that, he was good at his job. No one could take apart a bomb quicker. If running questionable errands for Morningstar ensured that he would keep his job – and maybe even earn a few bucks on the side – well then, good for him. He would just make sure to keep his hands clean. *All I'm doing is delivering this woman to the Pier ... as instructed by my nameless, faceless Pentagon contact.*

He trembled at a sudden realization. His contact – Simeon – was clearly using an alias, and Morningstar had told Pocks to never speak of their arrangement. Which meant – if he was arrested – he would be on his own. Morningstar would deny that he had sent him to do any of the things he was doing, and it was obvious the shadowy Simeon was off the grid. If Pocks got caught, there was no doubt in his mind; he would be hung out to dry. *So, don't get caught, Pocks.* He would need to ditch the town car as soon as he could, and then lose the disguise.

He had nearly reached the turnoff for the pier. He was getting more and more nervous the closer they got. He could see the agent with his gun on his lap. The man didn't trust him. But, then again, if the agent was dirty, Pocks shouldn't trust the agent. He wasn't sure of the truth, but he would assume that the agent was a bad guy. He would be ready to do whatever was necessary to keep the senator safe. He patted a pistol in his pocket and grinned. *Maybe I'll even get a commendation from this.*

He turned onto the road that led to the pier. His stomach lurched. No one was there. Though it was raining, he expected one or two people to be walking the beach or at least watching the waves from their car. It didn't feel right. *To hell with saving the senator ... I need to drop off these two and get out of here!*

He pretended to take a phone call, and then stopped the car. He opened the partition, looked over the seat, and, as convincingly as possible, said, "The manager of the hotel just notified me that the Pentagon called," he paused for affect, "...and I'm to drop both of you at a safe point on the pier."

Chapter 53
JACKSONVILLE, FLORIDA

1/6/04

Simeon was ready. The shot he had fired outside the hotel had had the desired effect. The senators had been forced to disperse, either to cars they had arranged in advance, or to cabs or buses ... anything to get away from the hotel. And, though he had been pissed that they had escaped the Sarin gas, there was a part of him that was glad. He was looking forward to his rendezvous with the senator. He had planned out every step of the next seven minutes, down to the fishing boat he had hijacked from an unsuspecting angler. The old man had left the boat unattended, and that boat was now docked only a few hundred yards away, just waiting for Simeon and Madison to take their journey out to sea. *And what a journey it will be.* He grinned, ignoring the rain as he knelt behind a row of palm trees near the pier. He would take his time with Madison ... allow her to appreciate his unique gifts. *There is so much that can happen when you don't care if it's a man or a woman.* He smoothed his hair under his cap, and rubbed his thighs. The very thought of it had gotten him aroused.

But, for now, it was up to Pocks. As Simeon saw headlights approach the pier, it looked as if the man had come through. Simeon didn't know Pocks; he didn't really want to know him, but he was glad to see that the man had done what he was told. *I hope he disabled the GPS.*

In spite of the rain, there had been people standing on the pier only minutes ago, but Simeon had gotten rid of them. He had walked the dock in a black raincoat, a hood over his head, ranting about " ... the end of days." He had the swagger of a man who was crazy ... and likely dangerous. The few who were there had not stayed long.

The car was getting closer. Simeon pulled a ski mask over his mouth and nose. *Showtime.* Underneath his hood, he had a black stocking cap covering his hair and forehead, and he was still dressed in the dark turtleneck and black pants. He slid on a pair of sunglasses. The rain was falling harder; it would help to hide him.

He pulled out his pistol and waited. He would kill the agent first, and then drag Madison along the shore to the boat. He would force her to row them out to sea, he would have his way with her, and then he would shoot her ... once in the head, once in the heart. *The first shot is for Jacob ... the second shot is for me.* He patted his phone in his pocket and grinned. *And I'll film every bit of it.* The Majority Whip of the U.S. Senate was about to spend the last night of her life with a master. *Who knows ... she might even beg me for more.*

~~~

Henderson had wanted to follow the town car, but there was no way; it had too much of a head start. But he had gotten the plate number. The rain was coming harder, so he found a sheltered bench about half a block from Beach Boulevard and pulled out his computer. Using his phone's hotspot, he logged into the hotel's valet parking information. He was stunned – and sickened – when he saw that an alert had been issued on behalf of the entire parking staff. He could find no details, however, so he went to the website of the Jacksonville PD. There was a banner moving across the top of the page. "Valet driver found gagged in

Grande Dames parking garage. A search is underway for all vehicles not present and accounted for."

Henderson's heart was racing. Maddi was in trouble. *GPS! The car will have GPS.* Using the software he had stolen from the Pentagon, he went to the airport town car website, and hacked into their GPS tracking system. He found a car that had been assigned to Larry Moses and looked for its location. *Dammit!* The car's GPS had been disabled. *Simeon is no dummy.*

So how was he going to find Maddi? *Her agent's phone!* All agency cellphones had GPS tracking capability, though they usually blocked it from everyone except administrators. He went to the site; he had gone there many times to check up on Maddi's agents. He hacked in, found Larry Moses' information, and then tried to hack into the GPS gateway. He couldn't. What he wouldn't give for the satellite hacking device that was buried in a stainless-steel trunk outside Gainesville. He stared at the screen. He would need a code to gain access. But how could he get it? There was only one person who would be able – and willing – to get him what he needed. He hesitated as he pulled out his phone. *You have to do it, Henderson.* He dialed the same number he had dialed minutes ago, and reached the same receptionist, who once again told him that Dr. Clarkson didn't take anonymous calls. Henderson said evenly, "The senator is still in danger."

There was a pause, and then he could hear her forwarding the call.

"Clarkson here."

"It's me again." He didn't need to elaborate. He felt confident that Hank had not talked to anyone else in the last ten minutes with charred vocal cords. "I need GPS access to the phone belonging to Secret Service Agent Larry Moses."

There was a pause. "Listen. I don't know who you

are, but—"

"Yeah, well, there's no time for that. Please ... get me the code. Send it to the same email." Henderson ended the call. He prayed that Hank would come through.

~~~

The driver had turned onto the pier. Maddi was doing her best to stay calm. Larry said, "This doesn't look like it will lead us to a safe point."

The driver didn't turn around. "I think a boat is meeting you at the end of the pier."

Larry frowned. He looked at Maddi and whispered. "We'll be sitting ducks on this pier." He knocked on the partition. "Take us to the police station now, dammit!"

The man shook his head. "Orders, sir. According to my boss, they come directly from the Pentagon."

Larry bristled. He pulled out his phone and was about to dial, when the driver stopped the car, opened the partition, and aimed a revolver at his forehead. The man was sweating and his lip was twitching, but it was clear he was comfortable with a gun. *The marines?* The man cocked the pistol. "Get out."

Larry hesitated.

"Take the senator and get out!"

Larry pulled Maddi from the back seat and shoved her behind him, as the town car peeled away. The rain was falling harder and she slipped in the mud. He helped her up, and then fired at the town car; the driver swerved and managed to get away. Larry led Maddi to a row of trees. He pushed her up against a wide oak. Maddi knew he was trying to limit the access points behind her. "Stay down," he yelled as he did his best to cover the area.

Maddi crouched to her knees. She was drenched, mud-soaked, and shaking. She watched Larry pull out his phone. He was about to dial, when a low voice about a hundred yards away said, "Drop the phone."

Larry hesitated. The stranger shot at a nearby rock, the sound echoing in the night like a cannon. Larry threw down his phone. The man put a hole in it.

Maddi crouched even lower.

Larry aimed his gun in the direction of the voice. "Who are you?"

"Drop the weapon."

Larry didn't move.

"Drop it!"

He dropped his pistol beside him.

"Kick it away."

Larry kicked the gun a few feet away and raised his hands. Sirens could be heard in the distance. He whispered over his shoulder, "Stay low. Help's on the way."

He walked away from the trees and onto the pier. Maddi wanted to run and stop him, but she stayed there, crouched by the tree. *He would just shoot us both.*

She heard Larry ask, "Who are you? What do you want?"

She peered through the branches, and, in spite of the rain, was able to see a tall, lean man step out of the brush. He was wearing a ski mask and dark sunglasses, and had a cap pulled low over his forehead. "Where's Madison?"

"Hiding."

"I see. Well, you might want to get her out here, because I'm going to find her either way, and you won't have much chance to help her if you're dead."

~~~

Henderson waited, staring at his laptop. *C'mon Hank!* Within a minute, a message appeared. He opened it and saw an access code. He memorized it and went to the Secret Service website. He hacked in, found

Moses' information, and plugged in the code. He clicked on the GPS. There was a thirty-second delay. A map filled the screen. He quickly oriented himself. The map showed Larry heading east to the pier, about a half-mile from the hotel. Henderson forwarded the map to his phone, and then shoved his laptop in his pack. He kept his eyes glued to his phone while he threw his backpack over his shoulder. It was raining even harder. He covered his phone with his jacket and ran to Beach Boulevard. He was about to hail a cab, when he stopped. The signal had vanished. Had the GPS been disabled? Had Larry turned it off? Henderson needed to hurry. He wasn't sure what had just happened, but he felt certain that if he didn't get to the pier within the next minute or two, Maddi would be dead.

~~~

Hank was pacing his living room. He had taken the call from the stranger with the raspy voice and – for reasons he couldn't explain – had given the man what he asked for. After all, the guy had been right about the threat at the hotel. Twelve guests had lost their lives, but it would've been a lot worse if not for the stranger's warning.

Hanover had called him soon after the attack. *"How did you know, Hank?"*

Hank had told him the truth. *"A guy who refused to tell me his name insisted that something terrible was going to happen to the senators at the retreat."*

Hanover had paused. *"That's weird."*

Hank had nodded. *"Yes, it is, sir."*

There had been another pause. Hanover had added, *"Let me know if he calls again."*

Hank stopped pacing and stared out the window. *He called again, Hanover.* But this time, Hank didn't bother calling his boss. No matter what Hanover might have said, Hank would have given the stranger what he wanted. Why? *Because he's been right so far.*

But it made him nervous. What if the guy was actually the enemy? What if the first intervention had merely been a ploy to gain Hank's trust, and the real goal was to compromise Maddi's agent? He shook his head. It didn't feel like that ... and Hank had learned through the years to trust his gut. It had helped him save a life or two when he was practicing medicine; he hoped it would serve the same purpose now.

He needed to talk to Maddi ... just hear her voice. *Where are you, Maddi?* For the tenth time, he tried her cellphone. Again, it went to voicemail. He threw his phone on the table.

He paced another minute, and then picked up his phone. He had to find a way to talk to her. *If I can't call her, then I'll call her agent.* He dialed the number for Moses' cellphone; a number he had written down when he had obtained the access code for the mysterious caller. It went straight to voicemail. He immediately dialed the Director of the Secret Service, Sam Allen. Before the man could even say hello, Hank said, "This is Dr. Hank Clarkson, Deputy Director of Homeland Security. I need to speak to Agent Larry Moses immediately."

There was a pause. "I'm sorry, Dr. Clarkson, but his phone's been disabled."

"Disabled?" Hank felt his heart stop. *What have I done?* "What do you mean ... disabled?"

"We were tracking it to keep tabs on the senator. About two minutes ago, the tracking device lost the signal."

"Where were they?"

"At the Jacksonville Pier." He paused. "We have officers on the way, and–"

Hank had heard enough. He ended the call and

dialed Hanover. Without waiting for a hello, he said, "I need to get down to Jacksonville."

There was a pause. "I was just about to send you. We've confirmed that sarin gas was used at the hotel, which makes this a bioterrorist attack."

Hank looked at the file on his coffee table. *I guess we've found the missing sarin gas.*

Hanover went on. "I'll have Jana arrange for a military transport plane immediately."

Hank ended the call and shoved the phone in his pocket. He ran into his bedroom and packed a bag. He stuck his gun in his holster. His hands were shaking. Maddi was with Larry, who was somewhere on the Jacksonville Pier ... *without any means of contacting anyone.* It didn't look good.

He zipped the bag and ran out of his apartment. He flagged down a cab and had it take him to Dover Air Force Base. The flight to Jacksonville would take about an hour. He checked his watch. *9:40 p.m.* Though he wasn't normally a praying man, he closed his eyes and whispered, "Watch over her, God ... please keep her safe." He sat back and stared out the window. God willing, he would be with Maddi by midnight.

~~~

Maddi was having a hard time breathing, and she didn't even want to try to stand. So, she continued to crouch by the tree. In spite of the rain, the man in the mask was holding his gun steady. Larry stared at him. "Shoot me, you piece of shit. The police are only seconds away, and you'll never find my protectee ... not before they get here, anyway." He paused. "You'll be prosecuted for killing a federal agent."

"And I'll enjoy every minute of it," the man said as he aimed his pistol at Larry's forehead. He was about to pull the trigger when a shot came from nowhere, hitting a post on the pier, less than an inch from where the masked man was standing. Maddi sunk even lower in the brush. She saw Larry dart behind a tree, and then turn to see where the shot had come from. The man with the mask ran for cover. Another shot rang out, again only inches from him as he vanished into the trees.

~~~

Henderson had reached the pier just in time to see a man in a mask about to shoot Maddi's agent. He was over two hundred yards away and the rain was coming in sheets. To fire a shot even close to him would be next to impossible. *C'mon, Phoenix ... help me out.* He aimed his Glock, careful to account for the rain, the distance, and the direction of the wind. He fired. He hit a post only inches from the shooter's forehead. He fired again. The man ran into the forest, and Henderson slipped into the woods after him.

As he sprinted between the trees and raced along the shoreline, he could see a boat tied to a post about a half-mile down the beach. He stopped and pulled out his night goggles. He clicked them to the highest magnification and was able to see the would-be assassin running as fast as he could to the boat. The man stopped and looked back. He was still wearing his hat and hood, but had removed his mask and the dark glasses. It was enough. In spite of the rain, Henderson was able to see the man's dark eyes and his narrow jaw. There was no mistaking it; it was Morningstar's right-hand-man ... Simeon.

~~~

Maddi was shivering by the tree. She was soaking wet. The sirens were getting louder. She felt muddled and confused. *Who was the second shooter?*

Larry ran back and knelt beside her. "Are you okay?"

She stood and brushed the mud from her dress. "I–

I'm fine, Larry. What about you?"

"I'm good. I'm pissed off, but I'm good."

Maddi looked at him and her heart broke. He had picked up his weapon and the rain was pouring off his forehead onto the shaft of his gun. She put her soaked arm through his and smiled. "You saved my life, Larry."

He frowned. "No; I put you in danger."

Maddi was about to argue the point when two police cars pulled onto the pier. The blue and red lights lit up the area like strobe lights. Larry took off his jacket, held it over her head, and walked her to one of the cars. He helped her into the back seat, and an officer slid in on each side of her. Larry got in front and used the officer's phone to call his boss. As the cruiser pulled away, Maddi looked out the back window, hoping to see the mystery man who had scared off her would-be attacker. Who was he? Where had he come from? *And why did he disappear?*

Chapter 54
WASHINGTON, D.C.

1/6/04

The call came in just after eleven. Morningstar was sitting on his couch staring at the TV, praying that Simeon's backup plan had worked and Madison was dead.

"It's Simeon."

"Is it done?"

There was a pause. "No, sir. Someone stopped me."

"What do you mean, someone stopped you?"

"A gunman came out of nowhere and shot at me ... twice. I heard sirens, so I had to get out of there, Father."

Morningstar gripped the phone, clenching his teeth as he stared at the TV screen, which showed smiles of the hotel workers who had somehow been saved from a horrible attack. With as much control as he could muster, he said evenly, "I see."

There was silence.

Morningstar added, "So what are you going to do about it, Simeon?"

More silence.

Morningstar yelled into the phone. "I'll tell you what you're going to do, you asshole! You're going to find out who *disrupted* your mission and you're going to take him out." He paused. "And then you're going to finish what you started ... you got it?"

"Y – yes sir."

Morningstar ended the call. Simeon and Pocks had failed him. Which meant that Madison would keep up her efforts to investigate the Silverton Arms deals. He paced the room, angry and frustrated. His soldiers had let him down. *If you want something done right, do it yourself.* But he couldn't do it himself. He had too much to lose. The success of the entire mission relied on his soldiers doing the dirty work, while he pulled the strings from high up in the citadel. And that citadel was deeply entangled with the Bentley Group and Silverton Arms, Inc. No matter what, he couldn't get caught, and he couldn't allow Madison to keep digging into the arms deals. He had to find a way to stop her. But now, after the failed attempt on her life, the protection surrounding her would be better than ever.

All at once he stopped. *What if ... instead of killing her, I give her something else to think about?* He grinned as he pulled out his phone and dialed. The call was answered on the first ring. "Simeon, it's me again."

"Yes, Father?"

"Have the ships left Africa?"

"Yes, Father ... about five days ago."

"Good. And one of them is landing in Charleston?"

"Yes, Father."

"Can you get a message to the captain of that ship?"

There was a pause. "Yes ... yes I think I can."

"Tell the guy that once he lands, he is to conduct his business in Columbia rather than Charleston."

"Columbia, South Carolina, sir?"

"Yes." Morningstar grinned. "It just so happens that Madison's brother runs a clinic downtown." He paused. "And I think he's about to get rather busy."

He ended the call. *That oughta' do it.*

Chapter 55
JACKSONVILLE, FLORIDA

1/6/04

Hank landed at the Jacksonville Air Force Base at 11:25 p.m. Hanover had called ahead for a driver. As he headed toward town, Hanover updated him on what had happened at the pier. Hank was in disbelief. *"So, she's alive?"* The answer had been quick. *"Yes."*

He was driven to a not-yet-opened Marriott, where Maddi had joined the others following her ordeal at the pier. As Hank's car pulled up to the entrance, it was clear the entire place was in lockdown. There were police cruisers surrounding the building, and no one was permitted through the gate without proper ID. Hank showed his badge and waited impatiently while the guard made a call to Homeland. His car was ushered inside, and he got out before it had even come to a stop. He ran through the doors to the front desk. Again, he was asked to show his ID. He held it up and said firmly, "I need to see Senator Cynthia Madison."

The clerk, who was wearing a nametag from the Grande Dames Hotel, double-checked the ID and nodded. "Let me make a call first."

Though Hank wanted to strangle the man, he understood. These same guests had just suffered a Sarin gas attack. The clerk couldn't afford to be lax with his security checks. Within seconds, the man nodded and got off the phone. He pointed to an elevator across the lobby. "Suite 525."

There were two policemen standing at the elevator and Hank nodded as he stepped inside. He pushed the button for the fifth floor, and was glad to see two more officers when he stepped off. He ran down the hall to room 525. Agent Collins was standing outside the door. He nodded when he saw Hank. "Hello, Dr. Clarkson."

Hank nodded. "Is she inside?"

Collins opened the door. Hank was about to walk in, when Maddi suddenly ran into the hall and hugged him. He hugged her back, glad to feel her body – alive and well – next to his. She had been the victim of a sarin gas attack. Not many lived to tell about it. He squeezed her even harder.

After a minute, she stepped back and smiled, her hair hanging in her eyes. "What are you doing here?"

He feigned a frown, gently brushing strands of hair from her forehead. "I heard there was a problem with some poison gas. As Deputy Director of Homeland Security, I'm obligated to fly down and investigate."

She grinned. "I see." She walked him into her room and they sat on the couch. Larry was standing nearby, and politely stepped into the kitchen. She looked at Hank. He could see her eyes glisten in the dim light from a table lamp. She was trying not to cry. He took her hand. It was shaking. Her voice broke as she said, "It ... it was awful, Hank. Twelve people died. I've asked Phil to try to get in touch with their families. I'd like to express my sympathy."

Hank squeezed her hand and scooted closer. "I'm just glad you're okay."

She smiled weakly. "Do we have any idea what happened? Who was behind it?" She paused. "And do we know who was shooting at us down at the pier?"

Hank frowned. "Not really. Tell me more about what happened at the pier."

Maddi tightened her jaw. "There's not much to say. A shot was fired while we were standing outside the hotel, and—"

Hank frowned. "A shot was fired at the hotel? I

didn't know that."

Maddi nodded. "Yeah, some guy yelled 'Allah Akbar.' I don't think they've found him. Anyway, Larry wanted all of us to get further away, so he called for our town car, and–"

"Who was driving?"

"The valet."

"You had an unvetted valet drive you away from there?"

Maddi frowned. "We had no choice, Hank."

He shook his head and sighed. "Go on."

"Larry told the driver to take us to the police station. He drove us to the pier instead."

Hank stopped her again. "Why didn't he do what Larry said?"

"It turns out, he was one of the bad guys. He pulled a gun on Larry, and forced us out of the car. He drove away before Larry could confront him."

Hank frowned. "So, you got into a town car with a driver that hadn't been vetted, the driver ignored your agent's instructions to take you to the police station, and then he drove you to the pier and forced you ... *at gunpoint* ... to get out of the car?"

Maddi nodded. "Yes." She shook her head. "And then this guy wearing a ski mask and dark glasses confronted Larry. He was about to shoot him when someone else fired at the shooter. He barely missed him."

Hank had gotten none of this information from Hanover. He frowned. "Someone else fired at the shooter?"

Maddi nodded. "Some Good Samaritan came out of nowhere and saved us."

Hank thought back to the phone call and the email he had received. *The same guy?* His cellphone rang. "Clarkson here."

"Hank, It's Hanover. I just wanted to tell you again what a good job you did today. I don't know how you knew what you knew, but if you hadn't acted when you did, this story would have ended a whole lot differently."

Hank sighed. "Thank you, sir. As I said before, it was just a tip, followed by a gut impulse."

"Well, take care of that gut of yours ... it's pretty reliable." There was a pause. "We'll talk when you get back to D.C."

"Yes sir."

Hanover added, "Oh, and Hank?"

"Yes sir."

"Remember Agent Beaker? I think maybe he's given you a hard time since you took the post of Deputy Director."

Hank frowned. "Nothing I can't handle, sir."

"Well, he stopped by to tell me how impressed he is that you saw this coming. I think his exact words were, 'The Doc got it right this time.'"

Hank laughed. "High praise."

"High praise, indeed. You're coming back tomorrow then?"

"I'd like to look into things a bit more. Maybe Thursday?"

"Sounds good. Be in my office Thursday morning, ten a.m. sharp."

"Yes sir."

The call ended and Hank tucked his phone in his pocket.

Maddi looked at him and grinned. "Did you have something to do with getting us out of that hotel, Hank?"

He shook his head. "I made a phone call ... that's it."

Maddi stood and he did the same. "I think you're

selling yourself short." She looped her arm through his and walked him into the hall. "Would you like to join me for a night cap?"

He smiled. He couldn't think of anything he would rather do. "Good idea, Senator. It sounds like you could use the protection of this beefy Homeland Security agent." But as he walked her to the elevator, he couldn't help but think, *And the protection of a Good Samaritan, as well.*

Chapter 56
JACKSONVILLE, FLORIDA

1/6/04

Henderson had watched it all. From a grove of trees not far away, and with the help of his binoculars and his laptop, he had seen Hank pass through the tight security at the Marriott. He had watched him run inside the hotel, and then, by hacking into the feed from the cameras in the lobby, he had seen him step into the elevator. He had switched feeds just in time to see the elevator stop at the fifth floor, and was able to see Hank run down the hall. He then saw Maddi dash out of her room and wrap her arms around him. He enlarged the screen, and was able to see the look in her eyes ... admiration ... maybe even love. Finally, he saw her pull Hank into the hotel room, not so different from what she had done when she and Henderson had spent the night in the suite in Providence almost four years ago.

Henderson saw it all and it burned right through him. The man with Maddi would never be him. No matter what he did; how many sins he atoned for, how many wrongs he righted ... he would never again hold her in his arms. He looked down at his hands. The scars showed even in the dark. He could feel them. They were always there ... like a toothache. A constant reminder of what he was and all he had done.

But Hank deserved the credit. Henderson couldn't have done it without him. If Hank hadn't acted on the email, Maddi would be dead right now.

But still he hated it. He missed her; he ached for her. It felt as if he had spent his lifetime aching for her.

Watching her with another man ... with Hank ... just made it that much worse.

He shoved the laptop and the binoculars in his pack, and threw it over his shoulder. The rain had stopped and the moon lit up the downtown. He checked his watch. *Eleven-fifty ... I'm late. I need to call Rozenblats.* He turned and walked south on Beach Boulevard, looking for a phone booth, thinking about all that had happened, not only in the past twenty-four hours, but in the past month-and-a-half. He had killed Al-Gharsi, had finally left Morningstar, had lost Lili, had gone to find her, and had returned to America empty-handed. But he had come back for a reason. He had come back to stop the man who was responsible ... the man who had saved Henderson's life only to ruin it ... the man who was preparing to create an apocalypse *"...the likes of which the world has never imagined."*

And now, that same man had tried to kill Maddi. Why? Did he know about Henderson's feelings for her? Had Henderson said her name when he had told the man his darkest secrets? If so, Morningstar had never mentioned her. Had he simply been waiting for the right time? It made no sense. Why wouldn't he have used Maddi – like he used Lili – to coerce Henderson not only to steal and lie and kill, but to stay in the fold forever? *He would have ... if he had known about her.*

He shook his head as he walked along the boulevard. Morningstar didn't know about Henderson's feelings for Maddi. *So why is he suddenly trying to kill her?*

Regardless of the reason, Henderson had been able to stop him ... this time. But would he be there the next time? Or the time after that? He frowned. *And will Hank be there to pull the necessary strings?* The only way Henderson had succeeded in saving Maddi's life was with the help of the guy she had just embraced ...

the guy she's about to spend the night with.

He saw a phone booth and walked toward it. So much had happened, and so much had changed. Maddi had changed ... Hank had changed ... and Henderson had changed ... a lot. They had gotten older and wiser ... he had become a completely different man.

But who was he ... really? He was no longer Martin Henderson, he was no longer Joseph, and he was no longer the assassin known as Phoenix. *Or am I all three?* After all, it was Martin Henderson who had reached out to Hank. And it was Joseph who had finally defied his father. And, last but not least, it was Phoenix who had led Henderson to Simeon at the pier, and had then shot at him from two hundred feet in the pouring rain, and actually got close enough to stop him.

He frowned as he reached in his pocket for coins. He should have killed Simeon when he had the chance. When he saw him by the fishing boat, he could have easily pulled out his Glock and killed the bastard. Why didn't he? *Where was Phoenix then?* In some strange way, he found himself feeling sorry for Simeon. He, like Henderson, had been duped by Morningstar. He was simply following orders. *Who knows what Morningstar might be holding over his head?*

And who was it that had helped Simeon? Who had driven the town car? The car had been abandoned less than a mile from the pier, and had been wiped clean. Henderson had tried to learn more about the attack on the valet driver back at the hotel, surprised when he learned the man's life had been spared. He had been gagged, tied up, and stuffed inside a dumpster, but he hadn't been killed. Simeon wouldn't have spared the guy's life. Whoever Simeon's partner was; he possessed compassion. *Definitely not a quality seen in either Morningstar or Simeon.*

Henderson stepped into the phone booth and

frowned. He had a lot to do ... and a lot to undo. He had destroyed families, a peace process ... *and the mental wellbeing of a woman I love more than anything.* Worst of all, Morningstar was still out there, pulling the strings of men like him, threatening them, forcing them to sell their souls ... to do what? What did he want in the end? Power? Control? Fame?

Henderson dropped the coins in the slot. He didn't know how, or when, or in what way he would turn things around ... all he knew was, no matter what, from that moment forward, he would be a force for good. He thought of Maddi – her smile, her enthusiasm, her resilience unlike anything he had ever known – and his heart ached. As he waited for the operator, he made up his mind. *I will turn this around ... and I will use Maddi as my compass.*

THURSDAY, JANUARY 8TH, 2004

"Scratch the earth, dig the burial ground,
Sense of time won't be easily found ...
... Is this the start of the breakdown?"

~ Tears for Fears ~

Chapter 57

Maddi stifled a yawn; she was exhausted. She was having a hard time sleeping for more than an hour at a time. The conference had ended early. Though the Marriott had offered to keep the guests for free, none of the senators felt like discussing politics, and they had disbanded and headed for home the following morning.

They had agreed to meet a day later, Thursday, which was today, at ten a.m. in the Senate chamber, to review what had taken place, and to consider legislation that would monitor more closely the transfer of all poisonous gases. Though Homeland and the FBI were already overseeing those transfers, Congress needed to feel like it was doing something. After all, twelve of its own had nearly been killed.

Maddi had spent the last twenty-four hours reviewing the entire tragedy in her mind. There were so many questions. Why had the senators been targeted ... and why had *she* been targeted in the end? Did the detour to the pier have anything to do with the Sarin gas attack? Was Al-Qaida truly behind it? The terror group had yet to claim credit. Who had picked them up in the town car? And who was it that had saved her from the shooter at the pier? Did she know him? Or was it just some vigilante who had been in the right place at the right time? She guessed she would never know. But, oh, how she wanted to. She wanted to look in the eyes of the man who had had the guts to save her, but had not wanted any of the praise such a gesture had warranted.

She had awakened that morning at five a.m. and, after a failed attempt to go back to sleep, had asked Agent Collins to drive her to her office. Which was where she was now, quiet and alone before everyone else arrived. She was doing her best to get back to the peoples' business. But she was distracted. She couldn't quit thinking about how close she and the others had come to dying. She closed the file she was looking at, stood from her desk, and strolled to the window. As she stared out at another gray day, she thought of how differently things could have gone. If the would-be killers had gotten away with the hotel attack, hundreds would be dead, the country would be in mourning, and the somberness that had surrounded 9-11 would have returned. Ten people died ... it was enough. The twenty-four-hour news stations had milked the tragedy, and Congress was about to enact legislation to do what was already being done. *There is only so much you can do to stop men who don't want to be stopped.*

She walked away from the window and went over to the credenza. She made a pot of coffee, staring out the window while she waited for it to brew. It was often like that in the morning before the sun came up. She would go in early to get a jump on her day, but would end up reflecting on all that had happened in her charmed, yet challenged life. Most of those challenges involved loss ... the loss of good men who had died violent deaths. A father who had been gunned down in the line of duty, a terrible man who had been killed in self-defense, a lover who had been burned alive in a hotel fire ... and a mother who had drank herself nearly to death, leaving Maddi and Andrew on their own to deal with all of it. Worst of all had been the murder of Al-Gharsi, while she was sitting less than six inches away. It seemed ironic; so much violence, yet she had physically been untouched by any of it. *As though I live in a bubble ... forced to watch while those around me die horrible deaths.*

She was startled by a knock on the door.

"Come in."

Phil walked in and laid a piece of paper on her desk. "This just came for you by special courier, Senator. I thought you would want to read it right away."

Maddi nodded. "Thank you, Phil."

He left the room and she poured a cup of coffee. She carried it to her desk, sat down, and pulled the piece of paper closer. She was about to sip the coffee when she stopped. She stared at the page, stunned as she read the paragraph in front of her.

"I'm not sure how to say this. I am sorry about your friend, Al-Gharsi. I wish I hadn't done it, and would give anything to take it back. I will do all I can to make it up to you."

Maddi's hands were shaking; she set the coffee on the desk. She couldn't move; she could barely breathe. She picked up the paper and turned it over, looking for some sort of identification. Who had sent it? Whoever he was, he was claiming responsibility for Al-Gharsi's assassination. But the authorities had all but proven that it had been the Omani leader who had done the killing, and then shot himself after the fact. She frowned. *Probably just some lunatic who's trying to get my attention.* But the man was *apologizing*. What sort of assassin apologized for killing his target? Maddi reread the message. *"I wish I hadn't done it, and would give anything to take it back."* Maddi shook her head. It made no sense. She shoved it aside, ready to ignore it, but then pulled it back in front of her. The words seemed genuine ... sincere. *Could it be?* She frowned. If so, then the idea that the assassin had been the Omani leader had been nothing but a con. Maddi felt sick. She grabbed her stomach with one hand and covered her mouth with the other. The murder of Al-Gharsi by the Omani had been the trigger that had ended the prospect of peace in a region that desperately needed it. But, if Al-Gharsi's killer was alive and well – *and sending me letters* – then that meant that the Omani leader had had nothing to do with it, and the loss of the peace negotiations had not needed to happen. Maddi's entire body had begun to shake. *What if that was the intent?*

She stood and walked to the window. Is spite of the fact that she knew it wouldn't budge, she tried to open it. She needed some air. The Secret Service had nailed it shut soon after 9-11 *"...for your safety, Senator."* That was what they had told her as they had pounded in the last nail. *Forget my safety ... I need some air!*

She paced the office, doing her best to regain her composure. She walked back to the desk and stared again at the memo. If Al-Gharsi's assassin hadn't been the Omani, then maybe she could tell the world and get the peace process back on track. She frowned. *Not likely.* Too much had happened as a result of the assassination. The bridges had already been burned.

Maddi walked to the door and opened it partway. "Phil, could you see if the FBI could find out who wrote this letter?"

"I'm already on it, Senator."

"We should have it checked for prints." He nodded and she closed the door. She walked back to her desk and was about to reach for her coffee cup, when she saw that her hand was still shaking. She stood and once again walked to the window. She thought about the words in the letter. If they were legitimate, then not only had Al-Gharsi not been killed by the Omani leader as the world had assumed, but the assassin was still alive ... and he was out there somewhere ... apologizing ... *to me!* Why? What did it matter to an assassin whether Cynthia Madison forgave him?

She clung to the windowsill, shivering as she realized ... *Because this man ... this killer ... knows me.*

Epilogue
Charleston Harbor

Friday, January 9ᵗʰ, 2004

The first of the three boats arrived at the Charleston Harbor in the middle of the night on Friday, January 9ᵗʰ, 2004. The captain, Abid Mensa, ordered his only shipmate to begin unloading the merchandise. The sailor, an older man named Kofi with bad teeth and a scar on his left cheek from a bar fight gone bad, smirked at Abid, but he got to work tugging the heavy bundles off the boat and onto the dock. There were three parcels, all about the same size, each one weighing well over fifty pounds.

As the old man threw the second bundle onto the dock, he glared at Abid and, in broken English, he whispered, "What is in here, Abid ... dead bodies?"

Abid looked at him and frowned. "Shut up, Kofi! You will draw attention."

Kofi grabbed the last bundle and threw it onto the dock. He walked over to Abid who was still at the helm, and held out his hand. "I get paid."

Abid batted the hand away. "Not until I do! I meet you here ... next week."

Kofi frowned. "Next *week?* What do I do 'til then? I have no money."

Abid bristled as he reached in his pocket and pulled out his cash, held together by a solid gold clip. He stared at the bills. One hundred, a fifty, and two tens. It was the last of the money he had gotten from the American, Jacob, four years ago. He held back the hundred for himself, and handed Kofi the fifty and two tens. "Take this. It will get you through." He paused.

"But I deduct it from your pay!"

The man stuffed the bills in his pants. He ran down the boat ramp to the dock, and then darted along the pier. He was quickly lost to the darkness. Though the Harbor was normally a busy place, and had been well-guarded since 9-11, Abid had learned from the two trips he had already made that the best time to dock was between two and three in the morning. The night shift was no longer paying attention, and the morning shift had not yet arrived.

Tonight was no exception. He looked around to be sure no one was watching, and then secured the boat. They had been on the small vessel for over a week; there was garbage and old food strewn across the deck. He would leave it for the seagulls. He made sure to leave nothing else, especially anything that might give away who he was. Though he was counting on the inspectors to ignore his tiny boat and focus on the bigger ones, he couldn't take a chance. No one could know that it was he who had brought in the shipment from Africa.

He stuffed the keys in his pocket, walked down the ramp, and stepped onto the dock. The bundles needed to be moved from the boat in case it was searched. Jacob had provided a place to hide them until Abid could sell the merchandise. He squinted his eyes to see through the mist. As promised, a large warehouse was only a hundred yards away. The old building was falling apart. Jacob had told him that it had been used in the past to store shipping supplies, but had been abandoned nearly five years ago, when they had built the new storage facility on the other side of the pier. He was to carry the bundles to the warehouse. He would use them as a sleeping bag until the morning light, when he would take them one at a time to sell, "... *in Columbia, not Charleston.*" The mysterious Simeon had radioed him as he had neared the harbor, and had told him to sell his wares out of Columbia, " ... *it's only about a hundred miles away.*" Abid had said, *"Why not Charleston, like we originally agreed?"* Simeon didn't know, and, at the end of the day, Abid didn't care. He would get paid either way. *A simple bus ride ... no big deal.*

As he lugged the first of the bundles to the warehouse, he couldn't help but wonder ... *What is so important about this merchandise, that Jacob is willing to pay me so much to sell it?* He tugged on the bundle as he neared the doorway of the warehouse. It didn't matter why Jacob wanted him to do it. All that mattered was that within a week's time, he, Abid Mensa, would be a very rich man.

Thank you for reading.
Please review this book. Reviews help others find
Absolutely Amazing eBooks and inspire us to keep
providing these marvelous tales.

If you would like to be put on our email list to receive
updates on new releases, contests, and promotions, please
go to AbsolutelyAmazingEbooks.com and sign up.

About the Author

Dr. Jill Vosler is a family physician whose medical studies took her abroad to the University of Edinburgh in Scotland and on to extensive travel throughout the UK and Europe. Her love for these places has flavored her novels, along with the many years spent as a deputy coroner under the guidance of her father, who was the county coroner well into his eighties. She has a keen interest in politics and a passion for music, but most enjoys traveling the world with her husband, John, and their son and daughter.

The New
Atlantian Library

24972500R00188

Made in the USA
Lexington, KY
20 December 2018